# Praise for *The Green Hell*

I remember when I was young my father had recurrent bouts of malaria. He was stationed in Australia, New Guinea and the Philippines during WWII. He never talked much about the war. Now I know why.

In *The Green Hell*, J Scott Payne paints a stark and sometimes horrifying portrait of this nation's campaign against the Japanese in New Guinea. Many young men were sent into the dense and dangerous jungle where they confronted not only the enemy, but malaria, dengue fever, skin ulcers, mosquitos, crocs, malnutrition and countless parasites.

This is a gritty read. Payne's crisp prose captures the jargon of the time and, with his meticulous attention to historical detail, he has created characters that are profoundly believable and complex.

But this book is not just about the United States troops. Payne also pays homage to the valor of the Aussies – those who were there before us and who carried on the fight long after we left.

If you are a student of history or, like me, just want to know what really happened to your dad over there, then this book is a must-read. Highly recommended for five bright, shiny stars.

-- Linda Watkins, author of the award-winning *Mateguas Island* Series

# # #

When reading this book, you feel like you are right there in the moment with the guys. It's written in first person, whereas my other reads aren't, so that you constantly feel like an observer. Not here. I can feel myself blowing the layers of flies off my bully beef.

– James Meeks, an avid reader and fan

## What readers had to say about the author's previous books, *Brought To Battle* . . .

- If you are a WWII buff, as I am, this is MUST read. I'm praying J. Payne writes another based in the same era.

- Books such as this should be given as recommended reading in high school as part of history class.

- Had to check the copyright date because the story felt like it had been written in the late 1940s or early 1950s due to the author's adept usage of authentic vernacular and slang of that period.

- I will read anything this author writes!

## . . . and *A Corporal No More*

Wow. I admit I wasn't sure where this book would go, but it didn't take long to suck me in. I was growing weary of book after book about Generals, Lincoln and battles. This book brought me a whole new perspective and appreciation for the working men of the Civil War . . . from both sides. I find myself wishing the chapters would never stop. Please Mr. Payne, do this again . . . and again.
--FrederickChristie

Payne's knowledge of the era gives this novel the feel of a first-hand account. He brings the story to a satisfying and surprising conclusion.
– Darlene Blasing

The author successfully portrays the life of a Union Army corporal and brings exceptional animation to a critical time in American history that scarred our great nation.
– Deanna Compton, author of *The Freecurrent Trilogy*

## Dedication

To Steve LeBel, a master of utterly critical publishing minutia, yet a kindly soul who somehow genially tolerates dunces such as me.

# The Green Hell

**A Novel of World War II**

J. Scott Payne

## Other books by the Author –

### Brought To Battle
*A Novel of World War II*

### A Corporal No More
*A Novel of the Civil War*

### One, Two, Three Strikes You're Dead
*A Brad Powers Mystery*

### The Green Hell
*A Novel of World War II*
Copyright 2017 by J. Scott Payne
All rights reserved

Cover design by
### H. William Ruback,
### InColor Digital Design

Cover photos by author and
courtesy of Shutterstock.com

Published in the United States of America by Argon Press.
ISBN: (CS edition) 978-1-944815-36-3
ISBN: (IS edition)  978-1-944815-37-0

Library of Congress Control Number Pending

J Scott Payne

". . . in every war, Americans learn the hard way. Right now this outfit is a bunch of pussies.

"They can march and shoot rifles. But they have no goddamn idea at all of what combat is. They'll learn . . . no, actually, the survivors will learn.

"There'll have to be a killing first."

# Author's Note

The young enlisted man telling this story of New Guinea may be grossly unfair to General Douglas MacArthur.

Or maybe not.

The narrator, a 20-year-old with three years of college, could not possibly grasp the problems that faced MacArthur in 1942. For instance, the general then had only three infantry divisions – a third the population of Peoria -- to defend an area roughly the size of the United States plus lower Canada

Two divisions were tough, combat-hardened Australian veterans. The third was an untested American National Guard outfit, many of its men just out of basic training.

The Aussies defeated two Japanese assaults at points roughly equivalent to Buffalo and Cape Cod. MacArthur counterattacked, sending part of his National Guard division against Buna, the enemy base on New Guinea – by analogy, somewhere around Montreal.

The ground shapes infantry tactics and nobody should have known that better than MacArthur. In the Philippines, he had seen the jungle break up and isolate his own forces, dictating the need for special training and great firepower.

Yet he never examined the far more hostile terrain that his green troops faced on New Guinea . . . let alone the deeply-burrowed jungle-wise Japanese veterans who outnumbered the Americans.

Perhaps events forced MacArthur to start his campaign like topsy. Certainly he pushed his neophytes into battle ahead of their supplies. His guardsmen not only lacked training and firepower, but also were on half rations. Moreover, they possessed too little of the ammo, quinine, needed to fight their most implacable foe, malaria.

MacArthur's staff apparently feared to trouble him unduly about these realities. Granted, he probably knew that New Guinea was a hellhole and that his troops weren't ready for it. Apparently he thought leadership could overcome such deficits.

And he seemed to think leadership merely consisted of giving orders.

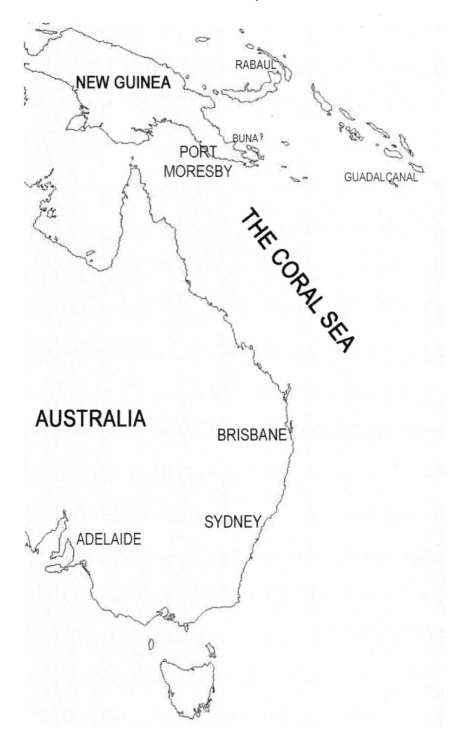

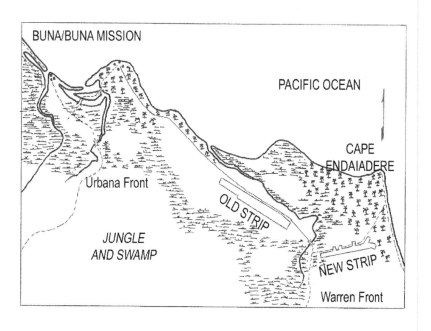

# Prologue

Kansas City (July 1959) – Dad picked me up from my summer job as a welder's helper and we stopped for a cool one.

Dad joined some guys at the bar yarning about WWII – 14 years past, but very much alive in their memories. A couple of stools down, my sociology instructor from last semester and I were arguing quietly. Two other men were bitching because Kansas City traded Bob Cerv back to the Yankees, so the A's would never amount to doodley squat.

I overheard Dad mention that the Navy had stationed him on Guadalcanal after its capture. He marveled, and not for the first time, at how Marines managed to defeat the Japanese, given the teeming mosquitos and disease-ridden jungles.

A quiet voice said, "I saw worse."

All eyes focused on a scrawny smoker at the far end of the bar. A grimy baseball cap shadowed pinched unshaven features that put him anywhere from 40 to 60. His sweat-stained denim shirt featured the little charred holes you get when using an acetylene torch.

Dad asked, "Where? The Canal?"

The man slowly shook his head side-to-side, squinting as smoke from his Winston laced his eyes.

Drawing beers, the bartender casually asked, "Well, where'd they send you?"

The man used his little finger to flick ash from his cigarette.

"New Guinea."

Somebody said, "Wow."

Another voice: "I heard it was pretty rough with malaria and jungle crud and all them diseases."

The guy stubbed out his cigarette and got up to leave.

"Naaa," he said. "New Guinea was the disease."

He paused in the door.

"It killed us faster'n we could kill each other."

# Chapter 1
# Reporting For Duty

Stepping out onto the arena's middle deck, Pop and I halted and just gaped, bunching up 10 other guys behind us.

The Cow Palace was so big it seemed to take a second or two for my vision to reach its far walls. It was the biggest building interior I'd ever seen and I think the same went for Pop.

We were conscious of a subdued murmur – sort of like a crowd waiting for the game to start. But instead of fans, the crowd was a few thousand soldiers lounging or trying to sleep in the stadium seats. And instead of a game down on the arena floor, three long columns of GIs – shirts off, OD T-shirt sleeves rolled up – were filing in vaccination assembly lines.

Behind us someone barked, "Make a hole!"

We all skittered to the side, making way for a tall, thick-shouldered staff sergeant. As he passed us he asked, "Anybody here got any college?"

Pop and I raised our hands.

"Anybody else? No?" He propped his butt on the low wall separating box seats from General Admission. "Okay, you others take this row of seats just behind this here wall."

As the others filed to the seats he snapped his fingers at us. "Your orders!"

With hands the size of coal shovels, he quickly paged through our files, muttering, "Aw, shit. As if I didn't have enough . . ." Glancing up with hooded gray eyes, he sighed and gave a resigned shrug.

"Okay, you two. Welcome to your new home – Headquarters Company of the First Battalion, 126th Infantry Regiment, 32nd Infantry Division."

He stood from the wall and added, "The name is Irish. You'll hear this soon enough so I'll just tell you now -- sometimes I can be a son-of-a-bitch, but I'm always a bastard."

I guess we both looked startled.

"Back in Nineteen and One," he said, "some poor broken-down whore left me on the sisters' doorstep." He paused. "They stuck me with Irish for a last name and Daniel for a first name. The whole rest of my time in that orphanage, the sisters and the kids called me Danny Boy."

With a look frosty as dry ice, he said, "Don't ever call me that. Ever!" He gave a slight grin. "I think those old knuckle-crackers hated me at first sight."

Pop nodded vigorously. "Oh, yeah, Sarge. I get it. I know allllll about Sister Mary knuckle-whacker."

At my puzzled sidelong glance, Sergeant Irish said, "Inside joke. You got to be a Catholic to understand. Now, which one is Mays?"

"Me, sir," I said.

"Don't you 'sir' me, young trooper! I ain't an officer, I work for a living."

"Sorry, sergeant."

"Yeah, okay. Just drop that basic training habit of calling NCOs 'sir'." He grinned. "It makes officers jealous."

Skimming our files again, he said, "And that means you've got to be Anthony Popalovski? Am I saying it right?"

"Yep. My friends call me Pop."

"I'm not your friend. I'll stick with Popalovski. And you both enlisted? You ain't draftees?"

"Right, Sarge," Pop said proudly. "We enlisted."

"Okay. You just got here from basic?"

"We paraded out this morning at Fort Ord," I said. "They bussed most of our company right up here."

"Have you qualified with rifles?"

Pop nodded. "Yeah, Sarge. I shot Marksman and Jimmy here shot Expert. They said he got one of the highest scores ever fired at Ord."

"They were telling us Japs have bad eyes," I said.

The sergeant gave a short bark of a laugh. "That's Newspaper bullshit. Believe me, the Nips are good with their weapons. Now, did you happen to qualify with M-1s?"

"No," I said. "We trained with the '03 Springfield."

"Great! Instead of Springfields, we have the M-1 Garand. Well, at least you know how to shoot and it's the same catridge. So now we've got to familiarize you with the M-1 and . . ."

Pop interrupted. "Wow, I'm ready for that. We've heard a lot about the M-1 . . ."

The sergeant interrupted. "I was about to say that we got to bring you up to the same training level as the rest of the battalion. So, either of you know the tommy gun?"

We both shook their heads.

"The BAR? Carbine? No? Okay, we can maybe familiarize you with those weapons once we board the ship. On the way to France in the last war, we sometimes practiced marksmanship off the stern. We'll see."

I asked, "So we're going somewhere on a boat?"

The sergeant gave me a pitying look. "See, Young Trooper, after the Nips hit Pearl Harbor they didn't have the guts to invade Conus. So we have to go way out thar on t'other side of the Pacific to kick their sorry asses . . . and, boy, we just cain't get thar by truck."

I felt my ears burning. "Sorry, Sarge. Stupid question. But I got one more. What's 'Conus'?"

"That's Army lingo for 'Continental United States'. Say you're stationed in Hawaii or Puerto Rico – you're in the United States, but you ain't in the continental United States – not in Conus."

Pop piped up. "So, why say 'Nips' instead of 'Japs'?"

It was my turn. "The Japs pronounce the name of their country 'Nippon.' 'Japan' is just our version of the word."

"Right," Sarge said. "So in our book they're Nips or Japs. We hear that both words insult them. That's how we piss the little bastards off."

He turned to me, "You speak Japanese?"

"Just a little," I said. "I was majoring in East Asian studies and I took a class in conversational Japanese."

"Might be handy," he said. "Okay. Enough bullshit. The exec wants me to fit you people in. We're understrength and they're sending you kids from Ord to make up our numbers." He paused. "So," he asked, "you boys had any infantry training at all?"

Pop said. "We heard our new outfits would train us."

The sergeant snorted and swept his hand in a broad arc taking in the panorama of stadium seating. "We're supposed to drill on fire and movement here in Row D of the fucking Cow Palace. Jesus! Did they teach you *anything* . . . digging foxholes? Grenades? Mortars? Radios?"

Pop grinned. "Sarge, we each got to throw one grenade. Mainly, we practiced marching to and from the rifle range, peeling spuds, bouncing quarters on bunks and shining shoes and boots."

The sergeant said, "Fuck!" He took a deep drag on his cigarette. "Either of you men in sports?"

"We both played college football," I said. "Pop was a tackle and I played safety. We were second-string juniors."

"Where?

"I played for Colorado," Pop said. "Jim here was at Washington."

"Okay, either of you type?"

"Yeah, we both do, sir . . . sergeant."

"Well, some good news for once. Okay, for now I'll keep you working for me. So, about face, march your asses inside and take a right."

He stepped to the doorway and yelled into the stadium's under story. "Benson! I'm sending you two new men. They're ours. Process them in and find racks for them. They type, so put them to work. I'll see you about it when the skipper and I get back tonight!"

He returned our files. "Give your files to Corporal Benson. We bunk in the horse stalls below this section of the stadium. It's stinky. Get you ready for the troop ship."

As Pop hoisted his duffle bag, he said, "Uh, Sarge? Any chance of a pass so we can go into Frisco?"

"Don't call it 'Frisco'," the sergeant said. "The locals don't like it. And no passes. We're on movement alert."

"Well, crap!" I said. "We haven't had a pass since we enlisted. I wanted to see China Town."

"Private Mays, you break my heart. You'll get a look at San Francisco when we go out under the Golden Gate. When we get back, I'll personally make sure you get a pass into town."

"If we get back," Pop said.

Sarge gave him a bleak look. "Yeah, well. Luck of the draw."

# Chapter 2
# Meeting FUBAR

During the next two days we caught only glimpses of the Sarge. He and several of the regiment's officers and NCOs were badgering West Coast military depots for equipment we were supposed to have received at Fort Devens.

Most of us got brand-new M-1 Garand rifles and we all turned in our old dishpan helmets for the new steel pots.

Signing us in was Frank Benson, a beer-bellied corporal and military bureaucrat with two speeds – slow and stop. After assigning us bunks in a horse stall reeking of piss and manure, he put us to work as clerk-typists. We began processing paperwork for dozens of new basic trainee graduates coming into the battalion.

At first Benson behaved like a real asshole. But he mellowed as we caught on to the paperwork -- pretty much dumb repetition. The one variation was that I had to type out an Emergency Travel Order for an officer whose wife back in Wisconsin was desperately ill. I had to make nine carbons of each page of the damned thing, so instead of hunt and peck on the typewriter, it was a case of hunt and pound. I was afraid that old Army-issue Remington Upright would fall apart.

When I handed his orders to him, the officer – a lieutenant who looked about 15 – was so pathetically grateful he reached out and shook my hand.

"Jeeze," Pop said, "at least he could have tipped you."

"Knock off that talk!" Benson shouted. "We're here to serve our people."

Once we settled in and Benson found us useful, he treated us more like coworkers. Being his own favorite subject, he'd talk our arms off when we questioned him about himself or the outfit. And as long as I got my work done, he let me use the typewriter to write to Beverly, my girlfriend.

He bitched constantly about the way Washington, D.C. had treated his beloved regiment and, by extension, the 32nd Division.

"It's a Regular Army FUBAR."

"FUBAR?"

"Men," he said, "those letters stand for 'Fucked Up Beyond All Recognition'. When we stopped laughing, he cautioned, "When ladies are around you say 'Fouled Up' instead of 'Fucked Up'."

"Oh, okay, Corporal. But what's so fucked up?"

"Our division, boys. Who ever heard of moving a whole damn division 3,000 miles in a damn week? That's what they done to us. It'd usually take at least a month, so you can see why everything is such a godawful mess."

Benson said it took maybe two dozen trains five days to move the 32nd from Massachusetts to California.

"Some trains got delayed along the way for repairs. So units arrived out here all mixed up. Able Company from one regiment gets stuck beside Fox Company of another regiment with maybe one platoon from Dog Company mixed in. Some of us is here at the Cow Palace and some units got sent to an island out in the bay -- No! No! Not Alcatraz! -- and some of 'em wound up at a dog track and even more is billeted for now down at Fort Ord where you men just come from."

He rocked his face in his hands for a moment. "All my files still haven't reached me -- Day sheets, inspection reports, strength reports, call logs, requisition forms, Disposition Forms. All of our regulations and training manuals. Christ on a crutch, boys, we're practically having to start from scratch!"

Benson was a cost recorder for a county clerk in civilian life and he also worked part-time as a janitor. Joining the Guard in 1935 seemed the high point of his life. He'd been an HQ paper-pusher ever since and was proud that the old man always trusted him -- and him alone -- to rig the lighting for dances at the armory.

He sighed. "Fellas, we used to have us real great dances . . . especially great for us bachelors all duked up in our dress uniforms. The gals really ate it up."

But he boasted that he also had military pride in his regiment.

"See, we're the National Guard from Michigan and Wisconsin . . . you know, built on the old Iron Brigade from the Civil War? And in the Great War, our boys showed the same kind of fight. They ripped right through any German line. That's how they come to call us the Red Arrow Division. That's why we've got that Red Arrow shoulder patch. Hell, after the war, Michigan's legislature even named a highway after us – the Red Arrow Highway!"

Benson said he was from a Lake Michigan harbor town named Grand Haven and that he enlisted when he was 22 because $12 a month helped put food on the table. Thanks to his court house background, he was head-down dogged with paperwork. His hard work earned him a whirlwind promotion to corporal which had him typing and filing at the armory office at least five days a month beyond the regular mandatory meeting schedule.

"For some guys," he said, "being in the Guard was kind of a social thing . . . you know 12 bucks a month could buy a lot of beer. And then, like I said, there was the dances."

He said everything changed in 1940, even before Germany invaded Poland and kicked World War II into gear.

"The War Department yanked us into federal service. We was the first and so suddenly we was a full-time Army division. The Army sent us down for the Louisiana Maneuvers. But that was planned and organized, see? Took six weeks for us to get there and it was only half the distance and half the men.

"Anyways, they run us all over Louisiana and Texas for damn near a year, partly filling us in with draftees like you boys."

I growled, "Look, Corporal, Pop and I are not fucking draftees! We volunteered!"

"Okay! Okay, Mays! Keep your shirt on! The point is we got into combat shape and weeded out all the old officers and NCOs. They even put the old division commander out to pasture.

"Now at first during maneuvers, we had nothing but old wore-out Springfields and even some Krag-Jorgesons from Philippine days. We was tacking together three pieces of lath for pretend machine guns and using Model A's for tanks.

"Well, at first, it was just us in the maneuvers. Then they sent two more divisions to work with us. And then they made us part of the Fifth Corps in the Third Army – tens of thousands of troops. And, my God, it was hot in summer down there. Whew!

"Sometime in there we heard Congress passed a law saying they can send us overseas."

Here, his voice would rise an octave in indignation, ". . . and then – *and then!* -- the bastards decreed we could be kept on active duty until at least six months after the end of the war. And the US of And we wasn't even *in* a war! How do you like that shit?"

He moaned that things just kept getting worse.

"When the Japs bombed Pearl Harbor, they broke us up to do guard duty all over the South.

"Our battalion for a long time was guarding some damned sulphur mines. Now can you imagine the Japs crossing the Pacific and then half of the US of A to attack a sulphur mine? Talk about a goddam Chinese fire drill. Jesus wept!

"Then, finally, the Army pulls us back together and ships us north to Fort Devens all the way up in Massachushits. They had us headed for the European Theater, so first they put our engineering regiment on a boat to go build barracks for us in Ireland.

"Well, no sooner do the engineers disappear over the horizon, than some jerk at the Flagpole in Washington, D.C., orders 'Abouuuut Faaace!'

# Chapter 3
# The First FUBAR

Corporal Benson told us the whole story at least six times and he always started the same way – solemnly shaking his head, side to side.

"So the whole damn 32nd Infantry Division – by then we was up to about 7,000 troops, give or take, but without our engineers, of course – so we had to turn 180 degrees and come clear the hell out here to San Francisco.

And, of course, maybe half our equipment ain't here and we're supposed to ship out at any time. It's just a rotten awful mess. A real FUBAR."

"Where are they shipping us?"

"It's secret."

He looked around and lowered his voice to a near-whisper. "I'm putting my money on the Philippines because the Japs really have our backs against the wall out there. But it could be Hawaii, first."

Then he got louder. "Of course, Jap submarines probably will be after us. And when we arrive – *if* we arrive -- wherever it is, it'll still be FUBAR with the different units all scrambled up."

Pop asked, "So, what's Sergeant Irish like?"

Benson rolled his eyes. "Well, he's Regular Army – kind of. So he don't fit in real well with a National Guard outfit."

"What do you mean by 'kind of'?"

"Well, first off, he's from Oklahoma. And being an Okie, he sometimes don't mesh too good with us Yankees.

"Second, he wasn't happy about being assigned to us." Benson looked around furtively. Almost whispering he said, "Don't let this get around but the sergeant's main problem is that he just don't think much of us guardsmen. He's got this 'up yours' attitude about us. Calls us 'Weekend Warriors' and claims we're just beer-drinking amateurs who don't train seriously.

"He really pissed off some officers by saying they ain't got the guts to give tough orders to their home-town boys. Personally, I think we shaped up pretty good in Louisiana, but he still looks down his nose at us.

"Third, when he gets mad, he's a damn blowtorch – and that just ain't how we do things in the National Guard."

Beyond that, he said, being a combat veteran from the Great War in France, Irish acted a bit snooty.

"He got two wound stripes in France and, after the Armistice, he did a hitch in the Regular Army in the Philippines and in China.

"After that," Benson said, "it gets sorta fuzzy. See, in the early 30's, Congress cut the Army 'way, 'way back. So I hear Sarge found a job with some warlord in China. He don't talk about it much. He calls the head warlord Chancre Jack.

"When the Japs invaded China, he joined the Chinese army to help them fight the Japs. They even made him a major. But he said Chancre Jack never would do anything but retreat. So Sarge quit and re-enlisted in the Army. Being's how he didn't go to college, the Army only took him back as a sergeant. It would have pissed me off, but he don't seem to mind."

# # #

Among the new guys who Pop and I processed in were two breezy characters from Los Angeles -- Julian Barkley and William Drexel. Sarge assigned them to HQ Company and they worked with us. I tried calling Barkley 'Julie" but he got so hot about it that I switched to J.B. instead. J.B. had been drafted out of UCLA.

Drexel was a plumber's son who apprenticed with his dad. He was close to graduating from business school when his friends and neighbors selected him for service with the U.S. Army.

The four of us not only worked as Benson's typing pool, but we also spent a good deal of time on the arena floor getting caught up on our shots.

You had to get the three typhoid shots at least a week apart, I guess, to make sure it would take. So we got the first two in basic and the last one, the booster, at the Cow Palace. And there were some other injections, but I don't remember what.

But I do remember it was a bit like being on one of those Boeing Aircraft assembly lines where Dad worked.

As my place in line got to the first medic, he swabbed alcohol on my upper arm and popped in a needle like he was throwing darts. The next medic squirted a syringe into the air, then mounted it onto the needle – and not being at all gentle about it -- and rammed the plunger in.

The next guy yanked out the needle and syringe. He'd say "Hold this!" and jab an alcohol-soaked cotton ball somewhere in the vicinity of the site. Then he pulled the needle off the syringe and the plunger from the syringe and put them in separate steaming trays.

The next move was ours. By the numbers -- roll down left sleeve, roll up right sleeve, three steps forward and then do a right face into to the next line for the next shot in the other arm.

We didn't like it. A few guys fainted right there in line. The medics weren't real happy, either. One said his arms and hands were so blasted tired he could hardly push in the plunger any longer. Too damn bad. My shoulders were sore as boils.

At least we didn't have to peel potatoes.

Incidentally, I found out later that in China, 'Chancre Jack' was the Old Army's derisive nickname for Chiang Kai-shek.

Oh, we finally got to see a little of San Francisco after all.

Damned little.

# Chapter 4
# Shipping Out

It was dark and the view out the back of a canvas-covered U.S. Army deuce-and-a-half truck is restricted to what the vehicle has just passed. So we got a very good look at San Francisco's street lights and the divider lines on the pavement.

That was about it.

Our tour of downtown started at some ungodly hour before dawn Wednesday, April 19.

Sarge roused us to load ourselves and our duffle bags aboard trucks which joined the convoy through downtown San Francisco to Pier 42. Oh, we sure got an eye-full of the pier. As dawn turned to day, we stood in long lines on the pier watching the ship's cranes lift aboard huge cargo nets full of duffle bags, and then a dozen or so 105 mm howitzers and many racks of M-1 rifles.

All of this was going on as GIs began filing aboard our ship, unit-by-unit while the rest of us waited.

And waited.

And waited.

At last, still amid masses of soldiers wearing backpacks, each with an entrenching tool (that's Army for a midget-size collapsible shovel), Headquarters Company, First Battalion of the 126th Infantry Regiment lined up at the foot of our gangplank.

Pop said, "Finally! Jesus, Mary and Joseph, we been standing on this damn dock for hours!"

Hofstra, a tall religious guy who wouldn't say 'honey' if he had a mouthful, agreed vehemently. "Sufferin' succotash, guys, this is really getting old."

Several boys cackled at his language and then ragged him. "Sufferin' succotash! Really? Honest to God, did you learn that from Daffy Duck or your Grandma?"

Trying to divert them from teasing Hofstra, I looked up the sides of our ship with its cruddy, slapdash gray paint job. "Hey, guys, it looks like we're going cross the Pacific Ocean aboard the the *S.S. Lurline*."

J.B. turned to me and snapped back, "Jim, you can just file that information under the heading of 'Deals, Big Fucking'. I just want to get aboard and get off my feet."

Looking amused, Sarge stood smoking behind Corporal Benson at the foot of the gangway. Benson yelled, "What the hell's your rush? You're gonna be on this here boat forever.

"Now listen up and listen close! As you come to me, stop and sound off with your name -- last name first. But don't start up the gangway till I check you off my list and give you the okay. Do you read me?"

Behind me Charlie Riegle muttered, "Oh, go fuck your list. This is such chicken shit! Honest to God, they're herding us around just like cattle."

"Hey, Charlie, you're finally catching on," Pop said, slapping his shoulder. "Why do you think they had us at the Cow Palace?"

Riegle snorted. "That's almost funny, Pop."

Though only 18, Riegle was an old-timer.

By that I mean he'd been with the regiment two years, and all through the Louisiana Maneuvers. Even so, he didn't give us the smart-assed static we got from most guardsmen. In fact, he seemed to idolize Pop and me because we both played college football -- Pop especially, because he was quite a bit beefier than me and about twice Riegle's size and four times his width.

Anyhow, he seemed to think we both were something special. We all thought about the same, I guess, until later in the year when the Japs whittled us down.

As I approached the gangway somebody said he heard that the *Lurline* was one of seven luxury liners taking us out to into the unknown.

Sergeant Irish gave a lazy grin. "Luxury liners?" In a deep bass, he added, "Ohhhh, yeah."

His cynical tone made me a bit nervous.

One-by-one the guys in our squad droned their names as they stepped up to the gangway:

"Muskiewicz, Stanislaus."

 "Hofstra, Eric."

"Barklay, Julian."

"Drexel, William."

"Svoboda, Anthony."

And so on, Benson giving a muttered repetition of the names as he searched for them on his roster. Then he'd check off the name and say, "Okay, get aboard."

As I stepped before him, I had a crazy inspiration. I snapped a short, stiff bow.

"Matsushita, Shigeo!"

Sarge, Riegle and Pop broke out in laughter. Benson searched his list for a second before giving me a bewildered look. Then, "Oh! Wise guy draftee. Give me your goddam name."

I gave another sharp bow. "So sorry – name is Mays, James. I no draftee! Sayonara!"

Sarge said, "Well, so Headquarters has its own comedian. We'll be sure to catch your act after we sail."

Benson said, "Just go tell it to Hirohito."

I told him, "That isn't how it's pronounced."

"I don't give a damn how you pronounce it, dammit. Just climb aboard!"

I eased the shoulder straps of my backpack for about the 90th time, and clumped up the gangway to rejoin the line, now queued along the shaded promenade deck instead of the dock.

Pop and Riegle closed up behind me, still chuckling. Riegle said, "Okay, Pvt. Mays, now just exactly how do you pronounce the name of Japan's little bastard emperor?"

"Not like we spell it," I said. "They call him something more like '*Hee*-rowsh-*toe*'."

The line started moving and we caught the odor of coffee and bacon. "Hey, maybe we'll get chow."

We wound through a broad doorway into what seemed like sheer blackness after the bright sunlight. The bacon smell grew much stronger. Practically starting to drool at the thought of breakfast, I followed the line into a passageway, then another turn.

Through an open door I caught sight of several officers eating and chatting at a long table. Some guy with captain's railroad tracks on his collars was sipping coffee from a gold-rimmed white china cup. A matching saucer gleamed on the snowy tablecloth.

"Keep moving!" somebody ordered. "And make damn sure you grip both handrails going down this ladder."

We descended the ladder facing away from the steps, and it was so steep that the handle of my entrenching tool kept bumping on the steps. Then it was another turn and down another ladder. And another and another. By then, I didn't know whether I was headed toward the bow or the stern.

We filed out into a wide echoing hold with a plywood floor on half of which the crew had tied down a dozen howitzers. All our duffle bags were heaped in a big roped-off mass in the center of the remaining deck. Sarge said, "This is home, men -- HQ Company's billet until we get where we're going."

"What about racks, Sarge?"

"This nice plywood deck is your rack. Find your duffle bag and use some of the stuff in it for bedding or pillows, like the overcoat." Riegle started to fumble out a cigarette.

"No smoking down here, soldier."

Speaking was a burly man in a flat cap and anchors on the collar points of his khaki shirt. "We're too close to the fuel bunkers. You can smoke out on deck during the day. But you have to wait until they announce that the smoking lamp is lit."

"Jeeze. Who the hell are you, buddy?"

The man, who looked a bit like a bulldog thanks to a flattened nose, thrust his head forward and glared. "Son, I'm this ship's chief. I'm a petty officer, just like a top sergeant in the Army. I know everything, right, Sarge?"

"That's right, chief. Your word is law on this ship."

"Well, can we smoke at nighttime?"

"No lights up on deck of any kind after sunset. Makes it easy for Jap submarines to spot us."

"Jap subs? At the dock in San Francisco?"

Sarge said, "You heard the man."

The chief nodded, grinned and walked away.

We looked around at our new home, dismay mingling with disgust. Pop, J.B., Drexel and I gave our helmets to Riegle to mark places for us away from passage ways so people wouldn't step on us. Pop and I played linemen, shouldering into the crowd to make way for the others. A full duffle bag weighs 65-70 pounds, and we were able to ram other searchers with them so that it only took about five minutes to round up all our bags.

We returned to find Riegle wrestling with a big palooka who tried to muscle in on our places. Riegle was a runt – all of 5-5 and weighing in at maybe 120. But even giving away 50 pounds, he was pure rawhide and farm-boy tough.

He had the oaf in a headlock and was hanging on for dear life as the guy started trying to slam him against the steel walls of the hold.

Pop said, "Hey, Charlie! Just leave go of that dumb bastard." Riegle did. The guy, red-faced and furious, turned to retaliate but then he saw us looming behind Riegle, grinning with our arms folded.

He disappeared.

"Thanks fellas," Riegle said.

"Aww shit, Charlie, you had him handled," J.B. said. "We just wanted to save you some time."

We had buddied up with Riegle because he had had a hell of a sense of humor and also because he showed us how to field strip the M-1 rifle.

"Guys, you just grab the rear of the trigger guard and pull back and upwards. The trigger group comes right out and then the stock slides off sweet as can be." He named off the parts as he disassembled and then reassembled them — "Bolt, operating rod, operating rod spring, follower and slide, the bullet guide . . ."

He also warned us to rock our hand up and out when letting the action slam shut. Otherwise, the bolt might try to chamber an important piece of anatomy. We especially appreciated that tip after Muskiewicz showed us his case of M-1 Thumb -- a deep black-and-purple perfectly round bruise portending the loss of the right thumbnail.

We no sooner got our blankets and overcoats out of the duffle bags than we heard a piercing whistle over the PA system.

"Now here this! Now here this! Lifeboat drills commence at 0600 tomorrow. Learn your routes by checking the schematic on your compartment wall! Morning chow will be served after we complete orderly -- repeat orderly! -- lifeboat drills."

# Chapter 5
# Loving The Lurline

Lifeboat drill was chaos.

They didn't issue inflatable Mae Wests for troops aboard the *Lurline*. We got those bulky cork life jackets and merely trying to don them was crazy. Everybody accidentally hit everybody else with elbows and forearms.

And trying to race three stories topside when twice your normal thickness became a street brawl.

They posted junior officers at the lifeboat stations to make sure the right units got to the right lifeboats. But the shave tails and first louies seemed just as bewildered as the rest of us.

As it turned out, with skillful blocking, we in HQ Company got to our boat station before anyone else coming up from the bowels of the ship. The guys at the boat station next to ours were ragging us. They were billeted in *Lurline's* ballroom. What's more, they had bunks – well, canvas racks stretched between pipe frames.

"How do you sad sacks like it down there in the bilges? We hear your accommodations are a bit on the Spartan side."

Riegle, who was a rabid fan of the football team at Michigan State College of Agriculture, took that lead and ran with it.

"Look, us Spartans can handle tough conditions. But you mommas' boys just can't seem to survive without princess-and-the-pea treatment."

Several of us had to form kind of a living bulwark to protect Riegle until Sarge and another NCO showed up to cool things down.

During the next drill, NCOs were posted to enforce the walk-don't-run rule. Things still got squirrely, but by the fourth or fifth attempt, the evacuation drill ran more like it should.

All of us in the hold, however, agreed with Drexel.

"Boys, if a Jap torpedo hits us, I ain't waiting in line like a kindergartener in a fire drill. I plan to be the first guy topside. And Pop, I expect you and Mays to block for me."

During a drill the next morning we discovered tugs had pulled our ship to anchor out in the bay.

Not a half-mile away was a Navy giant, a heavy cruiser named the *USS Indianapolis*. They said she and two smaller ships would escort us to our mystery destination which we called The Back of Unknown.

It took three damn days to load the entire division aboard seven ships. By then there were about 11,000 of us. We aboard *Lurline* had smoothed lifeboat drills to the point that they were less like a riot and more like a carnival funhouse.

During one drill, Riegle brought up an unspoken worry in all our minds. "Fellas, I don't mean to be a spoil-sport, but this here ship ain't got enough lifeboats to carry us all."

"Oh, bullshit," Muskiewicz said. "How do you figure that?"

"Hey, he's right," Svoboda said. "Just take a look around you right now. You think you can shoehorn all the people at this station in this lifeboat? Not nohow."

"That's right," Drexel added. "And besides all of us up here on the top deck, the promenade deck below us still is loaded with even more GIs. This ship is jam-packed. I hear she never carried more than 700 passengers. There's got to be at least a battalion of us on this ship – say 1,400 or 1,500 of us."

One of the boys assigned to the ballroom lifeboat was from San Francisco. He said his uncle was a Matson liner steward and that they usually carried 700 to 750 passengers.

"There, you see?" Riegle said.

Sarge held up a hand. "For God's sake, will you quit your bitching." He pointed out that the ship's sides were practically blanketed with oblong rafts, each with its own cache of food and water plus dye to help aircraft spot us.

"Look over there at the *Indianapolis*. They've got the same rafts on the sides of her turrets and her superstructure. If we do go down," he added, "there's plenty to float on until help arrives. Each raft can support six men in a pinch. They even got paddles."

(It didn't work out that way for the *Indianapolis'* crew in 1945 when a Japanese sub sank her in shark-infested Pacific waters.)

"Okay, Sarge," Pop said, nodding toward the ship's bridge. "So, what say you and I just mosey over to the front porch and tell the captain to keep an eye peeled for Jap submarines."

"Pipe down, Bluto. That's officer country. Those folks don't want enlisted people scuffing their carpets."

# Chapter 6
# Under The Gate

Late on April 22, we felt a brand-new vibration – something more than the ordinary quiet rumble of the ship's machinery.

We were underway at last, headed for the Golden Gate and pointed almost straight into the sunset . . . and they announced we had the honor of being the first U.S. Army division to deploy overseas.

My shipmates and I could have cared less about the honor. We just scrambled topside along with everybody else until humanity clad in olive drab packed the decks shoulder to shoulder.

Pop and Riegle and I wedged ourselves at the rail way forward near the port bow next to one of the ship's gun tubs. One of the crew's Navy party was going blue in the face trying to look nonchalant as he removed the gun's canvas cover.

"Hey, sailor, are those 3-inch guns?" Pop asked.

"Naaaa . . . twin 40 mm. Good for morale and that's about all." He pointed upward. "Might be able to bring down one of them."

A piper cub was passing over us waggling its wings. Meanwhile, a small flotilla of power boats paralleled our course, people waving. Maybe they were even cheering.

One lady – well, you never know in San Francisco but at least at that distance she looked like a woman – opened her jacket, put a hand behind her head and struck a model's hipshot stance.

Everybody on our side of the ship waved, cheered and gave wolf whistles.

"Knock it off, you guys! She's probably a Jap spy."

I thought somebody was joking until Riegle turned around and demanded, "Who says?"

"Me! Pfc. Eric Warner."

"And you think what, Pfc. Warner? She's Tojo's sister?"

Warner was a big bullet-headed bozo with thick shoulders and a single brown wooly eyebrow. In fact, he was the same guy Riegle earlier had in a headlock.

"Before they drafted me," Warner boasted, "I was working as reserve police officer in Wyoming. I was studying to be a detective and keeping up on the FBI's bulletins about all them Jap spies that we sent to the camps."

"Well, whoop de do," Pop said.

"Hey, guys," Riegle yelled, turning his head right and left and then pointing to Warner. "Get a load of our traffic cop! He enrolled in one of them matchbook school sleuthing courses so now Sherlock Holmes here figures the dame out there is a spy. And so what, Officer? You gonna take down the lady's name and address? Shit, the Japs probably already know about us."

Warner flushed bright pink. "Little man, that sounds like disloyal talk. You might want to watch your mouth."

"I'll say what I damn well please, you big ape!"

Svoboda, Hofstra and J.B. stepped between the pair. Pop said, "For Christ's sake, Charlie, settle down! You just talk too damn much for your own good. And Warner, just cool off. Maybe you was a cop, but now you ain't shit! Just another damn GI."

"One of these days I'm gonna pound that little fucker's ass."

Hofstra – who was even taller than Pop -- said, "By heavens, you better bring some help buddy." Then his language shocked all of us. "Otherwise we'll give you a stiff kick in your private parts. And when you recover you'll wind up in the brig."

He and Warner glared at each other even after one of Warner's buddies started to pull him away.

After we got them separated Riegle said, "That bastard reminds me of Alley Oop."

"Yep," I said, "he's a regular troglodyte,"

"A what?"

"You know, Pop, like in them *Alley Oop* Sunday funnies. A troglodyte is a cave man, a cave dweller."

"You tryin' to come on like some kind of interllectual?"

We just then began passing beneath the Golden Gate and I swear every face on the ship turned upward to take in the enormity of the bridge, and how far above us the roadbed was.

"Lord, what a sight," Hofstra said wistfully. "You know right about now I don't think I'd mind changing places with one of those prisoners back there at Alcatraz."

The two little escort vessels – we found out they were British corvettes on loan to the U.S. Navy -- already were well out toward the horizon.

*Lurline* was fourth ship in the convoy. The cool breeze off the ocean became stiff and chilly so that Riegle soon changed places to stand behind Pop and me. We made a pretty good windbreak.

It probably would have been smart to hold lifeboat drills as a way of getting people's minds off the finality of what was happening. Some of the kids probably hadn't been more than 50 miles from home before the draft sent them on their world tour.

But looking to the upper deck, I could see that drill was the last thing in the minds of the officers clustered up there. They peered back at the city as fixedly as the troops. And probably as wistfully. I know I felt a bit choked up and Riegle was wiping his eyes.

He was a long, long way from his folks' Michigan farm -- and getting further every minute.

Likewise, I was leaving Beverly far, far behind.

And it was even money some of us wouldn't come back.

# Chapter 7
# On The Bounding Main

The PA system boomed out that the troops' chow line was open, serving dinner, but the lads seemed more interested taking a last long look at their homeland.

Myself, I was getting hungry.

Now I want to note that I was a fairly experienced sailor, having spent many weekends crewing on sailboats out on Puget Sound. But for the most part, our outfit on the *Lurline* was a battalion of Midwestern landlubbers.

And that brought to mind one of my Dad's favorite stories of his service with the Second Infantry Regiment during Philippine Insurrection. He said that the day they embarked for the Far East, the whole outfit had a big breakfast of beans, cornbread and bacon.

"By the time we was out of that harbor, boy, you couldn't have put a pencil against the side of that ship without it was hit by a load of them beans coming down."

So I had the feeling that as soon as we passed between the Golden Gate's headlands, the ship would start reacting to the big Pacific rollers – and so would its Army passengers. Boy was I right.

Once out to sea, the wind sharpened and the ship's bow started a stately rise and fall. I'd say half of the soldiers ceased looking at the land and bent sharply over the railings.

I won't go into detail except to say the foredeck where we stood amid the cranes and lifting gear became an ungodly mess of cigarette butts and half-digested macaroni.

Soon, two of the ship's crewmen showed up with a high-pressure hose. They didn't actively try to wash any sick soldiers overboard. But, following their orders to flush off the deck, they didn't shift aim for anyone in the way, either. Some of the lads got hit by a hard, salty stream that, temporarily at least, shocked them out of their misery. But only briefly.

# # #

"Hey, Jim, what's the name of this ship again?"

"The *S.S. Lurline*."

"So what does 'S.S.' mean?"

"I think it stands for 'Steam Screw.' Refers to having steam-driven propellers rather than sails."

"Bullshit! 'S.S.' stands for 'Sickness Ship'."

"Okay, Pop, if it makes you feel better."

"It don't."

# # #

Sarge ordered me and Muskiewicz – the three of us unaffected by seasickness -- to accompany him to a meeting of NCOs and the battalion exec. To get to the mess deck which served as his auditorium, we had to weave our way through the five and six-high stacks of racks in the ballroom, already known informally as Stinking Sock Alley.

The major looked a bit green around the edges. Now and then he quavered – or stopped speaking to swallow because of some inner preoccupation. But he pushed on manfully.

"Look, men," the major said, "I know the troops' spaces are foul. But even if the boys are sick, you've got to put them to work to police things up. They won't like it, but it'll get them busy and it will help them get over it."

So we drove those kids to work.

"Now here this! Soldiers man your mops! Get out the buckets and clean up the goddam decks! And quit belly-aching! You don't have to like it -- you just got to do it. So turn to! Now!"

Being mere buck-assed privates, Muskiewicz and I couldn't give Order One to anybody, but Sarge had us set the example and then he bellowed at the other men to get up and get busy ". . . like Mays there, and Musky."

That earned us a several glares of pure hatred.

Like most of the men, Riegle moaned, groaned and pitched in. Uunlike the rest, he kept up a constant chatter. "I'm going to break a bottle of dirty mop water over the bow and rename this ship," he quavered, squeezing out a mop.

"She's going to be the *SS Vomitorium*. And now I'd appreciate some suggestions for names for the other ships."

"Come on, men," I shouted as I swirled those hideous gray mop strings around a multi-colored liquescent horror on the ladder steps. "Let's hear some new ship names."

In the end, our HQ Company clean-up crew rechristened it the Queasy Convoy, consisting of the *S.S. Retch*, the *S.S. Puke* and the Good Ship *Upchuck*.

We didn't presume to rename the *Indianapolis* because it seemed bad luck to demean the vessel that was there to protect us. Besides, it was Regular Navy and probably nobody aboard was sick.

The convoy had one bona fide troopship, the *USAT General Frank M. Coxe*. We renamed it the *USS Spew*.

That left two other Matson Liners to be christened the *S.S. Heave* and *S.S. Nausea*.

# # #

"Hey, Pop! How you doing today?"

"Yesterday I was afraid I'd die."

"Better now?"

"No. Now I'm scared I won't die."

# Chapter 8
# Into The Pacific

The further out we headed, the more seasickness tapered off -- except for a few extreme cases. Corporal Benson being one. Though a stout guardsman and heroic paper-pusher, our Corporal was a gastrointestinal panty waste.

Once topside, he feared returning below because he might start vomiting.

Once below decks, he feared returning topside because he might start vomiting.

And he was right.

We bought him soda crackers from the ship's store, but they couldn't quell his perpetual nausea. "Thanks, boys. I owe you. I do. I admit it. But I can't go -- *burppp* -- up there with ship tilting and rohhk . . . *ulp* . . . rocking like this."

I witnessed several instances of what, in explosives, they call sympathetic detonation. Basically it occurred when one guy would see another becoming sick and, thereupon, lose it himself. But in one case, I think the instigator merited some sort of special nautical decoration – maybe The Order of Neptune, with Paddle.

Now the chow aboard the *Lurline* was superb.

I am not kidding.

The ocean-going version of chipped-beef gravy on toast – known in the military as SOS for Shit on Shingle – was a thousand times better than its land-based Army version.

I'm serious. It was delicate yet savory – superior even to the Hot Roast Beef Sandwich at Pete's Diner back in Seattle. And I genuinely looked forward to it daily.

It seems to me it was the fifth day out that I was pushing my tray along the stainless steel rails in the lunch chow line, having just received my helping of SOS.

I was debating whether to have apple sauce or fruit cocktail for dessert when I caught sight of a young KP in the galley. He was deathly pale, with a vague greenish tinge. His face ran with sweat as he strained with something like a canoe paddle to stir an enormous pot of creamed chip beef.

Well, just then *Lurline* rolled sharply to port, digging into a big ocean swell, deep enough that green seawater roared frighteningly past the mess deck scuttles.

It was too much. The kid convulsed.

He attempted to clap his hand over his mouth.

*Oh no!* I winced, feeling his utter shame and agony as he spewed into the vat. But he recovered quickly, wiping his mouth with his forearm. Darting his eyes around and thinking no one witnessed what happened, he frantically stirred his contribution into the pot's depths.

Three men in line behind me, however, saw it all. You might say they fired a salvo. It was as if the *Indianapolis* had discharged all three turrets at once. They staggered out of the mess hall, leaving half-empty trays behind.

Men further back in the line also began drifting away.

After that, I always checked out the galley personnel before accepting my helping of SOS.

The seasickness epidemic pretty much dried up by the end of our first week, though the after-effects lingered. Suffice it to say that by now we renamed our hold Jockstrap Junction.

# # #

The further we progressed into the tropics, the more I thought about newsreel war films from China and stories about Japanese atrocities. We'd been seeing them off and on since 1937. Jap planes had bombed Shanghai and I'd seen the newsreel films of an abandoned toddler wailing in terror amid the blazing rubble.

The films also showed Jap troops binding POWs to trees and using them for bayonet practice. Likewise, we'd also heard some lurid stories about how they murdered Australian Army nurses.

We didn't know it at the time, but at just about this point in our cruise, U.S. Navy fliers were going head-to-head with Jap pilots in the Battle of the Coral Sea. Years later, I found that the battle took place uncomfortably close to our course. The convoy's skippers may have had an inkling of what was going on. But we were unaware of any danger.

In my case, however, ignorance was not bliss. Pearl Harbor was five months behind us. We were headed for war and I was worried about my own unreadiness for combat.

Sure, I shot Expert with a rifle. Somehow, though, I didn't think that fighting veteran Jap infantry would be anywhere as sedate as firing for record out at the rifle range. Once Pop and Riegle recovered from seasickness and could concentrate, I broached the subject to them.

We both remembered Corporal Benson talking about Sarge having seen combat and being wounded – plus his scorn for National Guard training.

As far as we could tell, none of our officers or even the other NCOs showed any concern at all. Officers, living two to a stateroom on *Lurline*, seemed to treat our voyage like a pleasure cruise featuring duplicate bridge.

Most enlisted men spent the voyage shooting craps.

# Chapter 9
# Floating Classroom

Pop and I cornered Sarge on the promenade deck, asking what we needed to know if we were going to fight and survive this war.

At first, he just shook his head. "Shit, I wouldn't know where to start," he said. "You kids don't know dick about infantry tactics. I just hope for your sakes we get some real training before we meet the Japs."

"So okay, Sarge, can you please clue us in on what's so special about the Japs?"

He gave us a very hard look. "Are you serious about this?"

"Hell, yeah! The more we know and the sooner we know it, the better."

He chewed his lip for a minute. "Okay, look. To start with, a lot of people in the states are contemptuous about the Japanese. But I'm here to tell you the Jap is probably the bravest, toughest, wiliest soldier on earth."

"Tougher than Germans?"

"Well, the German is a hell of a fine soldier. But he's Western, like us. He wants to survive. So if you trap him or surround him, chances are good that he'll raise his hands and yell 'comrade'.

"But the Jap never surrenders. He don't give a damn about his own life."

"No shit?"

"Pop," Sarge said, "a Jap may fear getting killed just like any other human being. But the Jap soldier will die rather than surrender.

He believes Japan has an unconquerable spirit and that he's a living part of it."

"Yamato-damashii," I said.

"That's right," Sarge said. "Those are the words. And I mean he really *believes* it right down to his toes. And what he really fears is that if he surrenders, it will shame his ancestors, his family, his kids and the whole damned nation – from the emperor right down to the janitor.

"You remember in the last war how Sergeant York got almost a whole company of German infantry to surrender? They were pinned down, and he was positioned above them, shooting them one-by-one, just like so many turkeys.

"Well, you might possibly pin down a Jap company, but it *never* will surrender. Never!

"You have to kill every damned one of them."

I'm sure our eyes widened. Sarge's words reminded me what I read in college about Japanese discipline and the lockstep way the Japanese learn and act.

Sarge said, "No kidding. The Jap soldier honest to God thinks it's an honor to die for his Emperor and that it's the ultimate disgrace to his nation if he is captured or surrenders.

"If you trap him, he absolutely will kill himself before he will surrender. If he's wounded and has a grenade, he'll blow himself to bits – and you, too, if you make the mistake of trying to give him first aid."

He paused and lit a cigarette.

"The other thing is that the Jap soldier is tough as a boot. He can endure just about any hardship. As a little kid, he slaves away in the family rice paddy. If he screws up – if he even talks back -- the old man beats the crap out of him.

"Jap army discipline is ferocious. Sergeants can walk up and slap a corporal or a private standing there in ranks – and he'd better stand at attention while it happens. So by the time he's an 18-year-old soldier, he and his buddies pretty can much stand up under cold, heat, filth, pain, rain, thirst or starvation.

"He's stocky and short – I'd say usually 5-2 to 5-5. But he's also strong as an ox and mean as a trapped rat. And he knows his jujitsu – oriental fighting, a real nasty form of boxing mixed with wrestling."

Pop asked, "Well, hell, what about us Americans?"

"Hey, we can be damn fine soldiers. We will be. But it seems in every war, Americans have to learn the hard way. This outfit is a bunch of pussies. They can march and shoot. But they have no goddamn idea at all of what combat is.

"They'll learn . . . the survivors, that is.

"But there'll have to be a killing first."

# # #

That started the first of almost daily conversations with Sarge. We'd all light up and he'd start talking, stilted and uncomfortable at first. But nobody can resist an attentive audience. When we'd question him, he'd relax and speak more freely.

He was a damn fine teacher.

After that first meeting, Pop and I and Riegle went to lean on the railing and stare at the ocean as *Lurline* pitched and rolled through it. We'd spot a school of flying fish tearing through the water and sailing on for maybe 100 yards.

I don't know what was on the other guys' minds. Sometimes I'd dream about Beverly.

I also was fascinated by the big, hook-billed Albatrosses. "Look at those damn things, guys. They got to have a 10-foot wing span and they just soar all day long maybe four or five inches above our bow wave. Maybe just touching a wingtip to the water now and then. But they don't ever need to flap those wings. They just ride the air currents along beside us. Wonder if they'll stay with us the whole way across."

Pop was a fan of terns. Now and then he'd snap a cigarette butt toward one. The bird, looking like a gull who'd grown up on Wheaties, would catch it in mid-air and then drop it in disgust for ordinary gulls' inspection.

As the three of us watched one afternoon, Pop rubbed his palms together. "I don't know, boys. You think maybe old Sarge has gone a bit overboard? He paints a real bad picture."

"Pop, the Japanese paint a pretty bad picture" I replied. "They've been kicking asses all over Asia."

"Yeah," Riegle said. "It looks like they might capture the Philippines any day."

"Yep, and it looks like they're about to go two-for-two because they already beat hell out of one modern western army in its own bastion . . . the British at Singapore.

"Pop, the Jap army has been in combat off and on ever since they occupied Korea back in 1910."

Riegle asked, "What are you talking about? What's Korea?"

So I gave them the benefit of my term paper in Modern Asian Conflict. When I tied it together with the Japs' invasion of eastern China in 1931 and then their 1937 invasion of Manchuria, even Pop started paying more attention.

"Well, there's got to be some way to stop the bastards," he said.

"Yeah," I replied. "And it looks like we're the ones that got the job."

I figured we were the cavalry showing up to save the wagon train.

It didn't work out quite that way.

At this point, we didn't know that some guy we never heard of – a general named Eisenhower -- had ordered the 32nd Division overseas because we were the only formed, half-way trained division available

And at this point, we didn't know two veteran divisions of Aussies already had arrived from Africa and brought the Japs' supposedly unstoppable army to its first screeching halt.

# Chapter 10
# The Big Heat

Sarge said we'd be smart to prepare ourselves for night fighting.

"That's the Japs' specialty, men. They are masters at driving you nuts at night. They harass you by firing off a few machine gun bursts from one position and then another. Then they jabber at you or rattle some cans, throw a grenade or two with those little knee mortars. They've got rifle grenades, too, just like we do.

"The main thing is that they try to keep you on edge and nerved-up.

"And while they've got you all hot and bothered about what's going on," he said, "two or three Japs might snake under your own barbed wire right into your position. Or he flanks you so that when he attacks, he's shooting you from behind – or maybe slitting your throat with one of them razor-sharp knives.

"And even if he don't attack, he creates constant commotion. At night in China," Sarge added, "the Japs could spook our troops so badly that a whole damn platoon would sometimes run off into the dark. Then you'd hear the Japs giggling and yelling 'Banzai!'

"Anyway, by the time it's dawn, you're so whipped you can hardly keep your eyes open.

"That's when the snipers start. You're just relaxing when you hear a thud behind you and your buddy has taken a bullet in the face."

### # # #

Pop called our sessions chalk talks, as in football practice. He and Riegle agreed with me that they were scary.

After Sarge dismissed us from one of his talks, we'd just go mull it over while doing the only thing that there was to do – find a place along the railings, lean on same and watch the ocean go by.

Oh, it was a relaxing pastime, feeling the roll of the ship and watching wavelets forming on the shoulders of our own bow wave. I could lose myself and my worries in watching the moving water change color – white foam, gajillions of bubbles and the deep gray-green inside the wave somehow transforming itself to dark blue – and all of it becoming a hard silver out toward the horizon.

Now and again we'd catch sight of a big ray soaring out of the water and doing a belly flop. The three of us would look at each other and grin. "Boy, I bet that stings!"

# # #

The little sub-hunting corvettes usually were almost to the horizon.

Once I saw a very young-looking naval officer making his way down a corridor and asked how the heck corvettes could protect us from subs when they were so far away.

He seemed impatient. "I can't tell you now. I'm in a rush. But I'll get back to you."

As he sped down a ladder, I heard a snicker behind me. It was Traffic Cop Warner. "Hey, looky here! It's Big Jimmy Mays the brown-noser, kissing up to an officer!"

Warner seemed to love giving the needle to everybody. I just stared at him until his grin died. He glowered and said, "Did that hurt your tender feelings, little Jimmy Brown Nose? You want to make something of it, Jimmy?" He raised his fists and rolled his shoulders.

I grinned. "Nahh, I don't think so, Warner. Not since I heard that you like to play Drop The Soap in the showers."

His face knotted and he shuffled toward me, dukes up and starting to bob and weave.

Like lightning, I reached out and grabbed his nose, pinching it hard between thumb and forefinger. Holding tight, I gave it a hard twist, too.

Warmer's ham-sized fists opened into a suppliant gesture. It made him look like one of those old museum paintings of saints at prayer – except he had no halo.

"Ahhh! Ahhh! Ahhhh!" he said, carefully turning his head with my grip.

Looking on and laughing, Riegle said, "Warner, you gonna be a nice boy, now? Or do you want old Jim here to keep twisting your schnozzola? He could make you look like Jimmy Durante. You know? 'Good night Mrs. Calabash, wherever you are.' Or he could just hit your nose like Moe does to Curly? *Boop! Boop!* How would you like that?"

I couldn't help it. Riegle's Jimmy Durante taunt made me start laughing.

"Ahhhh! Ahhh!," Warner said. "Okay, buddy! I'm sorry. Stop it, okay?"

"Buddy?" Pop said. "So you want to be Jim's buddy now? You mean that, Warner?"

"Ahhhh! Yeah! Yeah! I do. *Ahhhh! Ahhhh!* I'm really sorry! I really am. Please!"

I gave another hard twist and let go. Warner clapped his hands to his nose, trying to staunch the blood streaming down his lips and chin.

"Okay, Alley Oop," Pop said as we headed back out to the deck, "just lay off or the next time he's really going to hurt you."

Out on deck Pop asked, "Great trick. Where'd you learn it?"

"One of our coaches used it on a guy who thought he was real tough."

Two or three hours later, the officer – a Navy ensign – came walking along the promenade deck and spotted me. He astounded me by apologizing for rushing off. He'd been working on a problem pump in the ship's evaporation plant that produced fresh water, and that just wouldn't wait, would it?

Then he said corvettes had listening devices that could detect submarines. "They're steaming out there, say 6,000 to 10,000 yards from us, because that's where Jap subs would be is they were planning to attack us."

I'd read something about sonar months before and I asked if the devices were called hydrophones.

"I can't go into that," he said.

"Why, sir? It's a secret?"

He glanced around furtively. "No," he whispered with a big smile. "Because I don't know a damned thing about it."

As the ensign took off, Riegle said, "Well, how 'bout that? An officer who's also a human being."

"Ah, give him a year," J.B. said. "By the time they make him a lieutenant, he'll be just like the rest."

# Chapter 11
# . . . And More Training

Actually, some of the officers were quite decent.

A Lieutenant Woodsen in Heavy Weapons Company was a very pleasant guy. He gave us our first lecture about Japanese firearms – the tip-off, as if we needed one, that sometime soon we'd fight Japs.

He told us that the Japs had two main rifles named Arisaka – first, an old one being .25 caliber. That provoked some snickers from his audience.

"Now, men," he said, "don't pooh-pooh the Japs' .25 caliber. First of all, it's a hell of a lot more powerful than that little .22 you used at home to plink away at tin cans.

"Your .22 bullet weighs 40 grains and that puny little charge fires it off at maybe 800 feet per second. Technically, it could kill you if it hit the right place. But not likely.

"However the Japs' .25 caliber bullet – it's a 6.5 mm – is a whole 'nother story. It's a very long, narrow bullet with a very high ballistic coefficient. It travels at 2,500 feet per second. And let me tell you, men, it weighs 139 grains and if it hits you it's more like a 250-pound impact..

"And boys, if it hits square on it will go right through your steel helmet."

The snickers stopped.

"I see I've got your attention now," Woodsen went on. "The .25 caliber Arisaka is a particularly efficient weapon for snipers. For one thing, its report isn't much louder than a fire-cracker, so when machine guns and mortars are raising hell it's hard to tell where the sniper is."

He went on to describe the bigger 7.7 mm main infantry rifle, firing a bullet about the same as our M-1.

"Both Arisaka rifles are rather clunky, but they're extremely sturdy and capable of great accuracy. Their big drawback is that they're bolt action and can't fire as fast as your M-1."

Then he got into their machine guns – the Nambus, both light and heavy, with cooling fins on the barrels so that they could fire all day.

"The Japs call them 'Jukis.' It's their nickname. They're pretty good guns except that in real action with all kinds of dust and debris flying around, they tend to jam. That's because the Japs oil their cartridges so that all kinds of dust and dirt and crap adheres to them and gets into the gun's action.

"We hear Jap troops bitch a lot about the Nambu," he added, "but their generals don't seem to care because they can always order a banzai charge so they can get in close and fight hand-to-hand."

He discussed the Japs' mortars which were much like ours except for the little 50 MM mortar, actually kind of a grenade launcher nick-named the knee mortar.

"Fellas, if you happen to capture a knee mortar, for God's sake don't perch it on your knee to fire it back. It's absolutely not designed to be fired from the knee. In fact, the kick probably would shatter your knee."

On the whole, most of us stayed focused very intensely on what he had to tell us because we had just learned that General Wainright finally had been forced to surrender U.S. Army and Philippine forces to the Japs.

Afterwards, Sarge said the lieutenant failed to tell us – if, in fact, he even knew it -- that Japanese machine gun bullets were about 30 per cent heavier than ours.

"So the Nambu -- the Juki -- has a fairly slow rate of fire that makes it sound a bit like a woodpecker. But because the bullets are so heavy, they are lethal at a longer range and the wounds they produce can be even more damaging.

"Something else that the lieutenant didn't go into enough," Sarge said. "He mentioned snipers.

"Well, I'm here to tell you that the Japs use a lot of them and their snipers always try to hide in a high place. Now it's not natural for humans to look up – but when you're facing the Jap, you've *got* to look upward *all* the time.

"Spot the bastard and shoot his ass out of his third story window, or his tree, or his cliff, before he shoots you."

# # #

The further southwest the Queasy Convoy pushed, the hotter and more humid the weather became.

Topside was tolerable because the ship's speed usually caused a breeze of 15 or 20 knots across the deck.

But the breeze couldn't get below decks at all, especially since steel deadlights were welded over all the portholes. Life below decks was wet – thanks to condensation on the steel walls -- sweaty, odorous, boring tedium.

A lot of the men dealt with life aboard the slow boat to China by playing marathon crap games.

Except that after a time they announced we weren't headed to China. We were destined for Australia, everybody found that exciting -- though for all sorts of different reasons, the main one being that we actually had a destination.

In Pop's case it was different.

He heard that Aussie men refer to their women as Sheilas. You could say that the nickname gave Pop the itch. Less than three months earlier he'd been dating cheerleaders. Some of them, he bragged, would go all the way.

"If I'd been a fullback," he once mourned, "I bet I woulda had to beat 'em off with a stick. Even so, it was great. You always could at least cop a feel."

At that point in his monologue, he would sag and rub his buzz cut.

"But then the Japs had to bomb Pearl Harbor and I had to go get all patriotic and volunteer for the Army . . . and I don't think I've even *seen* a girl since then . . . except for a WAC or two. And they were ugly. I'm sure looking forward to making it with some of that Sheila stuff."

I'm certain that in his fevered brain – no doubt fertile with memories of *Sheena of the Jungle* comic books -- the word "Shiela" provoked visions of generously-stacked round-heeled females in leopard-skin bathing suits swinging from vines or perching on jungle limbs and crooking a red fingernail at him.

I admit that even with Beverly in mind, the thought of Sheilas excited me, too.

But then so did the notion of seeing another country and maybe even getting to watch kangaroos or Koala bears.

Some days we'd have a mandatory formation where an officer – probably just as horny as us -- would give us a cultural orientation.

"Now men, to most of us, Aussies have an accent that sounds English. But it isn't a true English accent and, for cripes sake, don't tell 'em that they sound English. They tend to resent the English even though they're proud to be part of the British Empire and they've been fighting like tigers against Rommel in North Africa. They're very, very tough troops. So don't insult them."

He said we'd find some phrases difficult to grasp, but that the Aussies liked us and wouldn't mind at all if we asked them to explain.

# Chapter 12
# The Doldrums

By our twelfth day out, the novelty of being on a voyage had worn off. And it just got worse.

Unfortunately, our course took us into a following wind. So with us traveling at 14 knots or so, no air at all moved over the decks. And what made it really bad was that the stack gasses curled down around us from the funnels in a yellowish pall – our own choking fog keeping pace with us.

At least the convoy was zig-zagging so that sometimes a change of direction would cause the cloud to kind of flow off one side, but never for long.

Not surprisingly, the *Lurline* became utterly rank below decks. We debated whether the ship ever could be suitable for ritzy passengers again.

"When the war's over," Drexel said, "they're just going to have to hose this baby out."

"Hose her out, hell," Riegle said. "They'll have sink her and they'll have to do it far, far away from land."

"Why?"

"Well, think about it, you jerk. So the bubbles rising from it don't blow across the beach and stink up the land with BO from the 32nd Division."

The ship had internal blowers which at least stirred the air a bit. But it was still stifling below decks. And we only got to shower in three-day relays because the ship's evaporation plant was too small to provide for so many passengers plus 250 crewmen.

And the showers almost weren't worth it because you had to stand in line for a couple of hours.

The crowding was so bad, we also had lines for the latrines, lines to get on deck and, now that seasickness was over, long, long lines for chow.

We all were ready for our cruise to end.

But it still was good just to lean on the railing and watch the ocean. Often times, at night we'd stay topside and try to find a place to sleep up on deck. Some of us also were assigned guard duty topside along with the sailors to make sure nobody was lighting cigarettes.

If you just had to have a cigarette, you went into an interior passageway and smoked there. Sometimes the tobacco smoke in the passages got so thick it was like inhaling with your nose in an ashtray.

On clear nights, I'd sometimes go topside and find a place to just lie back on the foredeck and watch the unbelievably brilliant stars. When the moon was down, the stars and the Milky Way seemed to create almost enough illumination to read.

When I was in the Boy Scouts, I earned Astronomy merit badge so that I still recognized lots of constellations – Draco, Cassiopeia, Orion and so on. Everybody knew the Big Dipper, of course – *Ursa Major* – and it added to my homesickness to watch it gradually edge toward the northern horizon.

The other neat things about spending the night on deck was seeing the incredibly bright phosphorescence in the water.

The *Lurline's* wake formed a glowing arrow right from the horizon behind us. At first I thought it was the reflection of the Milky Way, but the crew said a lot of glow worm-type critters lived in the sea and were lit up by the passage of ships.

And then some nights we'd get St. Elmo's fire. It looked just like dim flamed playing around the ends or radio antennas or the ship's cranes.

I kept thinking how much Beverly would enjoy the sight. Maybe if we beat the Japs by 1950 or so, I could use my back pay to take her on a real cruise.

Instead of standing and griping with a bunch of foul-mouthed soldiers, I could lean on the rail holding my arm around her.

# # #

Sarge again and again stressed, three rules in combatting the Japanese:

First, don't let the Japs smell you before they hear you.

Second, don't let the Japs hear you before they see you.

Third, never let the Japs see you.

"And now finally, men," he kept saying, "never ever forget old Sarge's Fourth Rule of Nightime Operations -- 'The night can be your friend'."

I don't know how many times he told us, "You got to learn to love the dark. Remember that. It can save your ass. When you move carefully in the dark, the Japs can't see you. And if you learn to move right, then they can't hear you, either.

"But, believe me, if you just sniffle or sneeze or clear your throat, they sure as shit can hear you. So you must stay very quiet.

"And you must trust your peripheral vision."

"Your what?"

"Men, it's like this -- in the dark, don't never look straight *at* things. Darkness plays tricks on direct vision. You get so you see things that ain't there. So, instead you stay alert and look slightly away so then you spot can motion for real out of the corners of your eyes."

Several of us took his words to heart and tried to train our night vision.

At night down in the hold, Pop would try to sneak up on me over the pile of duffle bags. I'd carefully and quietly move off in a corner or slide backward between the wheels of a howitzer and look to one side.

By damn, it worked! You *could* catch motion out of the corner of your eye. So then I'd try sneaking up on Pop. Pretty soon he and Riegle and I got Hofstra and J.B. to work with us.

We attempted to involve some other guys, but they always wanted to shoot craps or play poker.

One night, Hofstra – who really got good at the stealthy approach – pulled a hell of a trick.

. Thanks to the gamblers' focus on the dice, he managed to creep up behind Drexel and Svoboda and filch their winnings and then eel away from them in the dark.

Minutes later, Drexel and Svoboda started accusing the other players and the game broke up in a hell of a fight.

We crowed about it next morning when Hofstra returned the money, thinking it would make believers out of both. But they were still fried about what they said was a kid-stuff prank.

"Okay, you silly ignoramuses," Hofstra said. "You'll be sorry. Next time, I shall keep the money and send it home to Holland."

"Why would you send it to Holland? You're from Michigan."

"I'm referring to a Michigan town named Holland, you dummy."

# Chapter 13
# The Southern Cross

"So, Sarge, if we're attacking Japs," I asked, "just what do we do? I mean, do we just start walking toward them?"

Sarge said, "Mays, to attack you advance toward your objective, whatever it is. Period. Now there are things you do while advancing to protect yourself and we'll get into that.

"But the point is that whether you're walking or running or crawling, you assault by keep going until you find the enemy – and usually he spots you first and starts shooting."

"Well," I asked, "so can't we shell their positions first and kill them?"

"Sure we'll shell them. But as you'll find out, the earth is big place and guys who dig in make themselves very small. They hunker down in foxholes – or maybe in bunkers. So, yeah, we shell them. Or maybe we can even get planes to bomb them. But if they're in bunkers, boys, that don't do anything but make their ears ring.

"And," he added, "it really pisses them off."

# # #

I sometimes came away from our talks in a pretty blue mood. Pop and Riegle and J.B. and I would just go back to leaning there on the goddam railing, smoking, sweating and looking at the goddam ocean some more. It became boring but somehow seeing the waves seemed to help . . . at least it helped me. The waves and our crazy gang of dolphins diving and playing around the bow -- they didn't make me forget what we faced, but it helped me stow it in the back of my mind for a while.

A couple of times, I had to go off and be by myself – not easy on a crammed ship. But I found a lifting gear motor on the foredeck with a right angle in its housing. I could wedge myself in there.

I'd think about Beverly. Or sometimes, I'd dredge up memories of my few good football plays. My favorite was when the opposing quarterback threw to an end who was right next to me. He had to jump high to make the catch so all I had to do was upend him by grabbing his ankles and raising them to my shoulders. He came down hard – so hard that the impact jarred the ball out of his hands.

But the thing I always remembered was his left eye. I spotted it as I grabbed his ankles. It was wide with the realization he was about to wish he'd never been born. An instant later I heard the pop as he landed with his entire weight on his hand, either breaking his wrist or ripping its tendons. The defensive coach slapped me on the back and gave me an "attaboy."

The other memory that kept resurfacing was of my last meeting with Beverly. Bev was blondish and kind of plain – except when she smiled. Her smile just lit up the world. It was honest-to-God gorgeous, with luscious curves – curves that her slender figure almost matched. We went to a few movies together and kissed, but that was as far as she would go.

And I didn't try to push it, either. I'd heard all kinds of guys brag about getting girls to go all the way. But the thought of getting a girl pregnant – and I'd heard those stories, too – just flat terrified me. It would destroy our reputations and ruin both our lives.

Tears ran down Beverly's cheeks when I left for Basic -- the last time I saw her. She threw her arms around my neck and gave me the hottest kiss I'd ever had. Then, through her tears, she somehow managed to give me that smile as she demanded that I write to her.

All through Basic I did just that. And I prized the letters she sent me. I kept them in my duffle bag and the most recent one in my hip pocket. I read them often – really I had almost memorized them. Each still had a blessed hint of her perfume. We hadn't been in love, I don't think. But the further we steamed away from San Francisco, the more steamed I became about her. I guess she was someone wonderful to cling to.

I dreamt about her, of course. But sometimes -- thinking about Sarge's lectures -- sleep was impossible. I sometimes wondered if it wouldn't be better to just go into battle green and get wounded or killed right off the bat.

When I couldn't sleep because of those thoughts or the heat and the smell in the hold, it was diverting to go back on deck. The Southern Cross now was well in view with the Big Dipper hardly visible on the north horizon and the North Star disappeared entirely. I had asked the Navy Ensign how to find the Southern Cross.

He showed me a star chart and pointed it out. As we talked I sensed a fellow enthusiast and mentioned having the Boy Scout merit badge. It turned out he was a fellow Eagle Scout and a college football player, too  . . . varsity. We didn't go beyond that point because it's smart for enlisted people to maintain distance from officers – and I bet officers are told to keep their distance, too.

But it was refreshing to have at least a friendly acquaintance on the other side of the rank barrier.

# Chapter 14
# Crossing The Line

"Now hear this! Now hear this! This vessel is crossing the equator at 1100 hours at which time it will be boarded by the Emperor of the Deep, Neptune the Supreme, Ruler of the Waves.

"His majesty and his court, including his infant son, will examine and test the worthiness of those newcomers presuming to venture into his realm."

I'd read about disgusting tricks Neptune might pull – shaving you with a big wooden razor after lathering your mug with crank case sludge, or rotten eggs. And you had to kiss Neptune's disgusting 250-pound baby.

They rigged the court on the fore deck. My ensign friend was one of the initiates chosen to get the full treatment from Neptune, a fat petty officer wearing a mop for a wig and another one for a beard, and carrying a gigantic pipe wrench as a scepter.

Neptune told his court to thoroughly bathe several young officers, the ensign included, in a big canvas tub containing what looked either like very old chip beef gravy, or maybe detritus from the seasickness epidemic.

The ensign meekly walked to the bath, but then tripped two of the courtiers into it. His fellow initiates joined in and everyone but Neptune himself got a horrible bath amid roars of spectator laughter.

Of course, they couldn't hold a separate initiation for all 1,500 ground-pounders. But they had rigged hoses at most fire points and gave hard seawater showers to as many of us as possible.

This ceremony converted us to shellbacks from pollywogs. Dried saltwater certainly made you feel like you had a shell. Our new status also guaranteed a permanent welcome to visit Neptune's realm, likewise authorizing us to hold similar ceremonies in the future for other pollywogs.

Muskiewicz spoke for all of us when he said he was eager to be back on dry land and would rather not visit the deeps, welcome or not.

After all the excitement Riegle's sense of humor deserted him. In fact, he spoiled our mood when he suddenly was smitten with deep-seated homesickness. He blamed Traffic Cop Warner.

"When I called the bastard Alley Oop it reminded me of reading the papers after Sunday supper. Sis always tried to get the funnies first to read *Nancy*, for cripes sake!"

"Aw, you talk such crap, Riegle."

"Hey guys, I don't have much diversion. I can't play poker or shoot craps. Can't afford it because I'm having a big pay allotment sent to Mom and Dad so they can save it for me."

"Putting it in the bank?"

"*Hell* no! My family don't trust bankers after what those glassy-eyed sonsabitches did to us in the Depression.

"But what I really miss is the Sunday funnies. *Alley Oop*, of course. But I enjoyed keeping up with *Dagwood and Blondie*. And I always thought the *Katzenjammer Kids* were a screech.

"Yeah, I miss the funnies, too," Pop said. "My favorites were *Dick Tracey* and *Terry and the Pirates*."

"Jesus, Pop," I said, "isn't that pretty low-brow stuff?"

"Well so what if it is?" Riegle said.

"Funnies are part of my Sunday memories. It was the one day we'd all spend together trying to take it easy. Relax with the papers. Might not be too tired to listen to baseball on the radio."

He stared into space with a tear running down beside his nose.

Trying to soothe his mood, I asked, "So, anyway, who's your favorite character in *Alley Oop*?"

He grinned, "Oh I don't know, Jim. Dr. Onemug, maybe."

"Do you know who Dr. Onemug is supposed to be?"

"Who?"

"Onemug is the scientist Albert Einstein, the refugee from Nazi Germany. You know. Theory of Relativity and all that sort of thing."

"Who?"

"Einstein – that's the German work for 'one mug'."

"So who's Einstein?"

"Oh, shit. Just forget it. By the way, I hear there's a guy up in Stinking Sock Alley who has a *Batman and Robin* comic book that he rents out."

"Hot damn! What's his name?"

# Chapter 15
# The Cavalry Arrives

The Stinky Fleet bearing the odorous Red Arrow Division spotted land May 14 and the next day docked at Adelaide way on the south coast of Australia.

I think we all pictured wading through the surf into a desert loaded with kangaroos and scrawny black aborigines throwing spears and boomerangs at us.

So the sights – and, above all, the fabulous welcome -- were a startling surprise.

As the tugs maneuvered *Lurline* to the dock we found ourselves looking upon a big, beautiful city. Towering palm trees and dozens of church steeples gave it a jagged skyline squared-off by modern office buildings. On our way to our mooring, we also saw massive cranes dangling huge steel frames above a modern ship yard.

Far in the background we could make out the blue blur of mountains. No desert here.

But as sailors and dock workers tied us up, everybody forgot the mountains and churches.

We couldn't believe our eyes.

Instead of aborigines and kangaroos, the dockyard opposite our ship was jammed with maybe a thousand beautiful screaming, waving women . . . young women, gorgeous, curved blond and brunette and red-headed women jumping up and down and screaming and waving, their breasts jiggling so sweetly under their blouses. Maybe they thought we were the cavalry come to protect them from the savages.

"Holy crap," said J.B. looking down and waving back, "this makes me feel like I'm Tommy Dorsey playing in a giant nightclub."

But did we get to meet or talk with the Sheilas on the dock?

*Hell* no!

Not then, anyway.

We'd been 23 days at sea after eight damned long weeks of basic training – all with nothing but strictly male company. And our dirty bastard commanders marched us right past those luscious, smiling ladies with beautiful high-pitched voices who blew kisses and threw flowers to us.

Yessir, the damned officers put us on trains, very, very slow trains to army camps.

So First Battalion was a glum bunch that arrived after dark, still staggering with our sea legs, at a wide place in the road called Sandy Creek. They marched us and the rest of the 126th off the main drag to our camp – named Camp Sandy Creek, of course.

The 127th and 128th were sent 30 miles further to yet another camp.

We broke up into squads in the dark – black-outs were in force even though the nearest Jap was a continent away -- and groped our way into what seemed like some rickety, over-ventilated buildings. We found racks with crackly mattresses and hit the sack. For a change, at least we weren't sweating. In fact, it was so chilly, most of us dug into our duffle bags for our blankets.

# # #

If our arrival at camp was a bit of a comedown, dawn was fairly rude awakening.

First light revealed our huts to be air-conditioned corrugated steel structures with canvas roofs. The air conditioning was the foot of open space between the roofs and the walls. Perching in the rafters were sparrows and assorted other fowl. Our morning stirrings in their home caused them to squawk and fly off in panic, leaving some fairly generous deposits on us and our blankets.

Before we could even start a good grousing session, however, we were ordered outside in platoon formations. Each received a brief lecture. Our particular speaker was a leathery old Aussie corporal with a gaunt face and a jarring voice.

"Welcome mites! Glad to have yer heeh Down Under. Now, before you Yanks settle in, Oi want to warn you about a rahther large dynger – the Australian brown snike. He's a . . ."

Sarge interrupted. "Excuse me, Corporal. We're new to your accent. By 'snike,' you mean 'snake'? And 'dynger' is 'danger'?"

"Sorry, mate. You'll all learn proper English soon, Oi'm quite sure. But thet's roight on both counts. The brown snike – pardon me, the brown *snake* – is reputed to be the second most venomous on earth. He's quite a grumpy brute noted as being very short-tempered, indeed. And he's often found hangin' about farm buildings or any other plice, such as these loovely huts you're occupyin', where one loikely foinds birds or small rodents which is their mayne source of food."

He told us that the snake could be three to six feet long and not necessarily brown. "Whilst he's usually a uniform shayde of brown, he also can have speckles or bands, and can raynge from a tan to black, and orange, silver, yellow and gray."

Riegle said, "Well, shit, corporal, then it might not really be brown even though it's called Brown. Sounds like we'd better steer clear of all snakes."

"That's the ticket, mate. Especially at night. If you step out to use the necessary, Oi very strongly advise that you refrain from gaoin' about barefoot."

"Well, what if one of us gets bit?"

"Moi advoice would be to assume the supine position. Then put your hands together, steeple your fingers in a prayer-loik manner and employ your last precious minutes to moike your peace with God."

"Uh, what's the 'supine position'?"

"Tits up, son. Now, if you have no further questions, Oi'd best be off to warn your cobbers!"

We returned to our alleged barrack to learn that the mattresses on our racks were burlap ticking crammed with straw. Not at all what we'd had even in basic, and just about as soft and yielding as the plywood deck in the *Lurline's* hold.

As we got to know Camp Sandy Creek, we found it primitive in other ways. We shaved and showered in cold water, for instance. We had to share the showers with monster cockroaches. Some of the guys claimed the roaches gave menacing hisses when approached from the rear and were known to attack when wounded by careless heels or toes.

Now the mess halls had bread slicers just as our mess halls did back at Fort Ord.

The Australian version, however, produced slices of irregular width. Some slices would be almost thin enough to let light through while a neighboring slice might be two inches thick. The device's tolerances were so sloppy that on the next loaf, you'd get an entirely different slicing pattern.

The main concern, though, was that the guy feeding the loaves into the slicer had to be as careful as if he were working with a band saw in a furniture factory.

# # #

"Honest to God, Doc, that damned bread slicer like to took off my finger."

"Relax, Pvt. Riegle, you're not going to lose your finger. You'll be fine. Just keep a clean bandage on it. Next week I'll remove the stiches. When you run that machine again, I'd recommend using a stick to feed the loaf into it."

"No shit, Doc! I already figured that one out for myself."

# Chapter 16
# Down Under

In one respect, Sandy Creek pleased us. It had a tiny hotel – the Sandy Creek Hotel, in fact -- and that hotel had a tiny bar and that bar served beer.

Oh, it wasn't cold beer. And it was a bit flat compared to the Pabst that GIs from Wisconsin and Michigan were accustomed to guzzling.

But it did have a very nice, mellow flavor and, most important, it contained alcohol. Overnight, thirsting GIs drained the Sandy Creek Hotel dry, causing considerable consternation and grumbling among the firm's civilian patrons.

No other pubs, after all, existed in Sandy Creeks at the time

Fortunately, the hotel's management and the regimental motor pool teamed up to arrange regular beer runs to The Source, Adelaide. After that, the hotel provided all the beer that local residents and the 126th could consume together, plus all the outfits that arrived after we left.

The HQ motor pool always had loads of volunteers for the runs to Adelaide. That lovely city had both beer and, of course, Shielas, most of whom seemed entranced with American soldiers.

Granted, American submariners already had been welcomed – and warmly -- in Adelaide. But there just weren't that many of them.

And like them, we for the most part were good-looking, straight-backed, muscular kids in the prime of life who, moreover, spoke a vaguely similar language that, with some effort, the natives could understand.

Moreover, the few Aussie men in Adelaide couldn't be called competition. They either were well past middle age or were missing legs or arms thanks to combat.

What's more, unlike our veteran Aussie comrades, we weren't tortured – at least not at this point – by nightmares and daytime visions of our friends and comrades being shredded by mines or torn apart by artillery fire.

We had one other very unfair advantage. Our pay was far higher than the Aussies'.

As best we could calculate, an Aussie private received about $15 a month compared to $60 for us – which sum included $10 overseas pay. And in that day, you could enjoy some very decent dining for $2.

Pop and I once got a weekend pass combined with the assigned to make the beer run into Adelaide.

I stuck one of Beverly's letters in my hip pocket to keep me on the straight and narrow.

Didn't work.

I no sooner alighted from the truck than a gorgeous little red-head seized my arm in both of hers. She pressed her breasts to my arm and said I was a beaut. Then she proceeded to utter a sentence that I absolutely didn't grasp.

She and a very tall girl who latched onto Pop hauled us to a restaurant. They assured us that it wasn't "exy" which the girls said meant "not expensive." We could have cared less.

We spent a fine meal, a good many drinks and two hilarious hours trying to master each other's slang.

For instance, my little Shiela was called a "bluie." And that's because she had red hair. Strewth – that means "it's the truth," and no mistake, mate, and I don't know why.

I'm still trying to figure out "bonzer cove," which both Pop and I apparently happened to be. We guessed it was a flattering term.

We split up, going to the girls' places with the understanding that we had to be back no later than noon the next day.

We barely made it.

# # #

Once we encamped at Sandy Creek, our officers and NCOs had us hiking with full packs to tone us up after three weeks of leaning on railings at sea. We also started spending a lot of ammo at the range.

We who were new to the regiment at last got to load and fire machine guns. "You didn't listen, dammit! After you load a belt of ammo, you got to cock the machine gun twice!"

They drilled us in disassembling and cleaning those weapons – far more parts involved than in the M-1, including having the critical nuisance of headspace adjustments for the 1919 .30 caliber Browning machine guns.

They also taught us the care and feeding of the Tommy gun and the BAR.

Firing the Tommy gun was thrilling but a bit odd. In gangster movies it has all that flash and blast. But it's heavy as hell, so it dampens its own recoil to a mild seesawing of butt and barrel.

And while I liked the M-1, I loved the BAR. With that long barrel, you could really nail distant targets.

Funny, though, when you had it on a bi-pod, the recoil wanted to pull it forward away from you.

Unfortunately, the Army failed to supply us with the weapon that would have been most handy in the jungle -- the carbine, short, light, easy to handle and terrific for up-close work.

Much later, the Ordnance wallahs (Aussie for "fellows") showed us that with a small spring and some diligent filing, the carbine could be made into a very light machine gun that could fill a Jap bunker with 30 ricocheting bullets in about half a second.

Unfortunately, we didn't get carbines until after we began training for the Philippines . . . far too late for far too many GIs.

Sarge did his best by us.

Though we were only headquarters punks, he gave us lots of very practical instructions not only about digging in but also learning to recognize even the gentlest fold in the earth as good cover.

But we could tell he still was worried. He'd talked to some Aussies who believed we were going to an island named New Guinea which was all swamp and jungle.

# # #

After a 25-mile march, Pop and Riegle and I were taking off our packs and sweat-soaked shirts. Corporal Benson popped his head into the hut. "You men, get your duffel bags packed. We've got movement orders."

"Where we headed?"

"To a brand new training camp."

"Whereabouts is it?"

"Well, boys, General Harding hasn't gotten around to telling me which one yet. So, dammit, just get your duffle bags packed and hustle around and let everyone else know."

He gave a big grin as he started to walk out the door. "Oh, and I know you'll to love this. The old man gave orders to leave this camp in better shape than we found it."

"Well, that's easy," Drexel said. "All we got to do is step outside and shake the bird shit off our blankets."

# Chapter 17
# Moving North

Boarding the trains in Adelaide started a long, frustrating haul. Transferring 11,000 GIs to Brisbane – actually to Camp Tambourine about 30 miles south of Brisbane – grossly overloaded the Australian railways.

Some of the troops had to file back aboard Liberty ships and go to sea again.

The rest of us learned that the Australian trains not only were old and slow – running maybe 25 m.p.h. going downhill with the throttle wide-open -- but they also had differing track gauges from state to state.

This meant that over our 1,500-mile route – about the same as traveling half-way across the USA -- we had to get off our train at each new state, unload our gear, march across the state line to a new rail yard and wait for an empty train, load up again, and so forth.

It wasn't until then that I started to realize how huge Australia is. If you considered Adelaide to be analogous to New Orleans, then Sydney might be in somewhere around Mobile, and Brisbane near Richmond with Townsville being New York City.

The 127th and 128th Regiments only had to transfer twice – first where South Australia borders New South Wales and then again at Queensland, the state in which Brisbane, our destination lay.

Those of us comprising the bulk of the 126th Regiment ended up transferring three times – first from South Australia to Victoria, then Victoria to New South Wales and then New South Wales to Queensland.

As we waited for more rolling stock in New South Wales, Riegle started badgering an aged station master about why Australia's rail gauges were all different. The old boy enjoyed giving us a history lesson.

"You see, mate, the various stites heeh all started with quite different kinds of governments. Some was crown colonies and some was just prisons for felons what stole a loaf of bread in London. Any roads, they was the whole bloody continent apart from each other. Perth was in a different universe from Sydney. They had very little contact and nothing to do with each other, really.

"So when they started building rail lines, some got their steam locomotives and carriages from Mother Bloody England via South Africa. Others bought them from Japan and some from the US. They was all different, you see. There's bean a lot of noise about having standard tracks and carriages, but the stites can't agree about who's going to chuck all their own rolling stock costing millions of pounds in favor of the other stites. It's bean just too bloody expensive, you see."

When we at last arrived at Camp Tambourine we made two unpleasant discoveries.

First, a Jap submarine had torpedoed one of the Liberty ships, costing us our first casualty, Private Gerald Cable. Our commander, General Harding, renamed Camp Tambourine in Cable's honor; nice gesture, but not much help to Gerry Cable or his folks.

(It made me wonder if each time one of us got killed the old man would name something in our memories. Maybe Beverly could come to Australia to deposit some flowers at the Pfc. Jim Mays Memorial Boat Dock or the Pvt. Anthony Pavalovski Memorial Outhouse.)

The other discovery was that Camp Cable wasn't a camp -- just a nice semi-tropical stretch of land on Australia's east coast. So, instead of training at Camp Cable, we *built* Camp Cable, complete with its regimental tent cities, wells and water systems, latrines, showers, motor pools, mess halls, offices, firing ranges and all the rest of it . . . right down to painting rocks white to line the walkways into each headquarters tent.

I suppose wielding shovels and pickaxes and learning to mix and pour concrete -- and to paint rocks -- was beneficial physically, but it depressed the Sarge.

I heard him griping about it to another NCO.

"This is bad, goddammit. *Real* bad! Instead of construction work or standing guard on the damn beach, we should be running these kids through night maneuvers and infiltration.

"We also ought to hold live fire exercises. Not one of these new draftees has heard a bullet crack overhead."

His buddy, a first sergeant, replied, "Well, Danny, if the fucking officers don't give a rat's ass and the old man can't wake them up – and especially if there's no time allowed for training -- what are you going to do?"

"I guess at least I'm going to try training my boys on my own."

"Well, don't let the powers that be know about it."

Sarge asked for volunteers for a completely unauthorized special training and I was the first one with my hand up.

# Chapter 18
# Part-Time Training

We wound up with two squads from HQ Company – a dozen men each – leaving camp every night after dark.

Sarge would order us to go flat in some place that was rocky or thorny, or maybe beside one of those 10-foot sail-shaped termite mounds. Then every time he heard one of us scratch, sniffle, snore, burp, fart, or slap at an ant, or a mosquito, or try to wave away the gnats, he'd kick our butts.

"If you silly bastards can just learn to keep still and keep quiet, the night becomes your friend. Now, just start looking around carefully. Damn you, Riegle, use *only* your eyes at first!

"If you need to move your head, do it slow! Jerky movements tip off the Japs. They don't need to see you! All they need is half a glimpse or a sound and they'll fire a Nambu burst . . . that's three to five shots. And, young troopers, all it takes is one shot. Or they might toss a grenade your way.

"Either way, you're a slab of cooling meat. Got that?"

One night I noticed an extra man. I couldn't see his face, but he was tall and he moved like a cat. Once he took cover next to me. "Who are you?"

Sarge blasted me. "Mays, damn your hide, I told you no talking! Your M-1 there beside you? I want you to pull it up into firing position without making a sound. Take 10 minutes if you have to, but don't make a goddam sound or I'll kick your ass. And keep your yap shut!"

"Popalovski, for a guy your size, I think you're starting to get the hang of it. Hofstra, close your yap, I can hear your breathing a mile away."

The next night, of course, he buffaloed us by stressing speed, speed, speed.

"Men, now the thing is, once you get inside Tojo's position and you slit his throat or roll grenades into his foxhole, you've got to get out of there fast as a striped-assed ape. You run to the cover that you already picked out for yourself . . . run like hell and drop in there and hold your breath! Then you slowly resume controlled breathing."

"Sarge, what if somebody else is in their first?"

"Get beneath him. Hide!"

Here he gave a gravelly whisper.

"And then you just become part of the night . . . dark as a stack of black cats."

# # #

We'd drag back into our tents about 0100. We all were whipped. But it was hard to sleep because there was so much to remember. On the third night, I rolled out of the sack still in my skivvies and crept – more like slithered – to Sarge's tent. I just hoped I wouldn't meet an Australian Brown Snake along the way.

Once inside, I stole his .45 pistol. The noise of unfastening the holster strap's metal snap about made me wet my pants. But the sound failed to wake him. Then it seemed to take about five very slow minutes to ease the pistol out of that holster's creaky leather.

Right after reveille the next morning, I sauntered up to him. "Say, Sarge, I found this pistol last night. Thought someday you might need it."

He gave me a chilling look as he tapped the weapon on his palm. Then he gave a rare grin. "Mays, if you can do that again, I'm going to see the old man about you."

"Okay, Sarge. But meanwhile, who's the new guy with us?"

"None of your damn business."

The next night, I stayed off the duckboards, sneaking instead under the tent's side curtain. Slow-stalking my fingers spider-like, I touched the mouse trap he set for me. Once I captured and carefully compressed the striker bar, I held it -- and my breath -- and then slid the trigger aside. I eased the striker shut, first onto my index finger, then the fingernail, letting it close without a sound. Then I found the holster. Exploring, I also found a little bell he'd tied to it, depressed the clapper with my thumb, and verrrry carefully lifted it away.

Once I had the pistol, I slipped the mouse trap into the holster and slithered back into the night.

That's how I earned my corporal's stripes plus a weekend pass into Brisbane. Before I left on the pass, I asked Sarge again about the stranger who was training with us.

"I'm going to tell you," he said. "But first I'm going to read you a little Riot Act. You're a corporal now and you're going to get a pay hike.

"But as far as I'm concerned, it ain't a pay grade. You're now a non-commissioned officer – that means you're a leader. You set examples. You don't sit back and bitch with the rest of the boys. You're no longer just one of the guys.

"You don't wait for me to order your boys around. And if you don't lead, I'll bust your ass right back to private."

"Okay, Sarge. So who's the new guy? Am I responsible for him, too?"

"Jeez you're a nosey pecker," he said. "So I'll tell you. Just keep it to yourself. He's a first louie, name of Woodsen."

"Oh, yeah. He's the one who gave us the orientation about Jap weapons."

"Right. He's a Wyoming boy who put himself through college as a hunter. Now keep it to yourself."

# Chapter 19
# Basic Intelligence

As I said, Adelaide is a beautiful town with gorgeous ladies, but on this pass I avoided the Shielas. Not because I was such an upstanding guy, but because I wanted info.

I went right to the main library and made friends with the very sharp grandmotherly reference librarian. She helped me locate material, some of it unpublished, about New Guinea, aka Papua. I learned New Guinea, shaped a bit like pregnant dragon, is earth's second largest island . . . and by far the nastiest.

On Monday morning I was depressed and Pop wanted to know if I had a hangover. "Kind of," I said. "I did some digging on the place where we're supposedly going and just thinking about it gives me a hell of a headache."

Later I briefed Sarge . . . no, actually, I just spilled my guts to him because what I'd read scared the hell out of me. I wanted some reassurance.

"Sarge, it looks like the Army's going to dump us right into Satan's shitter. It's very hot and rains constantly and it's got more swamp than hard ground, except for the central mountain range where you can freeze to death at 13,000 feet.

"As for the jungle, dozens of missionaries and prospectors have trekked into it and never come out . . . or they've come out near dead of disease.

"Sarge, New Guinea has three different kinds of malaria, and some diseases I never even heard of -- stuff like dengue fever, scrub typhus, parasites called filariasis and leishmaniasis, that you can get on your skin or in your insides, or maybe both. Yeah, and yaws . . . that's where your damn skin ulcerates and just rots away, for

Christ's sake. They had pictures of people whose noses were eaten away. Nothing but holes between their eyes and mouth, poor bastards.

"Oh, yeah, and to top it off, the place also has some stone-age tribes that practice cannibalism. I mean, some of them tie their victims to trees and keep them there alive for a week or two as they slice off enough thigh or butt meat for each lunch and dinner. I mean, my God, what are we headed into? And why, for Christ's sake?"

He nodded soberly.

"The why of it, Jim? If the Japs control New Guinea, they can bomb Australia at will . . . or even invade. But if we control the island, then we threaten Rabaul . . . that's the Japs' huge naval base that anchors their south flank.

He paused. "That's the strategy. As for what it's like, all I can say is that if it's as bad as some Central American countries I've seen, it'll be real tough. Hot as hell, I bet. But as far as parasites are concerned, the docs have medicines that can handle them. The key thing is for you to get yourself ready mentally for it."

He tapped my helmet. "The heat, the jungle – you *can* handle them if you deal with them first in your noggin. Prepare yourself. Bitch about it. You know, if a guy can bitch he can get used to just about anything . . . that is, if he's ready for it. And you can be damn sure the Japs are ready for it.

"We'll suffer," he added. "That's life in the infantry. You just have to tough it out, but the Japs at first are toughened better than us."

He looked around pensively at a platoon marching past us, packs on, headed out for a hike. "So they're going to do a 25-mile hike today. That's nothing compared to 25 yards in real jungle. Some of these boys just ain't going to be able to handle it. Not at first . . . and then it will be too late."

# # #

A few days later, I had to run an errand to our regimental HQ. Just as I was striding up to the entrance to that tent, a lieutenant in starched khakis with knife-edge creases pulled back the flap.

Not to let me in.

Instead, he made way for a cluster of brass-hats trailing the big four-star commander himself, Douglas MacArthur, under the brassiest hat I'd ever seen. He had more gold braid on his noggin than a dozen Ritz Hotel doormen. At least three or four generals – one to three stars -- followed him, not to mention a flock of bird colonels. I never saw so much rank in one place.

Like a good soldier, I quickly hopped over the line of painted rocks to get off the walkway, came to attention, gave and held a rigid salute.

I couldn't help breaking the rules by following the general with my eyes as he walked past. He had that big corncob pipe and he glanced my way as he started to put on those sunglasses. He returned my salute with a half-assed wave of his pipe, like shooing away a fly. His eyes held as much expression as a glass of tap water. I've never seen such blank indifference.

*Damn. Now I know how a pawn feels.*

Walking just a few paces behind him was our division commander, General Harding. His head was down.

He looked furious.

# Chapter 20
# The Old Rah-Rah

A day later, General Harding himself gave us a pep talk.

We formed up on a broad theater-like slope facing a sign hanging between two huge trees. It was as big as a drive-in theater screen.

Honest to God, it bore cheerleading language – "Look Out! Look Out! The Mighty Thirty Second!" plus "On Wisconsin On Wisconsin" and "Michigan My Michigan" and "We Are The Badgers and Wolverines."

I don't know what it did for the Midwesterners, but being from Seattle, I didn't find it particularly galvanizing.

With a microphone and big speakers, General Harding indicated we'd go into battle soon.

He told how during World War I the 32nd Division came to be known as the Red Arrow, slicing through every German defensive line that had stymied French and British Armies for years. If we were to match our fathers' reputation, he said, we had to become killers.

We got the same pitch from General Eichelberger, a starchy looking older guy who was our corps commander. Both predicted we'd win fairly easily because Jap troops on New Guinea were worn out, starving and diseased.

Back at our tent we were moody.

J.B. said, "Some pep rally! I get the impression they think we aren't quite up for this."

I chimed in, "Well, the Sarge doesn't think so."

Hofstra said the general sounded like the coach of a high school team about to play the Detroit Lions.

"You can tell they don't think we're ready. They're trying to whip us up, acting like they're a bunch of cheerleaders."

"Only they don't look near as good," Pop leered.

Somebody had a copy of the division newspaper account about General MacArthur speaking to our officers. J.B. read it aloud, quoting MacArthur as saying we'd won the Australians' hearts. Then, deepening his voice to sound like an orator, he read a direct quotation of the general's words.

> "Always, the fellow who fights to the end, whose nerves don't go back on him, who never thinks of anything but the will to victory. That's what I want of you – and that's what I expect of you. It's possible that I won't see a great many of you again; but I want you to know wherever you go, it will be my hope and prayer that God Almighty will be with you to the end."

J.B.'s voice trailed off.

"Gee," I said, "that sure pumps up my morale."

Drexel said, "What an asshole! He wants us -- no, he *expects* us -- to fight to the end. Oh, yeah, but he ain't gonna have his balls out on the chopping block."

"What did he mean by 'the end'?" J.B. asked.

Svoboda spit. "You know damn well what he means. That old bastard thinks we're headed into a meat grinder."

That evening we heard General Harding had protested sending us into battle without jungle training.

General MacArthur overruled him saying "time is of the essence."

That news didn't help our outlook one bit.

# Chapter 21
# Arriving

Two weeks later, we found ourselves wedged aboard a C-47 with Lieutenant Woodsen, plus three engineer officers and some wooden crates.

Our destination was Port Moresby on the south coast of New Guinea.

The lieutenant said we were following Easy Company onto the island.

As an advance party for the rest of First Battalion, it would be our job locate a bivouac area for the follow-on troops. Two battalions of the 128th Infantry Regiment had already been moved onto New Guinea.

This was my first air travel except for a 10-minute ride in an old biplane at an airshow – cost me five bucks.

Flying was a very much a relief, because once we got some altitude, the air was cool and clean. For the first time I felt comfortable, far up out of the heat and dust at Camp Cable.

And the take-off thrill – the sudden lightened sense that you're off the ground – felt exactly the same in this huge cargo plane as in that old Curtiss Jenny biplane.

I was nervous, though, and our lieutenant looked every bit as shaky as I felt.

By contrast, Sarge's chin was on his chest and he seemed to be sound asleep.

Because we were headed north across the Coral Sea, I enjoyed peering down at the pale green shallows around the reefs alternating with the dark blue of deep water.

Pop tapped me on the shoulder.

"I don't know about you," he yelled over the engines' roar, "but I'm scared shitless about when we land. Are we going to be headed straight into combat? I hear there's already fighting going on in New Guinea."

"Beats hell out of me," I said, "but I doubt it. We've got our rifles but no ammo or grenades. I don't think they'd land us in the midst of a battle disarmed, do you?"

"Probably not . . . I hope not."

After about an hour looking down at the ocean, I leaned my head against the side of the plane. Following Sarge's advice, I mentally tried to prepare myself for the inevitable heat and misery to come.

*How do you prepare? You just count on it being utterly horrible and hope that maybe it'll be a relief to find out it isn't quite that awful.*

Soon the plane's steady drone and vibration lulled me to sleep.

Much later, somebody started poking my shoulder. "Hey, Jim! Wake up! I think we're here."

The plane was in a hard banking turn, so my first view out the windows was of a broccoli landscape − mile upon mile of green treetops looking welded together and appearing as solid as if you could walk on them.

Then we banked the other direction so that between the growing towers of brilliant white cumulonimbus clouds, I got my first glimpse of the island's snow-capped saw tooth center, the Owen Stanley Mountains, with hundreds of ax blade ridges and outcroppings so steep that they looked razor sharp

Swaying easily with the plane's motion, the co-pilot got up from his seat. Leaning to us through the cockpit doorway, he dropped his head phones to his neck and shouted over the engine noise.

"In about 15 minutes, men, we'll be on the ground. Sorry, but we have to descend fast just in case any Jap Zeros are in the neighborhood. And dropping our altitude that fast always makes it a bit bumpy. Air pockets, you know.

"Sometimes landing can be a bit rough, too, 'cause they don't always have time to fill in the runway craters real smooth. So if you got heavy gear in them crates, best you get behind them. Otherwise they could mash you against the bulkhead."

The engineers, who brought the crates, scrambled toward the tail. We were right behind them.

As we settled, J.B. looked at me and mouthed "Craters?"

I shouted, "Sir, do you mean bomb craters?"

The copilot nodded. "Yeah. Jap bombers hit Port Moresby every day or two and sometimes they clobber the airstrips. You'll see! But don't worry. They radioed us that there's no bombing going on right now."

"Thank God for little favors," J.B. said.

# Chapter 22
## New Guinea's Welcome

The co-pilot replaced his head phones as he withdrew into the cockpit and strapped back into his seat.

The plane bucked and squeaked as we hit air pockets. Several more sharp banks and now we were low enough to get a side view of the jungle atop a sheer slope maybe five miles away. It looked like a solid green wall interspersed with tall tree trunks.

We circled over a picturesque bay with several anchored ships and a scruffy-looking town on its shoreline. Another lower circle and we could see the town looked not scruffy but splintered and abandoned. A few banks later, and we flared and landed with a jar, bouncing and creaking.

The pilot braked and then ran up the engines to taxi off the runway, taking us past burnt-out shells of three cargo planes

The golden sunlight pouring through the cockpit windows turned gray as if someone had flipped a switch. I didn't pay attention because I was gathering up my M-1, helmet and musette bag, wanting to get on the ground to test myself in the heat.

The engines did a rattling shut-down as the co-pilot clambered back over the crates and our bodies. He swung open the wide double cargo doors and unfolded the ladder. Dozens of other planes were visible parked beyond ours.

Pop, the lieutenant and J.B. beat me to the ground and seemed to stagger. As I came down the ladder, I felt suddenly wrapped in a giant steaming barber's towel. My knees sagged and sweat instantly beaded on my face. Then I remembered Sarge. *It's a state of mind, Jim. Be ready for it. Embrace it when it comes.*

Embrace it, my ass! It was hugging me . . . suffocating me. I took a deep, damp breath and did the only thing I could -- started a heavy-footed plod toward the terminal. The building looked like somebody's idea of a bad joke – a thatched roof perched atop a dingy whitewashed frame sitting on dingy concrete pillars.

Then I discovered why the sunlight suddenly dimmed.

A solid curtain of rain roared across the terminal, virtually hiding it from view. It didn't so much fall as slam – warm water pounding our helmets and shoulders, instantly soaking us to the skin. It was like getting hit by a fire hose and plunging into a pool at the same time.

Through the downpour ahead of me, Pop and the lieutenant looked like vague ghosts in mid-air. Muddy spume rebounding from the ground hid their lower legs from view.

# # #

The terminal building at Seven Mile Airdrome was a big musical rectangle – musical thanks to discordant tunes of dozens of little water streams coming through the roof pinging, clinking, plonging, tinging, and plopping into cans, pans and wastebaskets sitting on tables and desks.

For an instant, a blue-white lightning flash illuminated the interior. I dropped my musette bag, propped the M-1 against a pillar and turned to gape at the cascade roaring around us. "Jesus! It's like being trapped under Niagara Falls."

Then I got an elbow in my back.

A muffled voice. "Here, mate! Be a good lad and hold this for me!" The speaker's voice was muffled by a spotted white face mask. He nodded toward two gleaming rings jutting out of a gory hole in a man's stomach. I grabbed the bloody handles of the doctor's forceps and he bent over, searching inside the red cavity.

"Raise them a bit! Good!" He was quiet for a minute. "Dammit! Light's no bloody good!"

My voice trembling, I said, "My God, it does get dark fast here."

"Welcome to the tropics, cobber. Now shift them to your left."

Somebody standing on the other side of the body pumped a Coleman lantern back to its brightest life and raised it. Glancing at the man with the light, the surgeon said, "Thanks, mate. There . . . I've almost got the little bleeder! Now hold on . . ." He quit talking as he worked with curved needle and thread inside that pulsating hole.

Watching him push glistening organs aside, I said "Jesus!"

"Righto, lad," he mumbled. "Put in a good word for all of us." Then his hands stopped. He grunted, "Bloody hell."

After a pause, he straightened up. "Okay, mate, he's gone. You can release the forceps." Shaking my head, I stepped away about two feet, accidentally putting myself back into the waterfall pouring off the thatch.

"Shit!"

As I recoiled into shelter, the surgeon told the man across from him. "Mike, thanks for trying." I could barely see the assistant, a stocky, shirtless black man, far blacker than any Negro I ever saw in the States. His only clothing was kind of a skirt.

"Righto, Doc," Mike said. "Sorry I be late."

"Not your fault. He was too late getting back to us."

"I didn't know this was a surgery," I said. "Where should we go to get out of your way?"

The doc pulled down his surgical mask and gave me an unshaven smile. "Well, a bloody Yank! Welcome! By any chance are you a sick berth attendant?"

"God, no! Just a rifleman."

"Well, no worries and thanks. This is only a surgery when we need it to be. He was carrying some scrap metal and didn't know it until he got out of his aircraft

"He's a pilot?"

"Was a pilot. Flew a P-39 – you chaps call it an Airacobra, I believe. He was just back from Milne Bay where he was chopping up coconut trees to take out sniper."

"He was what?"

Using the bloody mask, he wiped the sweat from his face. "You'll find out all about it soon enough. As to where you go, check with that WO over there."

"WO?"

"Right. Warrant Officer. Dave Oates. Dave runs things here at night."

The surgeon was the first Aussie soldier I met face-to-face and Oates the second. Both typified that hard breed. No matter how painful or miserable or hopeless the situation, every Aussie seemed to have been issued a permanent, leering go-screw-it grin.

I sloshed through the ankle-deep water on the floor to find Lieutenant Woodsen and Oates shouting at each other. The plane had delivered us to the wrong airstrip. Nobody here knew we were coming, what we should do or where we should go.

The lieutenant turned to us. "Sarge, the telephone to town is out and the last jeep is taking our pilots there. So I'll hitch a ride. You men hang out here and I'll get back to you soon as I find out what's what."

After the jeep took off in the downpour, J.B. asked, "So where can we sack out?"

Oates grinned. "Your luck is in. Port Oates Moresby usually is almost a desert. We don't get these rains that often. Either way, we kip on the floor. It's a bit like a bath. No mud -- not much, any roads."

# Chapter 23
# Getting Oriented

Sleeping in the run-off of a tropical downpour was like trying to doze in a tepid bath . . . not quite warm enough to enjoy, but not cold enough to force you to get out and dry off.

The main problem, though, was the mosquitoes. They sang and swarmed over every square inch of bare flesh. We all put T-shirts over our faces, but that didn't keep them from your hands or neck.

Just before dawn the rain stopped and a breeze sprang up, thoroughly chilling us in our sopping uniforms. When we got up and stretched, we discovered a foot problem.

Because he'd had the good sense to take off his boots and socks before turning in, Sarge's footgear was fairly dry.

Pop, J.B. and the rest us hadn't bothered. So as boot leather became saturated during the night, it swelled. It hurt our feet to stand and hurt like hell to take even two or three steps.

And we had some walking to do. The lieutenant succeeded in getting a call through to us, saying we had to make our way to the other airstrip which, according to WO Oates, it was about eight miles away.

"And mind you take your tablets before you hike," Oates said. "The mosquitos supped on you all night, so you need your Quinine."

He opened a glass jar and gave each of us two tablets. "One now, one tomorrow morning. One each morning thereafter. Turns you yellow, but that's better than coming all over yourself queer-like with malaria."

As we stepped outside I said, "Shit, Sarge, we can't hike in these boots! We'll end up with trench foot or something."

"Well, Corporal, then either get 'em off and try them without socks or go barefoot."

"Hell, I can go barefoot," Reigle grinned. "Went barefoot all the time on the farm."

Sarge turned his cold eyes on us. "One way or the other, we're moving out pronto!"

The boots were so soaked it was hard even to undo the buckles for the ankle collars. And it took some mighty heaving by Pop to get the boots off our feet. The socks came off to reveal feet looking like albino prunes.

But thanks to some foot powder, we at least got the boots back on. We draped the socks over our shoulders and then had to step out sharply, because Sarge already was a few hundred yards ahead of us

The air was hot, heavy and hard to breathe as we started our hike. The road at first was muddy slop. But in a half hour, the sun baked its surface into hardening cracks, first toasted our uniforms dry, soon afterwards making us sweat bullets.

Sarge took out a spare T-shirt and made himself a light turban tied in back and reaching just over his eyebrows.

"I recommend you boys do the same. In summer in China, the Japs did it and I'll bet they're doing it here. Keeps the sweat out'n your eyes."

"Well, what about your helmet?"

"Hook it over your bayonet. It's a nuisance, but your head's cooler, and your scalp don't itch so fierce."

The sun was drying the slit trenches along the road, handy in case Jap bombers came over or Tojo's troops assaulted out of the hills.

The area's occasional downpours had eroded the edges of the trenches so they looked like narrow mud baths topped by green scum – algae, maybe – and myriads of struggling insects. The trenches stank of decay.

"By God, I sure hope the Japs don't start bombing today," Riegle said. "I'm cruddy enough without having to dive head first into that."

"Yeah, you're cruddy and I'd appreciate it of you'd just stay downwind."

Riegle snapped, "Up yours, J.B. You sure don't smell like no bed of roses."

Svoboda growled, "Dammit, why don't you both save your breath?" They stopped wrangling.

We couldn't see the other airstrip because of the surrounding woods and scrub brush.

But one-by-one, a squadron of big twin-engine planes took off, soaring right above us in a circling climb toward the mountains.

"Gosh, guys," Hofstra said, "those look like our B-25s! You know, the Billy Mitchell bombers?"

"Well, zippity doo-dah," J.B. snapped. "Somebody grab a flag and wave it."

Sarge said, "What's the matter, J.B.? Heat getting to you?"

"Yeah, as a matter of fact it is. I don't mind warm weather. Grew up in it in southern California, but this place just seems to be wringing wet."

Fifteen minutes later three flights of sleek-looking fighter planes also roared above us – some bearing the white American star plus shark mouth decals near the nose.

Others were marked with the Aussies' red kangaroo. The planes circled in two groups, climbing toward the mountains.

Following with his eyes, Sarge said, "Boys, I bet they're headed out to intercept an air raid, so before too long maybe we'll all get to take Riegle's mud bath."

As the sound of the planes faded, Riegle again eyed the smelly slit trenches. "Sarge, if you don't mind, I reckon I'll take my chances right out here on the road."

Sarge grinned. "Bullshit, Riegle! I *do* mind. Your scrawny ass is official U.S. Government property and I can't allow you to risk it that way. If Jap bombers come, you dive! Head first! That's a direct order. Hear?"

"Awww, Sarge . . ."

I grinned and kept quiet. I was trying to hold up under the heat which almost felt solid.

Walking in it was an effort, like pushing through water. And the sun? Well, we were walking due west and the sun on the back of my neck actually was painful.

"How you doin', Mays?"

"No complaints, Sarge. I'm just sweatin' it out, Sarge. Just sweatin' it out."

I felt a blister working up on my left heel and noticed that our boots were starting to raise little puffs of dust in what had been mud.

"But hey, Sarge, how 'bout we take a quick break? My socks are completely dry and the boots seem to be getting there, too."

He nodded toward an approaching dust cloud. "Let's hold off a few minutes, Corporal. I think we maybe can hitch a ride."

# Chapter 24
# Meeting The Natives

A three-quarter ton truck – the Army calls it a weapons carrier -- pulled up and stopped, its dust plume settling around us.

The Aussie driver was a rangy old man in an open shirt and with a handkerchief tied around his neck. Tufts of snowy hair peeking from beneath his ragged slouch hat.

He told us he was taking pilots to the airstrip we'd just left and said he'd pick us up on the way back in "half a mo."

And so he did, also bringing along the shrouded corpse of the pilot who died in surgery during the storm.

"Call me Bob," he said as he braked beside us. "If you need transport anywhere around Port Moresby, just ask for Bob. Right now, there's naught else."

Like any driver, he eagerly filled us in on the local news. He said the American bombers we saw probably would cross paths with a Japanese raid likely to arrive in the next 20 minutes or so.

"The Yanks will be going to bomb Rabaul and the Japs are coming from Rabaul to bomb us."

Drexel said, "Looks like Sarge was right, Riegle. You're for sure going to get a mud bath."

The Aussie didn't get the joke and he chuckled when we explained. "No worries, Mates! The trenches are worth it. Muddy, but not near as bad as the swamps. No crocs for one thing."

"Crocs?"

"Yeah, mate, saltwater crocodiles. Huge brutes. They can get near 20 bloody feet long and weigh a ton."

Sarge asked him about the ground war.

Bob said an Aussie brigade and some American engineers had stopped the Jap invasion of Milne Bay cold.

Now those veterans from North Africa and the Middle East were cleaning out troops the Jap Navy had abandoned.

"The Japs Navy left behind big mobs of the bastards," Bob said. "Bloody fanatics won't surrender. So the lads have to dig them out one-by-one. Costly business."

Riegle asked, "So where's Milne Bay?"

Bob glanced at Riegle in exasperation.

"Crikey, don't you . . .?" Then he paused. "I'm sorry Cobber, early days. I forget you lot are quite new to these parts."

He told us that New Guinea stretched about 1,500 miles northwest to southeast -- a barrier covering Australia's north coast.

"Now the northwest end, which looks a bit like a head at the end of a badly bent neck, is right up near the equator. And you might say the southeast end of New Guinea down here, Milne Bay, is the arse."

He said the Japs had occupied several isolated spots on New Guinea's north coast, but that the jungles, swamps and the mountains -- New Guinea's spine -- were more or less keeping them there. The Jap attack on Milne Bay was an attempt to capture Port Moresby by doing an end-run.

"So how far from here is Milne Bay?"

"Oh, it's a bit over 200 miles down the coast southeast of us. There also was a bit of worry about the Japs attacking Port Moresby out of the hills. But first the militia and then some regulars bled them as they crossed the mountains.

"And it weren't the town they was after, you see. After all the bombing, it's naught but splintered buildings and shattered houses.

"No, what the Japs want is Port Moresby's bay and the airdromes hereabouts. That way they could easily invade Australia or just lie off and bombard its towns. Like they already bombed Darwin for no good reason but to terrorize people – just like they done in China and the Philippines. Bastards."

He paused but then brightened.

"Then last month your Marines captured an airdrome over to the east in the Solomon Islands – Guadalcanal, they call it.

"So the Japs attacking toward Port Moresby got orders to turn back, see. And much as I hate the little bastards, I pity them what turned back. They had crossed the Owen Stanley Range – the Kokoda Trail -- and were just a few miles or so away."

"Why pity those assholes?"

"If you get into the jungle, mate, you'll find out. It's just about the most rotten awful land God put on this earth. I know. Back in the 20s I tried some gold prospecting in two or three spots along the north coast. I was a tough young bloke, but it damn near killed me."

J.B asked, "What's so bad about it?"

"For starters, mate, you never can get dry. You work, eat, and sleep in mud.

"Now here on the south coast it rains quite often. But on the north coast, it bloody well rains nearly all the time – sometimes 10 inches in a day.

"And it's all rotten thick jungle and hot as the hinges of hell. Rots your clothes. Mosquitos sometimes get so thick you just wipe 'em off. Bloody bugs constantly bite you and the bites get infected and turn into jungle ulcers. The constant wet destroys your boots.

"Then, mates, there's the Kunai grass. It's got bloody big blades – six or seven feet long, they are – and it's got all these sharp edges. It just slices up your clothes and your skin.

"Poor bastards in our Seventh Division was shipped right here from North Africa. They was wearing desert shorts and the Army never issued regular trousers to them, so most of them what's been in the jungle – well, their legs is covered with sores and jungle ulcer. So they've had it very rough indeed.

"But let me tell you, mates, the poor damn Japs who crossed the mountains to attack Moresby . . . well, them ridges they had to climb are so steep you can't walk up them, you have to crawl upwards on hands and knees. And you crawl in tracks that's naught but mud, cause it's always rainin', see?

"And then -- once you get to the top -- it's straight down the other side into a gorge.

"And then at the bottom, the next hill is a stone's throw away. But to get there you got to cross a bloody little river, see, fed by mountain snows and rain. You cross on boulders that's covered with slimy moss. If you fall in, current sweeps you away.

"Then you start climbing again. So you can spend all day going up and down those two hills, and you ain't covered three miles on the map.

"There's just no flat land at all until you're out of the hills, and then it's mostly swamp . . . waist-deep, too, with leeches and ticks and crocs going for your goolies.

"Well, having come across all that, the Japs had to retreat all the way back through it again. The boys following them was finding Jap bodies by the dozens, all of them just skin and bone."

Suddenly, he hit the brakes and we skidded to a stop in a new cloud of dust. He pointed toward the mountains.

"See up there, lads? It's the Jap Air Force come to lay some eggs."

# Chapter 25
# First Attack

When Bob turned off the truck, we could hear the pulsating drone above us. The driver stayed in his seat. "Don't go for the trenches just now, chaps! Japs are fair way off, yet."

"That haze makes it hard to spot them." Suddenly my eyes caught them . . . two dozen silvery winged specks flying in three rigid V formations.

"Bob, you sure they ain't coming for us?"

"Nahhh, no worries. The little bastards can't see us from that high."

He laughed. "You know, headquarters say they've dropped a couple of thousand bombs hereabouts. About all they've done is tear up the town, but most of the folks had already moved back to Australia. So they make a lot of dust, plus a lot of splashes in the port. But thanks to the trenches, they have yet to kill anybody."

Big antiaircraft guns started cracking and black explosions began pocking the sky far aloft

Bob doffed his hat, trading it for a dishpan helmet. "Better keep your steel lids on, lads. Each one of those antiaircraft shells throws out shrapnel and it all falls down here whether it hits a Jap or not."

As we waited, Bob chuckled to himself. "You know, this minds me of a story that's been making the rounds. Before the trenches were dug, three blokes in a truck was driving along the road outside the town when bombs started falling.

"So the driver wallah and two other blokes jump out. With no hole or trench to shelter themselves, they dive under the bloody truck. But the driver was so scared he forgot to turn it off. Had it in low gear, you see, so it just kept bumping and sputtering along with the boys trying to crawl along to stay beneath it.

"Well, at first they managed to keep up because right then it was going up a slope, moving slow-like. But then it goes over the crest and speeds up uncovering them so they're crawling like mad to catch up."

We all grinned nervously, keeping an eye on the Jap planes. "Mostly," Bob added, "we don't go for the slit trenches until we hears the whistle of the falling bombs."

"So the guys and the truck weren't hurt?"

"Naah, mate!" Bob laughed. "The truck finally ran off the road and bumped into a coconut palm. Wasn't damaged at all. And you wouldn't exactly say the men were hostile fire casualties. But they scrabbled along the road so hard that they lost quite a bit of skin off knees and elbows. Had to see the MO for some sticking plaster."

"Now, look there," he pointed upward again. "Our fighter mob are having a bash at them."

One fiery dot was curving down trailing black smoke. Above it I could barely make out gnats darting among the bombers, presumably chewing at them with machine guns and cannon. Another aircraft exploded in a bright flash, generating falling smoke trails.

A few minutes later we faintly heard the whistle of falling bombs. Bob put the truck in gear and resumed driving. "No need for trenches, lads. Bombs are coming down quite a ways off."

Over his truck's rattle, we heard a steady overlapping drumming of explosions. It sounded like the drum-drum-drum of railroad freight cars telescoping together as the brakes come on.

Columns of smoke and dust bounded into view far to our west.

# Chapter 26
# A G2 Mission

We found Lieutenant Woodsen at the other airport. He was leaning over a stretcher talking with our old buddy, Corporal Frank Benson. Three natives squatted near the handles of a stretcher, while the fourth stood, carefully shading Benson's face with a huge tree leaf.

I didn't recognize Benson at first. The double chin was gone and so was his beer gut. His eyes looked sunken and anxious. In a weak voice he said, "Hey, Sarge! Good to see you." He drew a breath, his teeth chattering for a second. "Damn, and there's my helpers, Mays and Pop."

Sarge asked, "What happened, Frank? Wounded?"

"No, the docs say I've got a whopping good case of malaria. Had a temp of 105 first thing this morning, but now I'm freezing. Lot of the boys are getting it." His face glistened with sweat in the 90-degree heat, but he shivered like an aspen leaf.

Pop asked, "Didn't you take your quinine tablets?"

"Well, there's a little problem with quinine," Benson said. "You carry them in your pockets, but when you wade in swamps all day or get caught in these damned downpours, you wind up with a pocket full of mush. Right along with your cigarettes."

"Swamps?"

"Yeah, I told you guys this would be a FUBAR didn't I? I got stuck with Company E and Company E got stuck with building a road along some native track – nothing but a yard-wide path -- toward Milne Bay. It goes through dry ground on some plantations, but most of it was just jungle and swamps – forty fucking miles for starters!

"We had that Negro engineering regiment with us. And they had nothing but saws, shovels and axes . . . no bulldozers or graders have been shipped in to them yet. Jesus, it was rough – digging here, filling there. Ever try to fill a hole with muck that's sticking to your shovel? Just pure FUBAR, I tell you."

"Well, Benson," the lieutenant said, "we better let these boys take you to the hospital. Get well soon."

The corporal gave a weak salute as the Papuans gently bore him off. Sarge said, "Yeah, and we need to find some jars to keep our quinine tablets dry."

The lieutenant asked Bob to drive us to the port. And as we reached the town – up close it looked bomb-shattered -- he said, "Men, they've given us new orders. We're going to be a scout section for G-2."

Sarge asked, "Division G-2?"

The lieutenant swallowed. "No, GHQ at Brisbane."

"You mean General MacArthur, right sir?"

"Well, actually General Willoughby, he's G-2."

Sarge let out a breath, ducked his head and shook it.

I said, "Jesus, sir! Why us?"

The lieutenant glanced up. "Well, Mays, you're an Asian Studies major and you speak a little Japanese, right? And Sarge here had lots of experience fighting Japs in China. Any questions?"

"My God, we're the best they've got?" Pop and Musky and I just stared at each other.

"Yep," Sarge said. "When you start a campaign from scratch, that's often the Army way."

"So do we have a name?"

Sarge and the lieutenant looked at each other. Sarge grinned. "Sir, how about we call ourselves GHQ's Provisional I and R Squad."

"The what?"

"Intelligence and Reconnaissance Squad -- GHQ I&R for short."

"Right," Lieutenant Woodsen said. "Now the three of us along with Popalovski and Riegle will catch a boat over to a camp at Pongani. After we check in there, we'll catch a boat to some location near Buna where we'll determine the Jap order of battle."

We looked at him blankly.

Sarge said, "The lieutenant means we're to find out how many Japs are around Buna, what shape they're in and how well they're armed."

Then he asked, "So, sir, what about the rest of us?"

"J.B., Drexel, Hofstra and Svoboda will stay here to help with the supply boats that General Harding brings up toward Buna in the next week or so."

Muskiewicz asked, "Uh, sir, so what is Buna?"

"It's a small government settlement that has two airstrips and General MacArthur wants those airstrips. Once we capture them, our bombers and fighters won't have to fly over the damn mountains and through the storms. And they'll be able to carry bigger bomb loads and more fuel so they can hammer the Japs at Rabaul a hell of a lot better."

"What is Rabaul, sir?"

"It's a beautiful harbor about 500 miles away that the Japs captured from the Aussies. A lot of the Jap fleet is there and it's the anchor, you might say, for their southern flank in the Pacific."

"And where's Buna, sir?"

"Directly across the mountains from us."

"On the north coast, sir?"

"Right."

"In jungle?"

"Well, kind of on the edge of it."

# Chapter 27
# To The North Coast

If getting out of the plane at Port Moresby was a shock, setting foot ashore at Pongani was unbelievable.

We lost the sea breeze, of course, as our boat chugged in toward the beach. Without the breeze, the bright sun felt so hot it literally stung bare skin. If I'd had a magnifying glass, I could have set the boat deck on fire in about five seconds. The air was so hot you kind of avoided taking a deep breath.

Pongani itself was a tiny miserable village with no wharf or pier. Not even a makeshift dock.

So it was just a case of dropping five feet over the side of the boat into anywhere from three to six feet of sea water depending upon whether a wave was peaking or dying beneath you. Then you just worked to keep your footing as waves pushed you toward then pulled you back from the beach. Each time, you gained maybe a foot.

That was tiring.

The real drag, though, came on emerging from the surf with about 30 pounds of water streaming from your uniform, meanwhile shouldering 10 pounds of M-1 Garand and bayonet, ammo bandoliers, a full musette bag, cartridge belt, two canteens, entrenching tool and all the rest of it.

Once we got off the beach onto firm ground, we found it actually wasn't firm. The land just behind the beach was gooey mud about a foot deep. And once we got to the trail, we found it was slippery stinking pulp – an ancient, thick, putrefying layer of rotting vegetation. The buzz of flies was constant.

"Good God," Riegle said. "This is the kind of crap my dogs roll in."

When we dragged our butts uphill to the bivouac, we got another shock. Our friends of the Second and Third Battalion, 128th Regiment, were no longer the jocular, strutting, welcoming men we'd known from the Cow Palace or Camp Cable. They glanced at us and turned their faces back to what they were doing . . . listlessly sitting around scratching. Even their scratching seemed listless.

A leaning board sign told us in crude hand lettering, "Welcome to Fever Ridge."

The fact that the officers hadn't pulled down the sign was a statement of dead morale from the lieutenant colonel commanding to the lowest private. The only action around the place was the nearby bellowing and crash of bulldozers knocking down trees. The engineers were starting on an airstrip.

Black clouds were rolling down toward us from the mountains and we were wondering what to do when a weary-looking sergeant trudged up to salute Lieutenant Woodsen. "Sir," he asked, "may I direct you to the headquarters tent right over there?"

As the lieutenant headed toward HQ, Sarge reached out to shake the sergeant's hands. "Howdy, Steve? What are you boys doing here?"

"Not much, Dan. Just transforming C-Rations into shit. The Flagpole has had us here almost a month. We were supposed to launch an attack north of here at a place called Buna . . . but nobody has pulled the trigger. So our medics are getting lots of practice with tropical diseases and dysentery. Both of our field hospitals are overflowing. What about you boys?"

"We're I&R and ordered to do some scouting up around Buna."

"Hey, that's good to hear. Maybe they're finally going to get this show on the road."

Just then the thunder rolled and the rain roared down on us. The sergeant said, "That's New Guinea's north coast welcoming you with its Downpour of the Day." He led us to shelter in the administration tent.

"Our rations are running low," he said, "and worse, the quartermasters gave us a lot of that tinned Aussie bully beef. Except it ain't beef but real gamy mutton. Tastes rancid and sometimes it actually is 'cause the cans rusted through. The troops hate it. Main thing? Be careful when you eat. Flies are thick at chow time and so we've had a lot of dysentery."

It was still pouring when we broke for chow that evening. It shook me to see that some of the troops' boots were falling apart. And at dinner, we saw he wasn't kidding -- flies swarmed. In layers. The buzzing was audible. If you had a morsel on a spoon, it looked like a buzzing licorice sucker. You literally had to blow off the flies before you put it in your mouth.

"Jesus, this is disgusting!" Pop said, pursing his lips to spit out a fly after taking a bite of bully beef.

"Pop, are you bitching about a few flies?"

"Hell no, Jim! They're hungry. They've got a right to eat. It's just that this bully beef tastes like . . . well, I think it's mule meat that turned just before they canned it."

A week later we left the camp to return to the boat. We heard two battalions of the 128th were moving out for Buna and that we were to rendezvous with them there.

## Chapter 28
## Moving Toward Buna

By the time we left Pognani, we all had a bleeding rash of chigger or gnat bites around our necks and upper arms.

And nature was calling six to eight times a day. At times, it seemed useless to pull your pants back up.

By then we concluded that poor old Corporal Benson didn't know the half of it.

I think Riegle put it best.

"Men, I'd say the 32$^{nd}$ Infantry Division is buried up to its ass in FUBAR piled on huge mounds of TARFU (Things Are Really etc. . . .) at the peak of Mount SNAFU (Situation Normal, All etc. . . .)."

Ordinarily, I'd have grinned at his words as I did to all the other bitching that was going on.

But this time my morale happened to be in the toilet because of a very unsettling discussion that I had overheard in an adjoining tent.

One of the company commanders was telling an operations major that if he survived the war he'd apply for a teaching post at West Point or maybe on the faculty of the Command and General Staff College at Ft. Leavenworth.

"If I get the job, I'll design a course on how not to start a campaign and New Guinea will be my case study.

"No kidding, sir, I think that what has happened here is a crime just like Napoleon sending his Army into Russia without bothering to check with the weather man.

"General headquarters has plunked troops down in this green hell without a clear mission and left them here to rot for a whole damned month on half-rations and without clean water. A quarter of our men are too damned sick to move."

The major nodded. "I know what you mean. It reminds me of what happened at first in France during the last war. The initials AEF stood for 'Allied Expeditionary Force' but we soon changed it to Ass End Forward. You send in troops without supplies . . . well, headquarters eats high on the hog and the troops damn near starve."

"And get sick."

"Yeah. Headquarters is really dropping the ball."

Being an NCO, I had to keep my mouth shut, but I personally blamed General MacArthur.

I still do.

He half-deployed one of our regiments virtually without training, supplies or medical assets – and then let it sit in the jungle with nothing to do and little to eat. And in all the wet, the men's boots literally were falling apart at the seams.

Not understanding The Big Picture or whatever was going on, I just naturally figured Old Doug still was seething about how the Japs defeated him in the Philippines.

Then, I figured, the Marines *really* dented his ego by capturing that airstrip on Guadalcanal.

So, in my book, he was trying to play catch-up by rushing us into earth's worst jungle without supplies.

A few fishing boats sneaking along New Guinea's north coast couldn't carry enough ammo, food or medicine to support us.

And what really got me was that not one single piece of division artillery was with us in New Guinea.

I mean, we brought dozens of 105s and 155s across the damned Pacific – literally dozens of them together with their ammunition.

Those weapons' sole purpose was to support any attack by the division. But not one of those guns was in New Guinea.

Not a damned one.

As time went on, I got the impression our main support from headquarters was Doug's Daily Demand: take Buna immediately . . . at all costs.

We sure paid the costs.

Nobody, especially not headquarters, realized we faced and were outnumbered by a hardened, bitterly determined, veteran enemy masterfully entrenched at the fringe of an oozing, disease-ridden, bug-crawling sodden morass.

During the last year of the war, war correspondents wrote a great deal about General MacArthur's reputation for being solicitous about his troops' lives.

Frankly, I believe MacArthur was horrified that his rush in 1942 damned near destroyed the 32nd Division.

At one point he was quoted as saying, "No more Bunas."

But talk was cheap and his headquarters firmly controlled the war correspondents assigned to the Southwest Pacific Area.

# Chapter 29
# Contact

"Hey, Jim!" Riegle yelled. "We've got only 30 shopping days 'til Christmas."

I barely paid attention because I was scratching at the fiery itch on my neck.

He and I had just traded point so he was five yards ahead of me on the beach and the roar of rain and wind almost drowned his voice.

The downpour even flattened and muted the waves sloshing up and back on the sand.

"Right now," I called back, "I'd be real happy just with Thanksgiving."

Despite trying to joke, my morale was in the crapper.

For starters, we were supposed to have met up on the shoreline with the lead company from the 128th. But it was just the five of us and not another GI in sight.

Second, Japanese Zeroes strafed and destroyed our boat just as we got ashore and started unloading. Their machine guns butchered the crew, blood and gore immediately drawing sharks. We salvaged nothing but our rifles and a few bandoleers of ammo apiece.

Third, we were in a steam bath. November opens summer in New Guinea. Not that it matters because, at sea level, New Guinea always is hot as hell. Even the wind and rain felt hot.

So we were single-filing north on the beach, Riegle on point.

Lieutenant Woodsen's map showed us headed toward the east end of an airstrip built at right angles to the shoreline.

Maybe 300 yards beyond it was an older airstrip lying northwest to southeast, paralleling the shoreline. Between the old runway and the shore lay the Duropa coconut plantation, almost as big as the Lever Brothers Plantation back at Milne Bay.

We dubbed the two runways New Strip and Old Strip. Just a half-mile northeast of them the map showed us Cape Endaiadere, a point where the shoreline took a sharp bend northwest, leading to two beach settlements called Buna Mission and Buna.

Lieutenant Woodsen said we and the missing infantry company were to link up at New Strip with a second assault force -- another battalion of the 128th, advancing on a track more or less parallel to the beach, but a quarter-mile inland.

The two forces were to occupy the airstrips.

If resisted, they were to launch a two-prong attack – one from the beach, the other from the inland track. Once they secured the airstrips, our little I&R squad would check out Jap POWs and bodies and then report our findings to G-2's Order of Battle Section.

But we had no idea where either company was.

We couldn't call them. The Jap air attack had deep-sixed our radio.

We couldn't see the inland route thanks to a broad stretch of Kunai grass – razor grass the Aussies call it – growing at the high-tide line above the beach. Kunai grows eight to ten feet high in dense 20-foot clumps. The broad-bladed grass obstructed our view except for high jungle canopy maybe a half-mile further inland.

So far, at least, we'd heard no gunfire.

Lieutenant Woodsen told us G-2 believed capturing the airstrips would be a cake walk.

Supposedly, the Japs were diseased and starved, having gone through hell in retreating from their aborted attack toward Port Moresby.

Sarge was skeptical. "I don't like this, lieutenant. If Brisbane knows the Japs are in such bad shape, why do they need us to check them out after this supposed cake walk?"

"There's the problem," the lieutenant said. "G2 believes the Japs are sad sacks but wants verification."

"Excuse me, sir. But wouldn't the capture of the airstrips – or the failure to capture them -- verify or disprove G-2's opinion?"

"Sergeant, it doesn't make a lot of sense to me. For all I know, G-2 wants us to cover its ass. But we have our orders. And General MacArthur is putting on the pressure to capture Buna and these airstrips.

"I guess he figures that with the Marines controlling the airstrip over on Guadalcanal, and us able to use these airstrips we'd have the Japs in a real vice."

Sarge looked dubious. Same here. If capturing the airstrips would hurt the Japs so badly, why wouldn't they fight like hell to hold them?

"Okay, sir," I chipped in, "but without our radio, how do we get the word back to G2?"

"Corporal, for sure one of the assault companies has a radio. Besides, General Harding is supposed to bring supplies here by boat. We always can send our report back with them."

That was The Word as of 1200 hours after we dragged ashore like half-drowned rats.

Now at 1500, we still were scouting this beach all alone in what felt like a typhoon, Kunai up on our left, sea downslope to our right.

Other than wind, the only movement was flocks of little sea birds racing up and back in the foamy surf as it lapped up and back on the dark coarse sand.

Sarge called from behind me, circling his hand above his head. I trotted back to huddle with him and the lieutenant. The rest of the men took a knee.

The lieutenant, rain dripping from his helmet rim, nervously glanced around while scratching his own neck rash. "Okay, we've seen neither assault group and I don't want us to arrive at New Strip all on our lonesome. So I need a man to make his way through the grass to find out if we have friends over there."

Sarge frowned. "Sir, elbowing through Kunai that thick will be a bitch. They don't call it razor grass for nothing. It really slices you up."

"Yeah, well, it's probably only a few hundred yards. I need to know if we have friends over there. Who do you think would be best? Mays here?"

When Sarge said, "No sir, I'd recommend Riegle," I took a deep breath of relief. "Riegle's a lot smaller and can pick his way through the grass more easily."

Two minutes later, stepping carefully and using his rifle to push his way ahead, Riegle disappeared into the grass.

"Okay," the lieutenant said, "we'll just ease up toward New Strip and see what we see. I'll take over point."

Sharply, Sarge said, "Sir! Wait! You shouldn't do that! You're our only officer . . ."

"Don't sweat it, Sergeant. It's quiet and I'll keep my eyes open."

Sarge shook his head as the lieutenant unslung his rifle and took over the point position. He muttered "Dumb-assed National Guard."

As we walked north, we began catching glimpses through the rain of the tops of a forest of palm trees straight ahead -- overlapping masses of them, green fronds tossing in the wind.

We had to be getting close to the runways because the map showed the Duropa Plantation lying just beyond New Strip and lying between Old Strip and the ocean.

Suddenly, off to our left inland, machine guns started rattling.

Pop said, "Ohhh, shit . . ."

The other assault company apparently was over there after all and it was in contact with the Japs. More Jap guns started up.

Then came the faster stammer of our .30s, building the battle noise.

If nothing else, the Japs made it clear they would resist.

# Chapter 30
# Skirmishing!

"Come on, men!" Lieutenant Woodsen turned to look at us. He gave a wave. "Follow m . . ."

If the lieutenant had any dreams of battle glory, they died with him in that instant. A bullet hammered through the back of his helmet and exploded from his face.

Sarge shouted, "Sniper! Take cover in the grass."

Trying to sprint up the soft sand slope, I felt as if I were running in slow motion.

My eyes seemed riveted on the lieutenant's head, now the dark period at the bottom of a long, bright red exclamation mark in the sand.

Suddenly, bullets snapped past us and stitched the sand -- another Jap machine gun began its chugging rhythm to our front. The scare restored my focus.

Further back on the beach, Muskiewicz gave a little yelp – kind of an "ow!"

Terrified, I splashed face-down into a watery trough between two big clumps of Kunai. Pop yelled, "Stan? You okay?"

"Yeah, I think . . ."

Sarge yelled, "Everybody! Stay flat and hold your positions. If you see the bastards, shoot them. Otherwise, save your ammo."

Over the machine gun fire I heard Sarge's rifle bark twice.

The Nambu stopped firing. Briefly. But then it resumed.

Every time a machine gun bullet slapped through the tall grass above me, I felt myself cringe. Pop was close behind, but I felt panic-stricken and very alone.

Looking around, I almost crapped at the sight of a black mask five feet away.

It had two big bloodshot eyes and a terrified grimace. He was a native, nearly naked, black as the ace of spades, hair bushed out even wilder than Larry of the Three Stooges. He was shivering.

Riegle was prone beside him.

"It's okay, Jim," Riegle said. "This here's my buddy Adam. He's the other company's guide. He knows the area real good."

Crouched on his haunches, Adam cringed and jerked just as I did as each Nambu bullet zinged and snapped overhead. His shivering redoubled.

Adam was grinning or grimacing -- hard to tell because his teeth glistened reddish-black. The guy was a fulltime betel nut chewer.

Riegle and I started to calm down because the machine gun fire stayed consistently high. Cradling the M-1 across my forearms, I was wondering what the hell to do.

Adam got me moving. "Masta! Youpela come."

I shook my head, "What?"

Riegle said, "He wants us to come with him."

His voice trembling, Adam repeated, "Plis bossman! Youpela come bilong mepela. Bilong bom."

With that, he turned away, snaking on his belly along the shallow channel in which I took cover.

I couldn't help but see the calloused bottoms of his feet and how the big toe on each foot splayed out – almost like a thumb.

*Life without shoes, I guess.*

We followed him through the grass and moldy vegetation toward the stuttering Japanese machine gun.

Adam stopped abruptly and waved for me to ease up beside him. He gingerly tilted a broad blade of grass and pointed.

To our left was the seaward end of New Strip, all nice and neatly graded with a windsock whipping in the wind. To the right, 200 yards of naked beach.

In the scrub immediately to our right, the Nambu machine gun was blasting to the south down the beach.

Adam had guided us to a perfect position on the Japs' right flank.

The machine gun, heat waves rippling the air above its receiver and cooling fins, was hardly 50 feet away.

Its tripod sat on the crest of a muddy ditch near the side entrance of a bunker. One crewman huddled in the ditch, Sarge's work, I suspected.

The gunner, was firing a professional rhythm -- three shots, then five, then three, then five.

The loader, watching down-range, turned to fit a new ammo strip into the gun's action. As he did, he glanced over the top of the weapon.

He met my eyes.

# Chapter 31
## Stalled

The loader turned to warn the gunner, but I was way ahead of him.

Being right-handed and flat on my stomach meant I couldn't fire to my right, not without trying to socket the rifle's butt against my nose. I quick rolled onto my back, sat up, snapping knees and elbows together – my favorite shooting position -- and drilled the gunner before he trained the gun 10 inches our direction.

My second shot took off the loader's helmet and half his skull.

Adam slapped my shoulder. "Youpela tro bom!" He pointed to the grenade hooked to my cartridge belt, an Aussie Mills Bomb. They look a bit like our pineapple grenades.

"Bom! Plis masta! Youpela troem now!" He pantomimed throwing and – Duh! -- I finally grasped my first lesson in Southwest Pacific pidgin. *Bomb! Please, master! You fella throw him now!*

As I squeezed together the ends of grenade's cotter pin, Riegle yelled, "Jim! Throw the damn grenade, for Christ's sake."

I yanked the pin, reared to my knees, let the spoon fly with its ping and snap and lofted the grenade into the bunker door.

A Japanese soldier leaned from the entry and Riegle shot him just as he underhanded the grenade back toward us. It landed in the sand half-way to us. Riegle and I went flat. Adam disappeared.

Nothing happened.

The "bom" was a dud -- first of many over the next several weeks. Another Japanese appeared in the bunker door and I shot him.

Riegle and I raced to the bunker, arriving just as another Jap stumbled from it. I had the M-1 at high port, so it was simple to bash the rifle butt straight down onto his head. He collapsed atop his own rifle as if I'd shot him, even though I clobbered his helmet.

"I'll kill the little weasel," Riegle said, lowering his rifle barrel.

"No, dammit! Check the bunker!"

Rain drops hissed on the Nambu's hot barrel and receiver as Riegle first peeked and then carefully stepped through the bunker entrance. He stepped back and said, "Stinks, but it's clear."

I grabbed our prisoner's collar, pulled him away from his rifle and sat him upright against the back of the ditch. His head lolled toward filthy bandages on his chest. *No wonder he went down so easy.*

Sarge and Pop appeared behind us. "Now, how the hell did you guys manage this?"

For once, Riegle was at a loss for words. I couldn't answer either. I was still shaking.

# # #

Finally, Riegle asked, "Hey, where's Stan?"

"Dead," Sarge said. "Bullet clipped his leg artery. He bled to death."

"Shit!"

The fire-fight off to our left sputtered back and forth, though we seemed to hear more Nambu fire than American Brownings.

A GI, black with mud to the chin, sloshed in a deep crouch to us in the ditch beside the runway. It was Warner, the would-be cop.

"What the hell happened to you?"

Eyes wide, almost screaming he said, "Boys, it's all swamp over there, right up to your fucking armpits! Hey, I'm supposed to find your company commander. And Lieutenant Woodsen. My skipper needs to talk with them."

"Sorry buddy, there's no damn company," Sarge said. "We're just scouts. A sniper got Woodsen."

"Well, what the hell? My captain wants to talk to somebody who knows what's going on over here."

"Okay," Sarge said, "I'll come with you."

He turned to Pop, Riegle and me. "Corporal Mays, you're in charge. Don't relax. Keep alert for Japs infiltrating down the beach from the plantation.

"Be sure to check your prisoner for weapons and have Pop hoe out this bunker to secure any documents – maps, anything that looks like a diary, anything written.

"You know," he added, "this might be a good place to stow some of the supplies that General Harding's bringing."

"Yeah," Warner interrupted. "And for God's sake, see if you can get us some ammo. We're about out. Some of our machine gun ammo don't work and we got no mortar shells."

Sarge stopped him and turned to me. "Corporal Mays, your first duty is to tell the people on the boats to get word back to G-2 that these Japs sure don't look starved or diseased.

"And listen, make damn sure you stay low and keep your eyes peeled on those palm trees over there at the edge of the plantation. They're ideal for snipers. Sure as shit a sniper got Woodsen."

# Chapter 32
# Digging In

Each in a deep crouch, Sarge and Warner worked their way back inland along the drainage ditch next to the landing strip.

Looking over the Jap bodies, I decided Sarge was at least half right. Both the gunner and his loader were stout and heavily muscled. Their uniforms and gear looked fairly new and in good condition.

But the Jap who tossed the grenade back at us was scrawny and the one I knocked out looked almost skeletal. His uniform was raggedy as any panhandler's garb, and his brown leather belt was green with mildew. Wounds aside, one cheek looked abscessed and pus-filled.

He had a cheap watch, a 6-inch knife in a mildewed scabbard and a notebook filled with vertical columns of spidery calligraphy.

I kept the notebook for G-2 and stole the knife.

The blade was neat. Rather than being like a bayonet where both edges of a blade taper to a point, the business end of this one looked snapped off at a 45-degree angle. The result was an oddly slanted but efficient-looking point. Japanese writing decorated the blade and the edge was sharp enough to shave hair from my arm.

*A keeper. My first souvenir.*

The bunker impressed me too. From the outside, it merely looked like a mound in the earth covered, like everything else, by dead yellowed palm fronds, bamboo stalks and Kunai grass.

Inside, the Japs had worked as hard as they always do. It easily had room for seven men. They had cut out firing slits – three in front and two in back -- in the thick palm logs that formed the walls. The roof logs rested on sand-filled oil drums and were reinforced with rails. I figured it could stand up under fairly heavy artillery.

The smartest touch was two broad benches which ran the bunker's length. They were well off the floor so people could crouch or stretch out, feet out of the floor's mud slurry. I couldn't see why they fired at us from outside the bunker unless we showed up just as they were in the midst of installing the gun.

I examined the bunker again from the outside. It looked like no more than an unremarkable hump in a landscape littered with dead foliage, coconut husks and Kunai grass.

If you knew where to look, the firing slits were visible, but bamboo leaves, dangling fronds and grass blades broke up their outlines.

What I could see of the south end of Old Strip looked almost overgrown with yard-high grass, brush and bamboo. I don't know when it was last used by aircraft, but it looked as if it could have been a decade ago.

Returning inside the bunker, I peered north into the plantation through a reverse firing slit. I could see several mounds that might be bunkers, but no telling. The foliage and ground litter – refuse including six and 10-foot palm fronds -- could disguise them as ordinary hummocks in the earth. I also noticed a creek four or five yards wide, snaking in ox bows toward its mouth far up the beach.

It suddenly hit me that I should thank Adam for saving our asses, but he was gone.

Remembering Sarge's warning about infiltrators, I ordered Riegle to scout into the 300-yard area of scrub and beach between the end of New Strip and the ocean. I pointed out the creek.

"Don't cross the creek. Stay well this side of it. Keep low and under cover and, before you change locations, check up in those palm trees. Sarge says Jap snipers like high places. So stay under cover as you go."

"Oh, bull crap," Pop said. "All Japs are half blind."

"Hey, Pop," I said, "try to tell that to Woodsen or Muskiewicz. These guys we shot didn't have a single pair of glasses among them. But even if you're right and their eyes are bad, don't forget that Japan's lens industry is better than ours. I bet they mount damn good scopes on their sniper rifles."

That kind of sobered him.

Fifteen minutes after Riegle left on his patrol, I heard of rattle of machine gun fire in the plantation. He soon reported back, filthy with mud and sand but trying to act nonchalant.

"I got near the far edge of the runway where there's kind of a turn-out, or maybe a parking place for a plane. It's right near that wind sock. Didn't see anyone," he added.

"But then some Jap cut loose at me with a machine gun so I went flat and crawled back. I couldn't make out where the gun was. Couldn't see muzzle flashes – just tracers zipping past.

"I bet it was a bunker like this one," he said.

Then he laughed.

"I think the gunner screwed up by firing too soon and missing me. I sure heard a Jap yelling at the top of his lungs. I bet some officer was chewing that gunner's ass."

# Chapter 33
# FUBAR Again

When Sarge returned he said the company that made contact with the Japs was badly rattled.

"Every outfit is at its shakiest in its first fire-fight," he said. "And those boys had bad luck. They're a mess."

To begin with, he said, their long hike in the humid heat and the swamp had the men whipped.

"But then when the Japs started shooting, the boys found out that all the swamp scum – the algae and moss and crud – got into their ammo clips and that jams their M-1s. So right now they're more or less down to single-shot rifles.

"They couldn't see where the Japs were until they practically stepped onto their bunkers, so the Japs nailed a bunch of them. And they found the same thing we did – the few Japs they managed to kill looked well-fed and healthy.

He said the company's other problem was that rain or swamp or both swelled the fabric tape in their machine gun belts. "So the ammo wouldn't feed worth a damn and they could hardly return fire."

He stared at me for a long second. "Look, Jim, if I get the hammer, let headquarters know that fabric machine gun belts are no damn good here. They've got to start issuing link belt ammo. It don't swell up."

He gave a short snort of laughter. "Oh by the way, Riegle, your old buddy Warner just about had a conniption fit."

"What do you mean, Sarge?"

"Well, he asked me about something hanging from the side of his neck. Said it felt like a big hot dog."

"What, some kind of growth?"

He grinned. "Yeah, you could say that. It was a leech. It must have fed on him for hours because it was just about the size of a big sausage. I lit up one of those C-ration Chesterfields and touched the thing with it.

"It came right off and I handed it to him."

Sarge shook his head. "Guess I shouldn't have done that. He just went right off his rocker -- just bug-house nuts, hollering, screaming, clawing at his neck."

Sarge held up his fist with its steepled knuckles. "Had to cold-cock him."

"So what did they do about it?"

"Nothing. The medics already had their hands full with the wounded."

"Well," Riegle said, "maybe they could evacuate the bum."

Sarge gave a grim chuckle.

"He's just going to have to get used to it, Jim. Nobody's getting evacuated. The medics improvised a little field hospital – not much more than an aid station – about 200 yards back from the line. That's it.

"The closest road is still almost 30 miles away through solid jungle. The engineers won't get that done for a week or two. We're stuck here with very little fire power."

He looked toward the plantation.

"I'm just praying that the Japs don't counterattack. I'd say things can't get much worse."

But they did.

# Chapter 34
# ... And Trapped

We did our best to get ready for the Japs, setting up their Nambu to cover the gap between the runway and the ocean.

Before joining their ancestors, the Japs left us a nice legacy – some canned meat and fish, much more flavorful than either bully beef or C-Rations.

They also bequeathed to us three cases of their 30-round ammo strips.

Sarge knew how to work the gun, so we set up in their bunker with the gun at the firing slit on the bunker's reverse side.

We also used helmets to dig in next to the bunker. As we scooped out sand and soil, we discovered that rain and rising tide quickly turned our foxhole into a muddy bath.

"Hey, Sarge?"

"Yo."

"If the Japs built more bunkers, I think they'll all have to be mounded like this one because the water table is so high. I mean, we're only about three feet above sea level." I told him that I thought some of the ground irregularities in the plantation might be bunkers.

"At least they look as innocent to me as this bunker does from the outside."

"Damn good point, Jim. We'll have to spread the word about that. Oh, and Jim, I think you're missing something important."

"What Sarge?"

"The bunker you boys captured has firing slits both front and back. What does that tell you?"

"Well, that they can shoot both directions."

"No shit, Dick Tracey," he said. "What it really means is that they'll let, say, an attacking squad -- or just a patrol -- move past. And then start shooting them from the rear just as other bunkers start firing from their front. So – presto -- they've got a whole unit trapped under fire. And if snipers are in on it, then good luck to our boys."

It took a minute for the implications to dawn on me. "Sarge, maybe it would be better if the Japs attacked us instead."

"Right. But we're a little shy on ammo right now."

Luckily, they didn't.

They just spent the night shooting off and on in our direction and yelling nasty things. "Hey GI! We kirr you tonight!" and "GI, you die!" and "Hey, GI! Roseverrt eat shit!"

The few Republicans among us agreed but were ordered to keep their yaps shut.

Now and then the Japs sent up a flare or popped one of their knee mortar shells in our general direction. Occasionally they fired machine gun bursts. Just enough to keep you on edge.

Sarge reflected, "They're playing defense, waiting for us to attack. And it looks like they've got some new kind of gunpowder they didn't have in China. It doesn't give off near as much flash, so it's hard as hell to see their positions."

Late the next morning, rain roaring down again, we heard Riegle yell. Sarge had ordered him several hundred yards to our rear to keep an eye open for infiltrators.

He showed up at our bunker with two weary scouts from First Battalion of the 128th.

Deep scratches and mosquito bite welts had puffed up their faces so at first it was a bit hard to recognize Sergeant Elliott and Pfc. Hewitt. And they were slouching with exhaustion.

"I bet the rest of our company is stretched back on that trail a good mile," Elliott said.

"We just got out of that goddamn jungle trail, so the skipper's having First Platoon take a break on the beach. It's heaven compared to that fucking jungle!"

A few minutes later, their captain dragged up to huddle briefly with Sarge. Then, stooping in the Buna Crouch, the pair took off together to meet with the other CO.

Elliott and Hewitt stayed with me. Each used a cigarette to coax ticks off the other's neck and ears. "Look at that bastard," Elliot said, popping a thumb-sized tick from behind his ear.

"Man," Hewitt said, "I'm sure as hell glad I wore my spats. They are a pain, but they keep the leeches off your legs and they sure protect your ankles and calves from all them jungle thorns."

He unwrapped a bloody tee shirt from his hand to show me a cluster of deep punctures in his palm.

"I was stepping acrosst a log and lost my balance, so I grabbed this furry-looking tree to steady myself. Well, turned to be a six-inch layer of moss covering that tree's thorns.

"And I ain't talking rose bush thorns or raspberry prickers. I'm talking a tree trunk that's studded ever' square inch with black spikes like 6-penny nails and sharp as Momma's sewing needles. You know, like they use on canvas. Woke me right up, I can tell you."

They told us their company was late joining us at New Strip because their route was a narrow trail mostly either knee-deep in mud or under two to five feet of water.

"At first some of the boys were joking that we'd hit a river endways," Elliott said, "but it wasn't funny for long. Especially with the damned mosquitos. It's hard not to inhale the bastards when you walk through a cloud of them."

Hewitt said, "Man, I tell you we are one hell of a long, long way from Oshkosh. You know, sometimes we used to hike in the countryside and now and then we'd have to climb through a farmer's hedgerow . . . you know, where he'd throw all the rocks that he or his granddaddy plowed up. And the rock piles had all kind of saplings and brambles growing up around them? Know what I mean?"

"Sure," I said. Being a city boy, I didn't know what he meant. But what the hell? It sounded like a good story.

"Well, Wisconsin farm hedgerows are nothing! Nossir. You just pick your way through and you might get a few scratches from raspberry canes, but that was it.

"Well, shit, here the jungle along the trail is a damned wall, a solid brown-and-green wall. All them creepers and vines are all growed up twined together right out of that waist-deep water. You could have climbed it the same as a chain-link fence except for them spikey thorns."

"Yeah," the sergeant rolled his eyes and added, "and the damned leeches. Dirty black slimy bastards! Some was in the water and loads of them in the leaves overhead just waiting for us. They drop right onto you and just dig in and start sucking."

"Right," Hewett said. "And, just try to push off the trail into the jungle. Just try it! You bounce off all them creepers and vines and bamboo. You need a machete to get through, but of course we got no machetes. But even if you get through, you're just going up against more of the same.

"The jungle wall is miles thick, I bet. It's just a green hell."

"Well, couldn't your outfit find another route?"

The sergeant took over again. "Hell, no! We was lucky enough to begin with that the Air Corps flew our whole battalion over to Wanigela."

"Where the hell is that?"

"Just a little dump on the ocean," the sergeant said. "It's a village on stilts maybe 60 or 70 miles down the coast from here. First, they told us we was supposed to hike here from Wanigela.

"So they flew us in and we started the hike, but then our native guide boys and the Aussies discovered that some big river down there was flooded way, way the hell out of its banks.

"So the flyboys put us back in their planes and flew us load by load up to Pongani – it's a shithole we call Fever Ridge, mebbe 15 or 20 miles from here."

"Yeah," I said. "We know about Pongani. We spent a week there."

"Okay. Well, then you know they don't call it Fever Ridge for nothing. Bastards kept us there a month and their little hospital was overflowing with guys with malaria or jungle rot.

"Or some of them got dengue fever. That's a real bitch. They call it 'bone-break' fever. The poor bastards that get it walk like they was 90 years old . . . if they can walk at all, that is.

"Anyways, it's a real bitch of a hike to get here from Pongani. Got to cross four or five rivers, some by wading and some teetering on fallen logs for bridges. Lousy with bugs. And the heat! This beach is a damn nice change.

"Anyway, being's how it's just a single trail, I bet one of our companies is still swatting flies and mosquitos back on Fever Ridge.

"I bet it takes a week for the rest of the battalion to get up to here."

Just then Pop yelled from the bunker that the Jap POW seemed to be awakening.

# Chapter 35
## It Just Keeps Getting' Better

I used my flashlight to get a good look at the POW. His face was swollen and looked sore because of his infection and I bet he had a hell of a headache. But he wasn't letting on.

"Do you speak English?"

He just stared right past me with no expression at all. So I bowed deeply to the little bastard and said, "Konbanwa." Good evening.

The courtesy surprised him into a reflexive bow, but that was it.

Drawing on my tiny store of conversational Japanese, I asked him. "Sumimasen. Namae wa nandesu ka?" Sorry. What's your name?

He croaked, "Ishimoto."

"Ahhhh, Ishimoto-san! Arigato!" I bowed again and pointed to my chest. "Jimmy-san."

He bowed and his eyes showed a guarded interest. I pointed to his throat and then pantomimed pain in my throat. He nodded so I handed him my canteen. He drank deeply, grimacing at the chlorine taste of halazone-laced water. But he bowed again saying, "Domo arigato."

When I leaned with my flashlight to look at his infection, he cringed. I guess he feared we'd torture him.

I wanted a medic to examine him, but the medics were busy with our own people. So I just bowed to him and said, "Later, Ishimoto-san."

That seemed to puzzle him.

# # #

The skipper of the newly arrived company let Sarge code a message to G-2, which we learned now had moved from Brisbane in Australia to Port Moresby in New Guinea.

He reported our losses, our POW, the mixed condition of enemy troops and, finally, problems GIs were having with their own weapons.

G-2's reply was terse. U.S. weapons weren't its concern. It wanted us to deliver the POW to Port Moresby immediately and it wanted Japanese numbers – unit IDs and troop strengths. It would get us a new lieutenant in due course.

Sarge replied that G-2 could have the POW whenever it came to get him.

He then forwarded a report about our weapons to Operations and the Quartermaster. All the while he did a slow burn. Finally, he growled, "That useless bastard Willoughby."

"Who, Sarge?"

"I shouldn't bitch to the troops about higher headquarters," he said, "but I can't help it. Willoughby is MacArthur's G-2, his intelligence chief. He was a sergeant with the old Fifth Division in France. And now I bet his pouty little lips have a sweet lock on MacArthur's ass."

This kind of talk wasn't like Sarge.

"But who is he?"

"Brigadier General Charles Willoughby – except when I knew the prick he was Sergeant Adolph Something-Weidenbach, a German immigrant who joined the army.

"Being's how he was a Kraut, Fifth Division sometimes used him in interrogations. He got his name changed to Charles Willoughby, went to some military school, got commissioned and started climbing the rank ladder.

"Now here's the story that's making the rounds about him," he said.

"Back in August, the Japs landed a big veteran outfit just about where we are now. Their engineers constructed New Strip while their infantry hiked south through the jungle, and over the mountains straight for Port Moresby.

"Well Sir Charles, as Willoughby is called, pooh-poohed the threat. 'Naaah, Guys! Don't worry! Japs can't do it. Jungle's too thick. Almost impenetrable. No roads. Formed troops can't move through it or over those mountain trails. The trails are almost vertical, for God's sake.'

"I guess Willoughby forgot about how the Japs whipped our butts in the Philippine jungles . . . or that they advanced through 300 miles of jungle to capture Singapore. Anyhow, MacArthur bought what Willoughby was selling. So he had the Aussies send just a token force to block the Japs.

"First it was just militia and then a battalion of veterans from North Africa. The Japs outnumbered them, and overran them time after time. But the Aussies bled the Japs. Meanwhile, disease, lack of food and that gawdawful terrain nearly did both sides in.

"The Japs actually got within a few miles of Port Moresby. But when U.S. Marines landed on Guadalcanal, the Japs pulled back the remnants of their Moresby invasion force.

"Point is, Willoughby was just flat wrong. If it hadn't been for those few Aussies, the Japs could have done exactly what he claimed was impossible."

Sarge wiped the sweat off his face and gave a sour grin. "So then, that stupid shit turns right around and tells MacArthur that, oh sure! green Midwestern Americans can do what he claimed was impossible for veteran, jungle-trained Japs. Piece of cake.

"So now, instead of being here with us, the 2nd Battalion of the 126th is crawling north towards us over the mountains and through the jungles. And you know why?"

"Why, Sarge?"

"Because when MacArthur wants something, Willoughby cooks his reports to support him. Never mind the fact that trying to march through baking jungle and then over freezing 13,000-foot mountains is a man-killer . . . or that our own damn machine gun ammo won't feed.

"I tell you, I've got more respect for these blood-sucking leeches than that ass-kissing bastard."

# Chapter 36
## SNAFU Atop FUBAR

As a second company began deploying behind us on the beach, the rain let up. And we all took a hopeful breath upon hearing a faint rumbling bass – marine diesel engines, barges or maybe luggers, fishing boats the Aussies adapted for cargo.

Clapping his hands, Pop said, "Hot damn! Maybe it's General Harding with supplies."

He was right.

Unfortunately, the overcast cleared so that we received a surprise and very unwelcome visit from some other new arrivals.

A snarling roar announced a squadron of Zeroes -- at least a dozen of those silvery Japanese Navy planes, each with big blood-red meatballs on wings and fuselage.

They got right down at wave-top level, and as each zoomed past, it slashed the boats with machine gun fire. Their circular attack pattern went right past us, so low we could see the pilots' faces.

Sarge screamed, "My God, those headquarters idiots! They can't learn a damned thing. Didn't they hear how Jap Navy planes sank two British battleships last year?

"Jesus! Talk about shooting fish in a barrel!"

It sickened us.

Columns of spray practically concealed the boats and Zero bullets ripped plank-sized splinters into the air.

Men on the vessels tried to fire back with rifles and machine guns. But after each strafing run, fewer were left. Several boats burst into flame.

The Japs sank all of them.

We splashed out into the surf to help the survivors. I hauled in a foundering lieutenant colonel bleeding from small shrapnel wounds in his face and chest.

As I helped him up the beach, he gasped, "Thanks, buddy. Oh God, thanks loads."

For a minute he stayed bent over, hands on his knees. Once he got his breath, he looked back at the flotsam where the boats had been, he kept saying, "Jesus! Why'd the rain have to stop now?"

General Harding made it ashore unwounded with little more than his dog tags and underwear. Hofstra got to the beach about the same time.

Svoboda didn't. And Drexel's dad would have to find a new business partner.

Hofstra came out of the surf in about the same shape as the general. He was still shuddering as we peeled off some of our gear for him. We also got him some split-toed shoes from the largest Japanese corpse.

Hofstra said the first strafing run killed Drexel. He never saw what happened to Svoboda. "It was pure luck that anybody survived," he said.

I asked, "What all went down with the boats?"

Hofstra's language equaled the situation. "Oh shit," he said, "only about everything that matters – ammo, rations, radios, field wire for phones.

"We had an entire field surgery and lots of medical supplies and medicines. It's all gone. Every damned bit of it! The mortar tubes -- 60s and 81s -- plus all their ammo. Grenades."

"Well," I tried to reassure him. "Headquarters will send us some more."

"Really? I'd like to know how," he said.

"Well, I reckon on boats."

"What boats, asshole? We commandeered every single boat in Port Moresby."

# Chapter 37
# Getting Set

For about one minute after we showed him into the bunker, General Harding's face was ashen. He seemed to be in shock.

But I'll say this, the man had guts. He shook his head and took a deep breath. As he seemed to gather his thoughts, he made up a quick list and handed it to me.

"Keep this somewhere safe, corporal. These are the men of the boats who were firing back at the Jap planes. Several of them are dead and all of them deserve decorations."

He looked at Ishimoto.

"Now who's this?"

"That's our one POW, sir."

Harding nodded to the man. "Good. Let's see if we can get his wounds looked at. He might have some valuable information that we can use."

"Yessir." I jerked my head at Riegle. "Get us a medic, Charlie. General's orders."

Riegle disappeared and Harding asked, "What's your outfit?"

"Sir, we're from the 126th but GHQ designated us an I&R team. Right now, though, we're down to four men and our lieutenant's dead."

"Sorry to hear it," he said. "Where's your radio?"

"Sir, we lost it when the Zeros sank our boat two days ago. Let me go get Sergeant Irish. He's been in touch with both assault companies . . ."

"Assault *companies*? Corporal, there are three battalion assault teams – one's in column here on the shore, another just inland and another . . ."

"Nossir," I said. "The lead company in the second column only showed up here yesterday . . . that we know of."

"Well, for God's sake! Okay, where's your sergeant?"

Just then Sarge ducked into the bunker. "Right here general. I can guide you to either company. Meanwhile, I can fill you in on where they are."

"Well?"

"Sir, they just aren't deployed. They're pretty much stacked up back along the trails or here on the beach."

"Why aren't they spread out?"

"Swamp and solid jungle, Sir. This is all new to these kids and their NCOs and officers. They've never seen anything like it so nobody's patrolling just yet.

"Nobody can say for sure where the Japs are." Sarge added. "But knowing the Japs from China, I'd say that the only solid ground leads smack into their strong points.

"Sir," he went on. "I wanted you to know that I recognized the insignia on a couple of the dead Japs' uniforms. It looks to me like Tojo transferred some of these boys here from China. They're veteran troops."

Harding nodded and then peered intently at Sarge. "Weren't you the sergeant who served with Chiang Kai-shek? You were an officer with the Chinese?"

"Yessir, but that . . ."

"And you were in France in the last war?"

"Yessir. Infantry sergeant."

"Well, you're a lieutenant now, a first lieutenant. And as of now, you and your I&R team work for this headquarters.

He took a deep breath. "So, men, let's get this wreck back on track. Now, what outfit is over there inland?"

"Sir, they're the lead company from Third Battalion, 128th and they have a radio."

"Good, I need it over here now so I can get GHQ up to date and then start getting in touch with the attack columns."

Sarge said, "Very good, sir.

"Corporal Mays," he said. "You and Pop to haul ass over there and bring that company's radio back with all the batteries you can carry."

"We're on the way, Sarge."

Harding grinned. "That's 'sir' now, corporal."

I grinned back. "Yessir. Got it, sir."

# # #

Bending practically double, Pop and I worked our way along the ditch which now was nearly knee-deep coal-black mud.

As we struggled through it, Pop asked, "So, now that he's an officer, what do we call Sarge?"

"Hell, I don't know, Pop."

"Well, what if we call him Lieutenant Bastard? Remember when we met him he said he always was a bastard?"

"Yeah, but the other officers sure wouldn't cotton to that. I don't know. How about we call him Lieutenant Irish?"

"Or we just call him 'Lieutenant'?"

Later in the day when we were alone with him, our brand-new officer said he'd kick our asses if we called him Danny Boy – otherwise, he didn't give a shit.

He said even "Hey you!" would be okay, but that we'd better use "lieutenant" when around other officers.

In the end we chickened out and just settled on calling him Lieutenant Irish.

The captain of the inland column had a real dog-in-the-manger attitude about his radio.

He didn't dare use it because his own radio tech, the code man, was dead. Because of that, he couldn't safely contact his own battalion CO back along the trail somewhere.

Nonetheless, he wanted to hog the radio to himself.

So I suggested that Major General Harding might get somewhat bent out of shape if we had to go back and haul him to the radio. He saw reason and let us take the radio.

Humping that radio back to the general was one of the hardest things Pop and I ever did together.

It must have weighed a good 60 pounds so trying to keep it up out of the mud while crouching low enough to stay out of snipers' sights . . . well, football practice and basic training were a breeze by comparison.

At one point, I asked Pop to stop so I could stand up and ease my back. A second later, a bullet sang so close past my face that I felt its wind.

Like the captain, I saw reason. After that I stayed low as possible.

# Chapter 38
## Meeting The Enemy

Pop and I were catching our breath as the general and a surviving aide got busy with the radio.

That's when Riegle showed up with a medic. "I'm supposed to check out some Jap?" he asked.

Since by default I seemed to be the Unofficial Temporary Acting NCOIC Prisoner, I got Ishimoto to his wobbly feet and brought him out of the bunker to the ditch. "See what you can do for him. The general says we may need him."

The POW's eyes bulged when the medic knelt beside him with a set of shiny medical scissors in hand.

I held up a hand, palm toward the prisoner, and tried to sound soothing. "Ishimoto-san," I said, "it's okay. No problem."

He probably didn't understand, but he relaxed when the medic quietly repeated "It's okay" over and over as he gently cut away cloth.

"Well, my friend, looks like you've got some infection here. I'm just going to sprinkle some of our magic yellow powder on it." He dusted sulfa on the man's wounds and redressed them. He also gently cleaned the facial ulcer and applied sulfa to it.

Fifteen minutes later the medic told me that in addition to his shrapnel wounds, our POW was suffering dysentery and probably malaria. "He ought to be in a hospital. But that goes for damn near everybody. Feed him and keep him hydrated, he'll live.

"He acts depressed, though. We hear that's pretty common with Jap POWs. Supposedly they're so ashamed about being captured that they want to kill themselves."

Overhearing, General Harding said, "We need to interrogate him so we don't want any of that. Have him guarded at all times."

"Yessir. Uh, G-2 wants him, sir."

"Fine. He's all theirs whenever they come to get him."

# # #

General Harding's first task, once we brought him the radio, was to update MacArthur's headquarters.

Speaking in the clear, one of his staff told GHQ the Cracker Line was cut. It meant nothing to me, but Lieutenant Irish chuckled. "The general had his radio man use a fairly obscure Civil War situation to tell HQ where we stand – damn little food or ammo and the supply line ain't operating."

From the way General Harding acted, you'd never have known things were that bad. He may have felt discouraged -- I would have -- especially when GHQ reported that the tanks he requested had sunk. The barge on which they were being loaded went down blub-blub-blub under their weight . . . right at the dock.

"Damn!" was all he said.

He hid any doubts or fears, merely looking tired and now and sometimes seeming exasperated. He stayed businesslike and calm, just like one of my professors, even when swatting mosquitos, scratching bites and sweating bullets like everybody else.

So the rest of us took heart.

Now had I been in his shoes, I would have blown my stack when the commander of the delayed battalion finally reported.

Harding, however, welcomed him and listened attentively as the wretched man explained how mud and flooding all along on his assigned route slowed his outfit to a crawl.

"Sir, you just can't march at 120 per minute when you're waist deep in flood water or have four pounds of mud clinging to each boot!" The battalion CO also said the trek was too much for men who'd been on half rations while marking time on Fever Ridge.

The general calmly told the battalion CO that marking time was over. He directed him where to deploy his troops and to prepare for an assault in two days.

The battalion at least was able to bring along its mortar battery.

While waiting for GHQ to get back to him, the general asked how Riegle and I managed to capture the bunker. I told him how Adam, a native police officer, had guided us to the perfect spot.

"An ally, eh? Please see if you can locate him or some of his buddies. We could use their help."

It took Riegle about an afternoon to find Adam and bring him back. Two of Adam's friends tagged along. They looked just like Adam – short, broad-nosed, pitch-black skin, built like Charles Atlas, fuzzy-wuzzy hair, naked except for a knee-length skirt and hands and feet as hard as carved mahogany. They professed to hate Japs and to like Aussies but to like Americans even more.

General Harding's staff began arrangements to hire Papuans as stretcher-bearers and supply porters.

Riegle meanwhile managed to come up with some C-rations for Ishimoto. Later, he said the POW wanted to speak to me.

When I approached, the Japanese bowed deeply. "Jimmy-san, sank you drink, eat. Domo arigato!" Then he pointed to his knife on my hip and held out his hand. "Dozo!" Please.

I shook my head. "No, Ishimoto-san."

His face contorted and he thumped his forehead several times with his fist. He pleaded, "Dozo! Dozo!" Then he said "seppaku" while showing me stomach-slitting motions of ritual suicide.

*He wants the knife to kill himself, not us.*

I spent a hapless 20 minutes trying to lift his mood. Then I just changed to direct questions. I pointed to the coconut palm plantation. "Dozo, Ishimoto-san. Taksan Nippon heitai?" Please, Ishimoto. Many Japan soldiers?

"Hai!" He nodded vigorously, sucking his breath through his teeth. Then, using the throat-clearing noise Asians often employ for emphasis, he nodded and stressed, "Takhhhsan!" My Japanese didn't include "how many," so I scribbled the number 1,500 on a slip of paper and showed it to him.

"Iie!" he said, rapidly shaking his head no. He held up his right hand and spread the fingers, repeatedly dropping a finger then raising it then dropping it.

I called into the bunker. "General, sir? If I read him right, our POW here says we're facing 4,000 to 5,000 Japanese troops."

He came to the bunker entrance looking old. "You're sure, corporal?"

"Sir, I have only taken some conversational Japanese, but that's what he seems to indicate."

"Well," he said. "We really do need to get him to G-2. They may have a linguist. Even so . . ."

He turned back into the bunker. "Leonard, guess what the latest is."

A few minutes later, I heard the general swear for the first time. "Holy shit! He's serious?"

Soon, scuttlebutt had it that General Harding was white-hot. Not only had GHQ taken one of his battalions out of play by forcing it to march across New Guinea, but it also had just lent another battalion to the Australians. The Ivory Tower apparently ordered that outfit to march ten miles northwest through jungle and mangrove swamps to support the Australian assault on Buna.

Those orders bewildered me at first. Lieutenant Woodsen's map originally gave the impression that Buna was just beyond the two airstrips and plantation to our front. Yet now GHQ had the Aussies and the part of 126th attacking quite some distance from us.

It turned out they – together with the battalion trekking across the island for a month now -- were to assault Buna and Buna Mission, two tiny meaningless clusters of beach front dwellings nine damn miles north of New Strip and Old Strip.

The attack orders came along with a special cheering note from the Supreme Commander, Southwest Pacific, Douglas MacArthur himself.

"All columns are to be driven through to their objectives regardless of losses."

# Chapter 39
## "... At All Costs"

With dawn approaching, all we knew was that our mission was to attack and capture the airstrips. The assault turned out to be brief and brutal.

For us.

Having no artillery and few machine guns that functioned, the men of the 128th Infantry had no choice. Each simply had to fix his bayonet on his rifle, shove a clip into his M-1, chamber the first round, stand up and start walking north.

I was ashamed not to be part of the attack.

But glad, too.

We made out the shadowy forms of GIs moving in the ground fog and dim greenish sunlight filtering through the tree tops. As always, it was stifling. But right now no rain. No bird calls. The windsock at the end of New Strip hung limp.

Each GI moved in a slight crouch. The troops either carried their M-1 rifles diagonally across their chests or pointed the muzzles forward, stocks by their hips, fingers on trigger guards.

Three squads, well spread out, headed north along the beach past the east end of New Strip.

We were told that inland, at the far west end of New Strip, troops from the 128th would move north on narrow jungle tracks. From our bunker, we saw several other squads cross New Strip itself, moving toward the plantation.

Suspecting what lay hidden among the palm trees and Kunai grass, I got the impression that the plantation was holding its breath.

Then it roared.

Storms of machine gun and rifle fire flailed the attackers. As dozens of Nambu machine guns began their ponderous thumping, blue-white tracers clawed through the GI ranks.

Watching through our bunker's firing slits, Pop and I saw the fire cut down several soldiers instantly. Others staggered and then collapsed. Bullets knocked one soldier backwards into the creek. He disappeared, the weight of his gear pulling him under.

The instant that the firing began, perhaps a dozen scattered Japanese soldiers arose from forward listening posts and sprinted north into the plantation. Our men opened fire, killing some of the forward observers. Some GIs raced to get in among the plantation's trees, too. But Jap marksmen took them out one-by-one. Some of the men attacking toward the plantation recoiled to their own lines.

A squad near the east end of New Strip had disobeyed orders and sought the false comfort of sticking close together. Like most green troops, they didn't have the veteran instinct to stay five yards apart.

A merciless burst of Nambu tracers toppled them precisely in order just as if they were a row of dominos.

We rarely glimpsed muzzle flashes from the Japanese lines, just flying tracers.

Pop and I both had our rifles up. Together we nailed three of the fleeing Japs, but saw no other targets. Finally, out of frustration, we began shooting into the tops of closer coconut palms. Fronds whipped and twisted as our bullets smacked through them. Bright red elongated dots spattered down the trunk of one palm, but nobody ever fell from the tree.

Meanwhile, Lieutenant Irish scanned right and left with his binoculars, stopping to make notes.

It was all over in 15 minutes . . . except for the screaming from wounded men lying out in plain view. One man yelled, "For Christ's sake help! Jesus God, it hurts! Medic! Mediiiiic! Aren't there any medics for us? Where are you guys? Helllllllp!"

A medic with a red cross on his helmet and another on his arm, trotted with his equipment bouncing, to one of the wounded in the middle of New Strip. Just as he knelt beside the man, a harsh crack sounded – a sniper.

The medic jerked and collapsed beside the wounded soldier he set out to save.

It didn't take long for everyone to catch on -- Jap snipers were targeting medics. The medics wised up quickly, ditching brassards and helmets bearing the red cross.

The Japs appeared to be gut-shooting GIs. Men with those wounds could yell for hours until their voices gave out or they were lucky enough to die.

If any of our troops were still alive within enemy lines, they had hidden themselves.

# Chapter 40
# The Butcher Bill

Lieutenant Irish snapped us out of our shock. "Come on, you guys."

"What, Sarge?"

"Dammit, we've got to report."

We scuttled back four miles to General Harding's HQ. By the time we got there, he was meeting with the CO of the 128th.

"Look Colonel, General MacArthur this morning gave us a very specific directive to take Buna today at all costs. 'At all costs,' His words, not mine!"

The lieutenant colonel said, "Well, general, going against that kind of fire, I think we could lose an entire battalion without gaining 100 yards. It's just plain murder. You couldn't tell where the fire came from."

"Right," Harding said. "I don't want your outfit slaughtered, especially if we gain nothing by it. You know the 32nd earned its red arrow reputation in France for being able to cut through any enemy line – but what you don't usually hear is that it cost better than 11,000 killed and wounded. I don't want us to have that kind of butcher bill."

The colonel said, "He might come gunning for you."

"That's my worry, colonel. You just worry about your boys and your mission."

As the colonel left, General Harding nodded and turned to us. "Okay, Lieutenant, what can you tell me?"

"Sir, it's just like it was in France only worse. In France you at least could see the barbed wire and trenches. Here, you can't see much at all. Tracers came from at least eight well-concealed points in the eastern sector of the plantation alone.

"They're firing either from bunkers like the one Mays and Riegle captured, or covered trenches. Sir, I have to say that as long as the Japs have this kind of cover, 'at all costs' won't buy us a damn thing. It's trench warfare all over again."

Biting his lips, the general stared at him.

Lieutenant Irish spoke up again. "Too bad that we can't get the Navy in here to lay down a barrage. Just one cruiser or just a destroyer . . . they'd at least blast away some of the trees and ground cover."

The general shook his head.

"Can't. Navy's got its hands full trying to sustain the Marines over in the Solomons. We've got to do something on our own to pinpoint these bastards. I'm hoping we can get air support like they had down at Milne Bay.

"If nothing else, they can strafe these damned palm trees and take out snipers."

Lieutenant Irish said, "Well, if they could do some bombing in the plantation it sure wouldn't hurt. It would blow away some of that cover and bring down some of that timber."

"You're right," the general said. "But air support requires some damn good air control work. That won't happen overnight. We can see the planes, but they can't see us or our positions down here in all this lettuce."

Lieutenant Irish was quiet for a minute. Then he raised his head and looked at the general.

"You know, Sir," he said, "maybe there's something my boys and I can try."

"What do you have in mind, lieutenant?"

"Sir, do you remember that in North Africa the Aussies and British picked up an Arab word? They said we needed to 'take a shufti,' in other words to 'take a look'?"

"Yes, I remember."

"Well, sir, I think we can do just that for you."

# Chapter 41
# Taking A Shufti

I led the patrol.

But it sure as hell wasn't my idea.

Lieutenant Irish volunteered for the job, but the general said that he possessed specialized knowledge about Japs and their tactics – knowledge we needed. So he'd best stay behind and pick one of us to lead.

The lieutenant tapped me, claiming I was the Sneakiest Pete of the bunch.

It made me want to sneak right out of our headquarters. But I hadn't mastered the skill of simply disappearing right in front of my commander's eyes.

So I wound up pushing up this creek inside the Jap lines at 0200 hours with Pop and Riegle in trail. We hoped we'd get all the way back alive.

We'd rubbed mud on our faces, put on the dirtiest, darkest shirts we could find.

Hoping to break up our silhouettes, we covered our heads and necks with torn shirts from the aid station, threading them with leaves from palm fronds, bamboo and Kunai grass.

Hugging the banks, we crouched in the creek because, with the tide out, it was only tits deep.

I didn't want anything showing above the water but my head and the .45 in my right hand. I had Ishimoto's knife at my hip.

The creek was all ox bows and S-curves, winding left first, then right, then back, its low banks covered with brush and bamboo.

For the first time on New Guinea, I was happy about all the night noises – the myriads of buzzing bugs, the bellowing of crocs, piercing calls of night birds, the snapping of click-clack lizards or whatever they were, flapping fruit bats plus the land crabs that were forever rustling in the brush.

I hoped the noises would obscure the little gurgles that the creek's current created against our necks and shoulders. Stupid, I know, but I even welcomed the mosquitos' whine in my ears.

We started well after dark, wading off the beach into the ocean.

Then, chin deep, we cut north a good half mile in the surf – inhaling a fair amount of salt water along the way -- until we were at least 200 yards out from the creek's mouth.

From there we very slowly followed the creek for several hundred yards into Jap territory.

We moved against the current maybe a half hour when I experienced sheer terror well above my usual level of being scared shitless.

It happened when my right knee bumped something rock hard.

Now that didn't bother me.

But when the object started moving . . . and pushing against my leg . . . I damn near screeched like the choir's entire soprano section!

It pushed with immense strength and headed downstream.

And it was long enough that it took a while to pass me, something very rough and hard repeatedly hitting my leg under water.

*Good God, that's a tail? A croc?*

Something in the reptile's wake broke the surface of the creek right beside me. It rolled sullenly and slowly sank again, leaving behind the gagging smell of pure rot.

*Bastard must have been feeding.*

I didn't move a muscle until it passed. Didn't even breathe. Then I turned slowly and looked toward Riegle behind me and Pop behind him.

Their cover foliage was barely visible to in the darkness. Both were rigid. I signaled with my head and tried to slow my breathing and my pounding heart.

Meanwhile, it took supreme concentration to keep my sphincter's pucker setting at a full 100 per cent.

Riegle got to me first and started to speak. I clapped my palm over his mouth. "Close your hole! Not a fucking word. Understand?" He gave a jerky nod.

Then Pop arrived, starting to put his mouth to my ear.

Now Pop's bass whisper carries. I swear, when everybody's out on the range firing M-1s, you still can still hear his rumbly whisper over the bark of 30-06 shots.

"Jim! Was that what I think . . .?"

I hissed, "Quiet, dumbshit!"

We proceeded upstream through a long bend to a spot where the creek banks were higher and some thoughtful Japanese had dropped a bridge of palm logs across the stream.

Once beneath them, I ordered Pop to stay while Riegle and I crawled onto firm ground to take our shufti.

It seemed to me that the Japs would want some kind of defense near their bridge. They did. We found it in about a minute.

Singing was the tip-off. Reigle and I both grinned in fearful amusement, recognizing the rhythm and tune before we made sense of the garbled words.

Some hip Jap cat who should have been paying attention to duty was grooving to his own version of *The Bugle Boy of Company B*.

"A tooo ahtoo ahtooo didvahda tooo

"He bro eight to de bahh . . ."

The Andrews sisters he was not. Riegle put his mouth to my ear. "Let's kill him for butchering our song."

"Shuddap!"

Stomachs and faces to the mud, we maneuvered very slowly. It took a while to discover that the music came from a bunker that seemed twice the size of ours.

What's more, it had an antenna strung from one of its logs to the bole of an adjoining coconut palm whence it led upward into the night. *Maybe a headquarters.*

As we moved on, we heard men marching – at least two squads of Jap soldiers. They had their rifles slung and they were marching in step, hobnails on a solid surface, not 100 feet to our right.

We froze.

They stopped, stacked their rifle into tripods and stretched. Then they did a series of side-straddle hops, just like in our Daily Dozen. Once they finished their exercises, they retrieved their rifles and disappeared.

I mean it.

The SOBs just dropped out of sight.

# Chapter 42
# Sneaking Back

We edged very carefully toward the point where we last saw the disappearing Japs.

Riegle carefully came close and whispered. "You know what, I think they was marching on a real road. Not much foliage growing on it."

We came upon a deep ditch that looked about six feet wide and 100 feet long. A lot of boards and palm fronds crossed it, but it clearly was a ditch or maybe a communications trench that the Japs could use going from bunker to bunker.

It ran parallel to Old Strip.

We turned away and started moving south towards home. Big chilly drops began slapping our backs. And then it was a torrent. For once, we welcomed the downpour because it would cloak our noise.

As we made a big circuit, we got a whiff of latrines and then smelled cooking along with cigarette and cigar smoke, all coming from bunkers we didn't see.

We got a hell of a scare, too. The downpour also cloaked the sloshing march of a file, maybe a squad, of Japanese soldiers.

They were max ten feet away before we heard them passing. In the gloom and rain, we froze and didn't try to make out their faces. But we had no doubt they were Japs – baggy pants with tight-wrapped lower legs, short silhouettes, carrying rifles that looked far too long for their stature.

Most of them also were toting what looked like ammo boxes. Then, like the other guy we saw earlier, they just melted into the ground, one-by-one . . . another trench.

Taking a glance inside it, we saw what looked like a small artillery piece – slender barrel maybe five feet long emerging from a blocky action topped by a thick, curved magazine.

Figuring we'd done enough for one night I tapped Riegle on the shoulder.

"Come on, let's get up and walk. Just don't speak."

We covered no more than 100 yards, however, because we suddenly found ourselves sinking into ooze – some more of New Guinea's reeking swamp.

We had to half-swim, half-crawl to find the creek before we could float down to meet Pop still hiding beneath Bugle Boy Bridge.

The tide had turned, raising the creek level. It was a long cautious way back, but at least we didn't have to crouch. Once out to sea and far enough south to be behind our lines, we clambered up the beach just as dawn set the horizon glowing.

It took about 10 minutes and two Chesterfields to boost all the leaches from our legs, torsos and privates.

# # #

I reported to Lieutenant Irish that we had moved perhaps a half mile behind the Jap lines.

He asked lots of pertinent questions that firmed up my confused impressions. He said the gun that we spotted probably was a 25 mm antiaircraft weapon. In the end, I found his summation to be damned depressing.

"Based on what you guys report," he said, "here's what I'm going to tell the general. It looks like the Japs have constructed a very extensive bunker and trench complex and they might have it fully manned.

"It also appears to be defense in depth," he said, "with mutually supporting positions. And you say they seemed to have a road with a hard surface?"

I nodded yes and he mulled over his observations for a minute.

"If what you saw was typical, I'd say it looks like they've buried their defenses between New Strip and Old Strip and all through the Duropa Plantation.

"All those dug-in machine guns — let alone that 25 mm -- make New Strip and Old Strip absolutely useless to the Air Corps unless we capture the whole area. And then they've got a road to move units back and forth as they need them."

"So what you're saying then," I said, "is that we've probably got a lot of Japs waiting for us in an underground fortress."

"That's it, buddy. A regular Maginot Line."

"There's one other thing, Sir."

"What's that?"

"I may be off base here, but I think that the only way to get from New Strip to Old Strip is crossing that bridge or going through the plantation. Because it seemed to me that everything inland from the bridge and both runways is nothing but swamp."

Well, I was half-right.

What we didn't realize at this point — and obviously MacArthur didn't either — was that Japanese engineers not only cleared and graded New Strip, but they also constructed dozens of bunkers and hundreds of fighting positions near both strips, throughout the plantation and then north to Cape Endaiadere — where the coast bent abruptly west leading to Buna

Later we learned that they dug trenches, built bunkers and camouflaged fighting positions throughout the entire 10-mile coastal crescent extending from the airstrips to Buna.

It looked as if they designed it to repel invasion from the sea.

But considering that hardened combat veterans manned all those positions, their work was equally effective against attacks from land.

# Chapter 43
# At All Costs . . . Again

Being a mere corporal, I knew diddly about the conversations between General Harding and GHQ. But any dunce could tell that our boss and his bosses were at odds.

We all knew MacArthur was demanding that we capture Buna and the airstrips immediately, never mind any details about swamps or bunkers.

Meanwhile, General Harding was ordering the commanders of his battalions not to get their men uselessly butchered

I don't know if GHQ just refused to believe what we reported after our patrol or if they just didn't give a rat's ass. Maybe the problem was Herr Willoughby. Whatever the case, GHQ just kept ordering Harding to take the objectives "regardless of cost" because "time was of the essence."

MacArthur applied more pressure by sending his own chief of staff, General Sutherland, to browbeat General Harding.

I overheard their shouting match while I was busy digging a headquarters well. (Go down two feet and you got crystal clear water. Just don't forget the Halazone tablets.) General Harding was much the shorter, quieter man but I thought he gave as good as he got.

He blasted Sutherland.

"Bullshit, Dick! And stick your threats up your butt! I damn well will not relieve *any* commander. Why? First, because GHQ keeps meddling with *my* command, and superseding *my* orders and it's just causing sheer chaos. And, second, GHQ has kept about half my command out of my control. So why the hell would I have the faintest reason to dump men who are kept out of my control?

"And, finally, Dick, you can tell General MacArthur that my officers have been doing as well as anyone could expect under these conditions which, I might add, GHQ could do a great deal to alleviate by getting supplies to us.

"Finally, I don't want my boys to pay the 11,000-man cost that the 32$^{nd}$ paid in 1918."

As I left, General Sutherland -- a sarcastic and nasty SOB – was growling something about "If you can't get these guys moving, we'll find someone who can."

# # #

General Harding's sentiments were fine with me, especially now that Riegle, Pop, Hofstra and I were sent to temporarily replace casualties in a company at the west end of New Strip. A sergeant commanded the platoon to which they assigned us. His CO disappeared in the last attack.

"Was he shot?"

"Hard telling," the sergeant said. "Maybe the crocs got him or maybe the Japs shot him and the swamp rats ate him."

"Swamp rats?"

"Yeah. Big fat bastards. We've noticed that they feed on corpses. Look, boys, don't worry about them. If you're dead, something's going to eat you and you won't give a damn what it is. Right? So just worry about the Japs and stay alive."

He passed us to Third Squad – seven survivors of the original dozen. They looked somewhat like pirates -- dirty, gaunt, hollow cheeks, eyes sunken, scruffy beards and uniforms in rags.

They were pale and two of them were shuddering with chills.

"It's malaria," one said. "They can't give us nothing for it and they got no place in that shithole of a hospital, so might as well be here."

The squad leader was a corporal, a little guy with his upper lip curled in a perpetual sneer. His boys glared at us when he demanded whether I was taking over the squad.

"Nope," I said. "You know these guys and you're all veterans. So you're in charge. The four of us would like to stay together, that's all. Just tell us where you want us."

The corporal told the squad his commander-sergeant had briefed him to attack at midnight.

"No more of this walking tall shit," he said. "We're going to attack quiet-like on all fours. You can even submarine like we used to do in football, right down on your gut.

"But when we see them, we're up and on them. Fix your damned bayonet. You'll probably need it. Clean the ammo in your clips, 'cause otherwise your M-1 jams.

"And you new guys! No fucking smoking once we move up. Jap snipers love it. You can't see them, but they sure as hell can see you lighting up with your Zippo. Personally, I don't give a rat's ass if a sniper kills you. But the bullet might hit one of us and that would really piss us off. Got it?"

His men nodded grimly.

"Oh, the other thing -- don't trust the grenades. Sometimes they just don't go off."

# # #

We moved up to the line about 2330, my heart pounding so loud -- whup-thup whup-thup – that I feared Japs could hear it. I also was terrified that I'd chicken out -- and was just this side of doing it.

At 2400 we heard the attack signal, three pistol shots. The attack began immediately but I think it started as one the quietest assaults in the history of war.

We moved out on all fours, pushing quietly into pitch darkness along the muddy tracks. To keep together, each had to keep a hand on a boot of the guy ahead.

Finally, somewhere off to our right along New Strip a Nambu started coughing. From its *bap-bap-bap-bap*, those brilliant blue-white tracers chased above us, clattering in the branches and vines overhead.

A mortar flare popped above us and we froze.

At first, the flare just made things worse than the darkness. Rocking back and forth above us in its little parachute, the flare created moving shadows that seemed to put every leaf and vine in play – even the bushes and rank grass in which we lay seemed to move.

But that sickly green light helped me spot a single stationary object, a black rectangle maybe three feet wide and a foot high in a low mound 30 feet off to our left.

Clusters of palm leaves dangled over it, their shadows shifting back and forth with the flare's oscillation, but the rectangle stayed rock steady – had to be a bunker firing slit.

Remembering our training by Lieutenant Irish, I hissed to Pop slowly turned my head and nodded to his left

He slowly nodded and cautiously moved left as I let Riegle and Hofstra know. I shifted right.

Submarining – moving on our bellies with Hofstra and Riegle behind us -- we shoved inch-by-inch through a matted tangle of thorns, leaves, brush and vines beside the trail . . . and then both of us sank more or less face-first into a deep pool of mud.

# Chapter 44
# Operation Crud

Well, no, it actually wasn't mud – nothing that nice.

We were floundering about in decaying semi-solid vegetation – kind of like the sodden remains of a head of lettuce that you've left in the fridge for a month or two.

Except rotten lettuce usually isn't populated by the little moving things that skittered away from us.

On reflection, I'd say that assorted bats, snakes, toads, fist-sized snails, monkeys, frogs, parrots, sloths and other jungle critters had died and fallen into that depression – but only after first being required to shit in it.

After that they decomposed, adding to the mix of dead lily pads, algae, expired vines, fungus, dead leaves and rotting branches. It was a real, *real* ripe bath, with the rich color and thick texture of a chocolate malted.

It just wasn't chilled.

But it was deep enough that with my feet still behind me on half-firm ground, my arms were barely long enough to touch bottom. To keep from drowning, I had to push with my rifle to lever my head above the putrid liquescence.

*Good luck keeping my M-1 clips clean.*

Beside me, Pop sputtered, "Waugh! This stinks"

By now the flare was out, though tracers continued arcing around the jungle. I spat out a mouthful of muck and wiped my eyes. Then I got my feet under me and, crouching low, began a slow-motion frog walk through the waist-deep morass.

The suspected firing slit verified itself by exploding in light and fury, muzzle flash and tracers ripping from it. For a second I thought I was a dead man, but it all flashed past me toward the trail.

Maybe the gunner was nervous. Anyway, he stopped shooting almost as soon as he started.

Practically beside the firing slit, a slimy giant reared out of the muck -- Pop making a tackle's long reach as clots of filth plopped off his sleeves and shirt. He shoved his grenade through the firing slit into the bunker.

Two-three-four-five. Nothing. Another dud grenade.

Three shapes scrambled, yammering ferociously, from the back of the bunker, tearing over its top toward Pop. I shot one and the other two were on him. As they thrashed in the scum, I couldn't shoot again for fear of hitting Pop. I started to push toward him when Riegle yelled, "Look out, Jim!"

Then I had my hands full of Jap.

My attacker was little, but my God was that bastard strong! It was just savage gutter fighting. I tried to bash his head with my helmet but lost my grip on it. His attempt to head-butt my face glanced off. We both growled in clenched-teeth fury because slime made us too slippery to get a solid grip on each other.

I yanked at his shirt and the rotted khaki just ripped away at the seams. He gave an explosive shout and jammed the meat of his hand into my mouth, apparently wanting to twist my head right off my neck.

Dumb move.

I imagined myself a croc, and bit down with all the strength in my jaws. He yelled again, yanking that steely hand away.

My greater weight enabled me to roll his head and shoulders under the surface of the mire.

I thought I could drown him but somehow he wiggled around enough to kick me in the nuts, forcing me to take a sudden bow . . . face down in the muck again.

He locked a rock-hard grip on back of my neck, but then it just went limp and disappeared.

I could stand again. I could breathe again.

Not seeing the Jap, I let myself collapse against the face of the bunker. I was too whipped to even wipe the ordure from my face. Pop and Riegle joined me. Pop was wheezing and pulling with him a Jap whose neck he held locked in the crook of his arm.

We stayed low, half-lying on the bunker's slanted face, because the night was alive with gunfire, tracers flying everywhere – crimson American vs white Japanese.

I finally gasped, "Hey, Pop? That guy? Is he dead?"

"What guy?"

"The one you're dragging under your arm there."

"Oh." He released the body, letting it float. "Yeah."

I looked at Riegle, "What the hell happened to my guy?"

"I bayonetted him and Hofstra bashed his head with his rifle butt. Twice! He was one tough bastard."

"Yeah," Pop said, flicking rot from his face. "They were real hard-asses."

"Where's my rifle?"

Hofstra said, "Jim, I bet it sank in this . . . uh . . . stuff."

"Thanks a lot."

"Hey, Jim, I didn't lose it! You did."

"No, Stupid, I mean thank you – you and Riegle both -- for saving my damned life."

"What do we do now?" Hofstra asked.

"Let's get back to the trail."

We started toward it. Hofstra eased up onto the trail and machine gun fire blasted through him, left to right, knocking him on his side.

Hofstra gently rolled onto his face without a sound. We ducked back into the muck.

Pop had spotted the muzzle flash.

Riegle said. "Let's flank 'em and take the bastards out."

"Are you crazy?" Pop whispered, loud enough to be heard in Tokyo. "There's probably two more bunkers ready to hose anybody trying that. Ever hear of interlocking fire?"

Just then, with the usual roar, New Guinea dropped one of its patented tropical deluges on us.

"*Now* can we try it?" Riegle asked.

We tried grenades first. All three of us threw a grenade toward the bunker. Two exploded and the shooting stopped.

The Japs, it turned out, weren't inside a bunker at all. Instead they had mounted their Nambu below one of those domes of slender roots supporting some kind of jungle tree.

The roots were close together, but not enough to screen them from grenade fragments.

# Chapter 45
# The Malaria Assault

Slithering in the dark like slime-coated lizards, we eased past another bunker's face and tossed our last three grenades inside. One exploded.

It did the job.

We hauled the Jap bodies from the bunker. As it started to rain again, we stood in it, faces raised, taking a cool but welcome shower.

We took over the bunker and I stood first watch.

I didn't want the dreams.

# # #

Waking up at dawn was a cold cast-iron bitch. My ears were roaring and I was shivering. Just getting myself to my knees was a dizzying, staggering effort. *Malaria, I bet.* The instant I started to rub my eyes, I quit. At least three well-engorged ticks had fastened themselves around my eyes.

Pop was now on guard. I whispered, "Hey, Pop."

"Yeah, Jim."

"How about firing up a butt and getting these ticks by my eyes?"

He opened the little tin box in which he kept his Lucky Strikes. As the lighter illuminated Pop's face, I could tell he felt rocky. His normally round mug looked craggy and was running with sweat. H was shivering, too.

Meanwhile, Riegle moaned and twisted in his sleep. Pop gave me the cigarette after he persuaded the ticks to drop. Then we started to work on each other's leaches.

As we did so we made a sickening discovery and both nearly vomited. The downpour had washed a lot of the dirt and crud from us, but every fold in our clothes was filled with its own a little wiggling squad of maggots.

Riegle's clothes, too.

"Frantically brushing at his sodden clothes, Pop said, "Auggggh! For God's sake where did they come from?"

I had my shirt off, flapping it to get rid of the creatures. "How the hell would I know? Maybe from that slime bath that we were taking last night."

It took quite a while for us to settle ourselves down.

After that, we had to awaken and then calm Riegle. Being a farm boy, he didn't find the discovery quite as revolting as we did, but it still shook him.

# # #

"Sack out Pop," I said. "I'll take the watch."

"Naaa, I'm okay. I just wish we had some food."

"God!" Riegle said. "How can you even think about food now?"

"At least we're fairly clean," I said. "The rain rinsed off a lot of that crud."

"Not enough," Pop said.

We should have been cocky. We had killed Japs in two bunkers, captured their Nambus and now held a toehold near the west end of New Strip.

But the squad now was down to five men – three for our bunker and two for the other. Our sneering corporal tottered toward the rear some hours ago, a muddy field dressing covering the mangled side of his face.

At first light, we spotted him -- face down in the muddy track behind us, not far from Hofstra. Rats were busy at both corpses.

That's when we also got our first daytime look at the surface of the muck pool in which we had fought. It contained the bodies of the Japs we killed, and older corpses, all seething with a white wiggling crust of you know what.

We named it Maggot Marsh.

So I was in command of two bunkers, having no idea whether we were inside or beyond our own lines. We didn't dare speak above a whisper.

Worse, I didn't know what to do other than watch for Japs in the jungle curtain and keep an eye peeled for snipers.

"What are we going to do?" Pop asked.

"I was just telling myself I don't know, so I can't tell you."

Riegle sat up. "Well, MacArthur's orders are for us to capture Buna at all costs."

"Right, Charlie! And if you want to press on toward Buna, be my guest. Pop, you want to go with him?"

"Up yours, Mr. Corporal, sir."

"For God's sakes," Riegle said. "I wasn't saying *we* should do that! I just think it's time for somebody to take over from this squad. Wouldn't you say so?"

"Yep, and I think maybe one of us should go back to see if we can find HQ and tell them what the situation is. But I don't like the idea. I bet snipers have the trail covered. We better just wait until they send some people up here. If they don't, we'll take off after dark."

Pop stretched out and Riegle and I were peering through the firing slits at the jungle when we heard airplanes.

The jungle canopy screened them from view, but their sound grew nearer and then they began circling.

"They sound like fighters, but not like them Zeros," Riegle said. "Their engines sound different to me somehow. Hey, do you suppose we're finally getting some air support?"

We had the impression at least three or four fighter planes were cruising overhead. "What the hell are they waiting for?"

At last, the sound of one engine deepened to a roar and it zoomed above us. Then came two crashing explosions well to our rear.

"Shit," Pop said. "They're bombing our rear area, so they must be Japs. And where the hell is our goddam air force?" Two planes repeated the performance and then switched to strafing runs.

The jungle always causes weird echoes – not to mention monkey screeches and bird whistles– so it's always hard to know where noises originate.

But I'd have sworn the strafing was at the beach end of New Strip, over by the coconut plantation – which meant they could be our planes. But, again, it was a hard to tell with the malaria beating the drums in our ears keeping rhythm with our chattering teeth.

"Hey," Pop said. "When we clear out, don't forget to bring Hofstra's dog tags."

"Just one," I said. "You're supposed to leave one with the body."

"Yeah," Pop said. "But how do you know the crocs will leave the body?"

# Chapter 46
# Operation Cutthroat

Turned out that it was an Air Corps FUBAR – or maybe a GHQ TARFU.

"Those cocky fly-boys sure didn't know our dispositions," Lieutenant Irish told us. "It ended up looking like they were trying to bomb our own field hospital. But thank God the bombs landed short."

We found the lieutenant in mid-morning after a below-strength squad finally relieved us.

The lieutenant wanted to know everything we had done, and applauded us for staying flat on the ground. "That's your only choice when we've got no artillery."

When Pop asked what he'd been doing, Lieutenant Irish gave him an icy look. Pop hastily started to apologize.

"Don't worry, Pop," he said. "I'm bent out of shape because I had to play court all day to GHQ feather merchants.

"One of them was Lieutenant General Sutherland hisself, MacArthur's chief of staff. He was here and I quote, to assess leadership of American troops in this sector, end quote."

I grinned. "Yeah, I've seen that arrogant bastard. He and Harding had a real brawl. He wanted Harding to relieve a bunch of battalion and regimental commanders. What did he have to say this time?"

"Well, the general seems to think we have morale problems."

"No shit? Really? Why on earth would anyone say that? We're all very happy. Just look at us. Wait, sir! Was General Sutherland by any chance wearing starched fatigues?"

Lieutenant Irish chuckled. "Nope. He had on khakis with all three stars on the collars -- real sharp creases in the pants and shirt. Them creases lasted about ten minutes after he got out of the plane into the humidity.

"Anyway, he said that our men shouldn't be slouching about – those was his words – unshaved and with such lousy posture. He told me everybody should be clean-shaven and have their heads up, shoulders back, chests out. You know. Parade ground stuff.

"I explained it's pretty tough for the troops to shave without soap or razors. He snapped at me that the troops are responsible for furnishing themselves with such gear.

"So I came right back at him, 'Well, general,' I said, 'you see we're a little skimpy right now in the PX Department and none of these boys has been near civilization for a month or more.'

I also said malaria might have something to do with the men's posture."

"So he asked me, 'What do you mean by that, *Lieutenant*?' laying real heavy stress on my lowly rank. So I said, '*Sir*, it's kind of hard to march like a parade ground soldier when you're half-starved and running a temperature of 103 or 104.'

"So then he asked what I meant by half-starved and I explained we've been on half rations or less ever since we've been here. Nor have we received further supplies of quinine."

"Jesus," Pop said, "is he even in the same world as us? So how close did he come to the plantation?"

"Oh, he didn't. I had to hike back to meet him at Dobodura."

"Where the hell is that?"

"Oh, it's a new depot located about 10 miles inland," he said.

"The Air Corps found a natural airstrip there and have improved it so, with the help of hired porters, supplies finally are starting to get through to us here.

"Meanwhile, some of the fighter squadrons have transferred to Dopodura from Port Moresby. We hear they're really starting to raise hell with the Jap Zeroes and Jap shipping.

"They also said a squadron of B-25s will start operating out of there in a day or two. They plan to raise hell in Rabaul which is a big Japanese naval and air base and supply center."

"Sir, what was with the bombing and strafing we heard yesterday? Was it Japs?" The lieutenant looked pained again.

"No, not Japs," he said. "They were P-40s from Port Moresby, courtesy of the U.S. Army Air Corps. They didn't seem to know dick about how to find targets in jungle.

"General Harding gave their ops people a royal chewing. He asked them to please refrain from helping until they can be sure they're not helping the enemy."

"Well did they kill any of our people?"

"I heard they killed 17 or 18 men in the 128th but I don't know for sure."

Just then we heard airplanes, not fighters but the heavier sound of bombers.

It was a flight of B-25s tearing low along the shoreline. "Look out," Pop said. "Looks like the flyboys are attacking us again."

Lieutenant Irish said, "Maybe not this time. I think they've got a spotter." He pointed toward a slowly circling little blue plane that looked nothing like a P-40 or an Airacobra.

The spotter circled New Strip and Old Strip twice and then dropped a red flare into the center of the plantation.

Coming in low, three B-25s bombed the marker, shattering some trees and sending others sailing. As a fourth bomber approached, a cluster of yellow flashes tore apart its nose. The plane side-slipped, pancaking into the ocean.

After a minute, Lieutenant Irish said, "Well, it looks to me like they've got more than one of those 25 mm guns you spotted."

"Back to Sutherland," he said, "I think he's holding the knife that GHQ is getting ready to shove into General Harding's back."

"Why, for Christ's sake?"

"I'd say that it's because a week ago, GHQ told all the war correspondents that, thanks to General MacArthur's brilliant strategy, American and Australian troops now have moved into attack position and are about to assault and capture Buna.

"So, all the newspaper and Movietone boys want to fly over here to get pictures of us heroes and all the Japs we've killed.

"But they're being told it's too dangerous 'cause we're still in the final assault phase. Besides, they're keeping it secret so the Japs won't find out."

Riegle said, "Wait a minute, sir. GHQ is telling the press they can't come over here because the Jap Army might figure out from the *Detroit Free Press* that we're trying to capture Buna?"

"Yeah, more or less," the lieutenant said. "It would be funny if it wasn't so stupid.

"And I'd say," he added, "that if General Harding doesn't hand Buna to General MacArthur in a day or two – you know, to fit with his publicity plans -- he'll get the ax."

# Chapter 47
# Operation Misery

A mean, scarred-up old sergeant at Fort Ord told us one day that in combat every infantryman can count on being hit.

His words went in one ear and out the other until the first time I witnessed how bullets fly by hundreds of thousands once combat begins.

Count the tracers and multiply by five, get me?

Anyway, during my first sight of combat, his words came back.

"How in hell," I asked myself, "can you *not* get hit?" After that I tried to forget about it, because the alternative was worry yourself crazy.

But then we made our fourth or fifth "at all costs" assault, this time toward Bugle Boy Bridge between New Strip and Old Strip. The bridge was a perfect choke point, or what one of the officers called a fatal funnel.

That's when the old sergeant's words came back with double force . . . along with some Jap bullets that hit Pop and winged me.

The problem was that any attack toward the bridge came under Jap fire from our right within the plantation. Showers of bullets also tore at us from the left in the jungle to the west, and fire from in front of us, too – from the bunkers and trenches around Old Strip itself.

Finally, Jap fire came from above, courtesy of the snipers who tied themselves into the tops of the trees.

And sometimes, of course, it came from behind us. Some Japs in bunkers had orders not to shoot but to wait until we passed them – and to start chopping at us from behind.

We knew our assault was stupid, but without artillery, it was the only possible way.

Anyhow, this time it was dawn and my squad was advancing north – actually, we were crawling lizard-like – into the plantation toward the bridge. Other squads were to our right and our left.

The nine of us in my squad were trying to work as a team because I had bellowed and stormed at them the night before about how to support each other.

"You bastards keep your eyes peeled to the right and to the left *and* upwards to the tops of palm trees. And you're doing this not just for your own good, but for all of us -- your buddies, too.

"Well, gee, Corporal, how are we supposed to do all that and fight, too?"

"Son," Riegle chimed in, "you just better start doing it and keep doing it. Because if we don't shoot them, those slant-eyed sonsabitches sure as hell will pick us off, one-by-one."

"Yeah," Pop added, "and if your neck ain't aching by the time we're done, you haven't been doing your job."

On this assault, Pop decided to carry a Tommy gun. "I figure it's perfect to bring down snipers from palm trees. A .45 slug stops anybody, and, at 600 rounds per minute, Tommy here puts a lot of .45 slugs where they need to be. Real fast, too."

I warned him a Tommy gun isn't the easiest weapon to use when you're flat on the ground.

See, it's got this long magazine which tends to dig into the earth if you hold the weapon upright. So Pop had to push it along the ground left side down until he'd have a target.

Then his idea was that he'd whip up 13 pounds of gun and magazine and start blasting to his front or straight up into the trees.

"I might have malaria," he said, "but I'm still strong enough to do it."

At least we had some help this time. One of the battalions had dialed in its mortars around the bridge itself. The black explosive plumes might help morale, though I suspected most of the enemy fire wasn't actually coming from anywhere near the bridge itself.

For the first time, we also got what seemed like some pretty effective strafing runs by fighter pilots trying to comb snipers from our trees. The P-40s came in right down on the deck so that with a tremendous roar the bullets from their six .50 caliber machine guns shredded the tops of coconut palms, occasionally even blasting the top from a tree.

As the planes tore overhead, those big empty shell casings cascaded among us. Next, torn palm fronds came sailing to the ground.

Inching along, I spied what looked like a possible firing slit in a bunker. It was hard to tell for sure -- malaria was blurring my vision. But I was low-crawling to try to flank it. Through all the rattle and noise, I heard Pop yell from my right, "Hey, Sammy-san!"

"What? Can't you see I'm busy."

"There's a Jap in the tree just ahead of you."

"Well, shoot him, dammit!"

"I can't! He knows I'm after him and he keeps ducking back behind the trunk. I'll keep him covered and maybe if you slide off the left a bit you might get a bead on him."

So I moved left and kept rolling onto my side to look up into the tops of the palms.

On the third or fourth try, I spotted him. He was bare-chested and wearing only his khaki pants and white sweat band around his forehead. His attention seemed focused on Pop.

Aiming was instantaneous and reflexive – looking through the peep sight lined up with the front sight blades, post on his head, then lowering the sight picture to his knee because I'm aiming up-hill.

I pulled up the slack on the trigger and squeezed.

I was so locked in I didn't feel the rifle go off. But the instant before I fired, I saw him take aim straight down.

I think we fired simultaneously.

# Chapter 48
# Medical Evacuation

Pop roared in pain and fury, "You baaaaastard!"

He rolled over onto his back, raised the Tommy gun and fired a burst up at the Jap.

He only knocked down a couple of coconuts and chopped splinters from several others.

Meanwhile, the Jap – killed by my M-1 shot -- fell from the top of the palm, and then stopped abruptly to dangle in mid-air, limp hands down and head dripping, snubbed by the six-foot line tied to his left ankle.

The sniper's Arisaka fell to the ground, a good 80 feet, sticking muzzle-first into the soil.

Pop emptied the rest of his Tommy gun magazine into the dead sniper, possibly making himself feel better while ripping the corpse to tatters

"Pop, what's going on? Why the hell are you shooting up my trophy?"

"Trophy? Congratulations, Jim! I'm very happy you got a trophy. Now get over here and help me dress my wound and get to the medics."

"He hit you, Pop?"

"Hell yes. The fucker damn sure shot me. Felt like somebody dropped a cinder block on my left leg . . . point first."

I started to crawl back toward Pop, but a medic raced out from behind a thick palm, grabbed Pop's collar and hauled him back into shelter. I jumped up to join them.

The medic rolled Pop to his right side and used scissors to cut away the left pant leg revealing a ragged blue-edged hole in Pop's thigh.

Blood was welling out of the hole which looked enormous to me -- and scary because of all the dirt and palm tree crap in it. "Good God," I said.

The medic frowned at me and shook his head. Shut up, Buddy. He immediately started with his professional prattle.

"Aw, hell, this ain't so bad. Bullet went right through and you can thank your lucky stars it was one of them little .25 caliber rounds. Might have creased your femur. Not much more damage than that, though. Just like a big skeeter bite!"

"Bullshit," Pop snapped. "It hurts."

"Well, of course it hurts. That's a good sign."

"A good sign of what?"

"That you're alive, dammit!"

The medic kept chattering as he snapped open Pop's first aid pouch, got out the red tin with its little Sulfa packets, tore one open and sprinkled a cloud of the powder onto the big hole

He kept chattering. "Just relax. I'll get you patched up real quick. Now this here is the exit wound.

"Yep, now over here in the back of your leg is this neat little entry wound. Gonna field dress 'em both and give you a little shot."

Pop tried to be witty. "Hey, Buddy, don't you think I've had enough shots for one day."

"Yuk. Yuk. Yuk," the medic said. "Why do I always wind up with wiseacres like you?"

He injected a morphine syrette into Pop's good thigh. "You're lucky buddy. We didn't have any morphine at all until two days ago."

"Good. Now can you set me up with a pretty nurse?"

"On that score, friend, you're shit out of luck. The only nurse we got right now is even uglier than me."

"Pop, you poor bastard," I said, "looks like you're going to have to take pot luck."

"Aww, Jim, go screw yourself," Pop said. And the three of us chuckled.

We should have been looking for the bad guys instead of clustering together shooting the breeze.

That's why the Juki burst hit the medic and me.

I heard the thumps and saw three bullet holes punch into the medic's fatigue shirt. They slammed him backwards, knocking off his helmet revealing thin sandy hair. I was still looking at him when something that felt like being triple-teamed by a center, guard and tackle all together – each maybe swinging a sledgehammer.

# # #

I came to, lying on my back, head swimming, and still looking at the dead medic's hair.

I stared up into the trees for a minute, trying to gather my wits.

"What happened?"

"Jesus," Pop said, "they shot you in the side."

"No shit." I turned toward him. "Can you see my guts?"

"No, lots of blood, though."

Though fading with the morphine dose, he tried to help secure a field dressing around my waist.

Now as these things go, it wasn't a bad wound. Just bad enough to get me a little vacation away from New Guinea's north shore.

Oh, I don't mean to say it didn't hurt. It hurt like hell . . . enough so that you want to get up and walk out of the theater every time you see some Hollywood star's clenched-teeth act in cowboy and Indian movies.

The worst part was trying to pull Pop behind me as I crawled back to our lines.

He's big and the morphine made him goofy, so he was no help at all. And both my malaria and blood loss wasn't helping me help him, especially with the pounding in my ears and chest.

Finally, I just kind of curled up next to Pop and went to sleep beside the creek. I really didn't want to try crossing it . . . something about keeping Pop's dressings dry

The next I knew, I was on a stretcher being carried by four of those little Papuan supermen.

Those guys were only about 5-5, but they were all muscle and damned considerate. One of them gently laid a huge leaf over my face to keep the sun out of my eyes. "Mipella tok you slip now, bossman. Slip. Sliiiiip."

"Where's Pop?"

"Don't know boss. You slip, okay? Slip now."

Maybe I did sleep.

I do remember lying for a while in our little temporary jungle hospital. It fascinated me to see a surgeon standing ankle-deep in mud as he sutured a hole high on the back of a guy sitting on his operating table.

About every five seconds, a runnel of blood would stream from the hole down the guy's naked back. Just before it would reach the patient's belt, a nurse wearing plastic gloves would intercept it with a rag near the belt and then wipe it up and away.

Lying there with my head pillowed on my arm, I told the doc his stitching work looked great, "Just the way mom used to darn Dad's socks."

The doc glanced at me and nodded, eyes crinkling above his surgical mask.

Either a doc or a medic dressed my wound and sent me on a day-long trek through the jungle and swamps to the division's new field hospital at Dopodura.

Half way through that hike, the pain started to get to me in a big way. Plus that, one minute I would be quaking with chills and the next sweating buckets.

If my stretcher had been jostled a lot, I don't think I would have made it. But those Papuans seemed to have arms of steel and PIE truck shock absorbers for legs.

When they set me on a rack in the hospital tent, the only thanks and reward I had for them was my Zippo and an unopened pack of Lucky Strikes.

They nodded and returned huge grins

Squatted beside me as the rain thundered down on the canvas overhead, the leader took out one cigarette and lit it and the four of them and I passed it hand to hand.

All of us were happy to be out of the rain and – for now, at least – safe from the Japanese,

I was running a high temp the next morning, so that got me a place on the dawn flight to Port Moresby.

The medics said that the Nambu bullets came maybe a half inch from missing me.

I sincerely thank God I only sustained a couple of rib meat gouges instead of the injury inflicted on the guy in the next stretcher in that hospital.

He was a big handsome kid. Something had struck him about a half inch above his nose, leaving a perfect little hole.

Blood kept oozing up out of the hole and spilling into his left eye.

Some medic or nurse would come over and sponge away the blood. The patient just kept staring up at the tent ceiling. I don't think he was even blinking.

I tried to talk with him. "Hey, buddy. How you doin'?"

At first I figured maybe my words were slurred and he couldn't understand me.

But a medic glanced at me and just shook his head.

# Chapter 49
# Evacuation

Blinding white thunderheads building along the north shoulders of the Owen Stanleys made our flight to Port Moresby about as rough as a cross-country jeep trip. A couple of times it felt as if my stretcher and I together bounced two feet off the plane's floor.

The medic on board had his hands full when two stretcher cases started screaming. Plus that, a lot of us became air sick, so the plane soon smelled like a locker room right after a long summer day's practice.

After we landed, both the pilot and co-pilot looked a bit green around the gills. The rest of us – Pop included -- were ready to claw our way out of the fetid aircraft

But the medical team at the Port Moresby airstrip ran like clock-work. The plane's propellers still hadn't stopped turning when a pair of three-quarter ton ambulances backed up to the plane. As they lifted our stretchers out, a bare-headed doctor in an OD T-shirt looked at our casualty tags.

After checking each, he said either "Tenth Evac" or "Station."

At least I think he was a doctor. A stethoscope dangled from his neck. When I nodded to him, he forced a quick grin, glanced at my tag and said, "Station."

He sent Pop to Tenth Evac.

As they carried me into the ambulance's shaded interior, I asked a medic what the doc meant by "Station."

"Oh, it's a hospital," he said. "The 117th. They're keeping you here because your wound ain't real serious. Bad cases go to Tenth Evac where they get some quick treatment and then get shipped off to one of the big hospitals in Australia."

When the medic said "hospital" a comforting picture bloomed in my mind – air-conditioned, white walls and ceilings, beautiful leggy nurses in tight white uniforms, neat caps and white shoes, quiet linoleum floors in spotless wards with antiseptic odors, and beds with white porcelain head rails and crisp white sheets. Even steak dinners.

The 117th turned out to be a dozen long, open-sided sheds made of rusty corrugated iron. They had plywood floors that boomed when the nurses or doctors walked on them . . . in their brown combat boots.

Ten sheds were patient wards, each with ten Army-issue cots, each tented with its own mosquito netting. The sheets were white but hardly crisp because we malaria patients soaked them with sweat. As for the air-conditioning . . . well, it was nature's -- 80 at night to 95 in the day. Breeze stirred through the sheds, but the netting blocked most of it.

At least our nurses were women. Unfortunately, their uniforms were baggy Army fatigues matching their boots and OD leggings. Working virtually around the clock, they looked dog-tired and weren't what you'd call glamorous. But just seeing them enter the ward was wonderful because of their gentle, soft, caring eyes and wonderful generous smiles.

My first week was pretty foggy thanks to malaria plus the after-effects of morphine and surgical anesthesia.

The drugs seemed to intensify some of my run-on nightmares about the long crimson exclamation mark a Jap sniper painted on the beach with Lieutenant Woodsen's blood.

The surgeons said my wound was superficial, but slow in resolving possibly because I kept getting fever bouts. When able to get up and totter around at first, I needed a cane because my balance wasn't all it could be.

It turned out my brand of malaria – *Plasmodium vivex* – was a variety that caused chill-fever-sweat bouts about every 48 hours.

But once quinine began taking effect I could stand without splitting headaches . . . though the buzzing in my ears was louder than all but the biggest mosquitos.

It surprised me to find that only 21 of us patients had wounds. The other men – the 117th had 100 patients all told -- suffered malaria or dengue fever, or both, often complicated by pneumonia and dysentery. Tape worms were also a problem because the parasites' larva entered the body through feet left open by disintegrating boots.

Most of us also displayed garish purple patches anywhere from ankles to faces – gentian violet, applied to our fungal infections. We called it war paint, with the wishful thinking that the colors would scare the Japs into retreating.

I overheard an Aussie Army doctor tell one of his American counterparts that tropical disease was decimating the allied forces.

"In North Africa and the Middle East," he said, "malaria was present, but with nothing like this prevalence. The primary disease was dysentery, gyppy tummy, you know. And not too much of that.

"But when whole Commonwealth brigades and Rommel began bashing at each other, we'd be cutting and stitching 'round the clock in surgery for bloody days and nights on end.

"Here in New Guinea, disease is the thing. Not quite two regiments of your chaps are in action. Some of them get wounds requiring surgery, of course. But the number is low compared to North Africa.

"Yet for every wound we get, we see five malaria casualties. It was a crime to send these men into jungle without a reliable supply of quinine. And we often find quite a lot of jungle ulcer because every flamin' insect bite can get infected.

"In point of fact, the malaria rate is almost 100 per cent and it certainly retards the pace with which wounds heal."

# Chapter 50
# Recovery

One broiling afternoon, I minced my way to the Day Room – the hospital's alleged entertainment shed.

The entertainment was stale tea, a radio, a weak fan, several card tables, jigsaw puzzles and a library. The books – mainly westerns and detective stories -- were dampish, disintegrating paperbacks. The humidity caused puzzle pieces to swell so that they wouldn't fit together.

Just as I sat down to read, I saw a familiar face -- our old Aussie driver. He ducked in through the entrance carrying a restaurant-sized coffee urn. "G'day, mates. No more tea for you lot! Now you can enjoy your own java thanks to the Savos."

"Savos?"

"Yeah, Australian Salvation Army. They got it from the States, or maybe their Doughnut Girls stole it from your Army mess. Who in blazes knows?"

He trotted back out, immediately returning with three large cardboard cartons. "Here's the coffee, mates. The rest is up to you. I don't know how the bloody thing works."

Because it was in the 90s, a scalding cup of coffee was about the furthest thing from my mind. So I yelled, "Hey, I remember you. You're Bob, right?"

"S'right, Mate."

"Would you happen to be driving any place around here where the breeze would be a bit stronger?"

"Do you have permission to leave hospital?"

"Yes," I said. "I just gave it to me."

He gave me his toothless grin and nodded. "As a matter of fact, cobber, I've got to stop at the Ivory Tower and then make a run up on Paga Hill. Always a bit of breeze up there. I got two more loads to bring in. So, pop out and get in the truck."

When he started the truck he said, "First the Ivory Tower."

Bob explained that Ivory Towner was the troops' nickname for Government House, the elegant New Guinea governor's mansion overlooking Port Moresby's harbor.

"This is General MacAuthur's sanctum," Bob said as we arrived. "And that's the bloke's motor car." He pointed to a gleaming black limousine with the license plate USA-1 just above another bright red plate with four white stars.

"That's a Wolseley -- one bonzer automobile," Bob said.

"Damn," I said, "It's sure got big headlights."

"Yeah, and an ace engine under that bonnet."

I peered around hoping to catch a glimpse of The General. We'd heard he liked to lounge about in a pink kimono with a black dragon embroidered on the back.

No luck.

On to Paga Hill, shaped like an inverted cereal bowl, which also looked over Port Moresby's harbor. Stop No. 1 was the Papua Hotel. It was a weary-looking flat-roofed building with its jalousie windows cranked wide.

A large sign proclaimed it to be doing business as Supreme Headquarters Southwest Pacific Area. Two sweating guards stood with their M-1s outside the main entrance. Several OD sedans were combat parked out front, each with a front bumper holder for red plates featuring one, two or three stars.

Bob dragged two Army duffle bags indoors – each apparently packed with mail. When he returned he rubbed his nose, said, "Phew -- well, General Sutherland's doxie is on duty today. I'm surprised you can't smell her."

"His what?"

"I'm talking about a captain – Woman's Army Corps. She does double duty as the general's mistress."

"The general is doing the bump with a WAC? No big surprise, I guess."

"Yeah, but mate, she's an Aussie, and her poor bastard of a husband is in a Nip POW camp. Anyroads, the brass hats here pushed all the levers and pulled all the strings, so now she's a bleedin' officer in the U.S. Army. Works there during the day as a receptionist and works at night under General Sutherland, if you get my meaning."

"What a bunch of crap."

"Right you are, sport." He was quiet for a minute. "The thing I don't see is why he goes for her. She ain't much of a looker and has no . . . no . . . well, no class, as you Yanks might say. And you can smell her bloody perfume from a block away. Makes me sneeze.

"Okay for some, I guess."

Bob fired up the truck. "So much for the post. Let's go find some fresh breeze. I know just the place."

# Chapter 51
# Recovering

He took a road circling south around the hill which opened to the Pacific Ocean. The trade wind found us -- a stiff breeze of the sort we felt while aboard the *Lurline.*

"Oh, man, that breeze is a treat."

"Too right, cobber."

We pulled up to a structure that looked a bit like a bunker sunk into the sloping hillside. It was probably 20 feet wide and had a thick concrete roof. But instead of a firing slit, its interior was wide open to the ocean's horizon. I could dimly make out what looked like a giant brass binocular back inside it. Bob took a package indoors and returned with a pipe-smoking Aussie Army lieutenant who limped badly.

"Corporal Mays," Bob said, "I'd like you to meet my nephew, Leftenant Teddy Elphinstone.

The lieutenant rolled his eyes said, "Christ almighty, Uncle Bob. Ease off."

I saluted and in my best Australian accent said, "G'die, Sir."

He grinned, "Just blow the formality, Corp. I'm a mere reservist. Welcome to the fortress."

"What is this place, anyway?"

He grinned. "We are the gun battery that sinks the bloody Jap Navy if it ever dares approach King George's majestic Port Moresby."

I pivoted on my cane to look around. Perhaps 200 yards down the steep slope, I could see the top of another concrete slab roof, a long gun barrel jutting from beneath it.

"Just the one gun?" I asked.

"No, we have a second about 400 yards further around the hill."

"Big caliber guns?"

He grinned again. "Well, these things are relative, of course. If the Japs should send destroyers against us, our two six-inch guns up this high could reach them well before they got in range with their five-inch guns. We'd scupper them in short order.

"On the other hand, if a Jap Takao-class cruiser or perhaps a battleship popped up over the horizon, we'd make very vigorous phone calls to the air bases for the boys to bomb up and pitch in immediately."

I said, "Gulp!"

He said, "Right!" and then laughed with Bob.

The lieutenant was recovering from wounds to his legs last year. "I got pranged in an air raid at Rabaul and was lucky to be evacuated before the Nips captured it. I was with the infantry then, but now they permit me to keep my hand in as a coastal artillery wallah."

He noticed the bandages beneath my open shirt and asked how I was wounded. During our windswept conversation, I told him of our frustration with Mills bombs.

"I think you're lucky they all aren't duds," he said. He blamed the grenades' failure on North African sunlight.

"The bombs came to us with the 6th and 7th Divisions," he said, "but they originally were assembled in Mother bloody England. When screwing the fuse and detonator into the bombs, the girls in the munitions plants – God bless 'em all – painted the threading with varnish to make them water tight. Unfortunately, desert sun and heat causes the varnish to break down.

"That didn't matter in Libya or Egypt or Palestine. But when in a swamp or a bloody rain forest, water can seep in so that you might as well throw a rock at Tojo. It's a wonder any of them works."

As we chatted, an OD sedan bearing a one-star plate stopped next to our truck. Two American officers got out and I recognized

General Waldron, also a survivor of the strafing on General Harding's supply boats. He was short, skinny and had deep hooded eyes. The other, a major, was tall and beefy.

As they passed us, the lieutenant and I came to attention and saluted. They returned the salute and the major asked, "What's your business here?" He made it obvious he'd like us to leave.

Lieutenant Elphinstone said, "Sir, I'm today's duty officer at this battery."

The major started to speak again, but General Waldron interrupted pleasantly. "I'm an old artilleryman, lieutenant. Tell me about your battery."

They launched into a deluge of technicalities – 6-inch, 45 caliber guns, maximum range 18,500 yards. World War I weapons but in excellent condition, fired only for ranging purposes. Same shell dimension as the U.S. 155 mm.

". . . bet you had a hell of a time getting them up here and mounted."

"Oh, I wasn't in on that sir. I was still in hospital."

The general looked at my cane. "I take it you've been over on the other side of the island."

"Yessir. The docs tell me I'll be going back in a few days."

"The best of luck, Corporal."

"Thank you, sir."

# Chapter 52
# Recovering

*They charged, tearing through the bush toward us, looking exactly like their Yellow Peril newspaper cartoon caricatures – buck teeth, pencil-thin moustaches, squinting slant eyes behind glasses with inch-thick lenses barely visible under their soup-bowl helmets.*

*But they weren't little.*

*Every one was a six-footer – a bona fide White Tiger – except their officer, a scrawny whip-thin evil-looking little man with an infected cheek but running strongly, holding his shining samurai sword in both hands over his head, poised to swing it either right or left at my neck.*

*Warner was running right there in the middle of them, charging at us, carrying an Arisaka all his own. He was coated with mud but a police badge on his chest was partly visible through the filth. Gross swollen leeches dangled from his earlobes like grimy jewelry. He had Beverly with him, her dress torn from one tender white shoulder. He was yanking at her wrists that were bound in handcuffs.*

*She was terrified. "I'm not with them, Jimmy" she screamed to me. "Not with them . . ."*

*Every rifle mounted a wicked-looking two-foot bayonet and they were plunging toward our chests. We all were firing – Pop, Sarge, Hofstra and Riegle and me. Pop was throwing grenades too, but they just bounced off and disappeared in the mud.*

*Our machine gun actually was working right, pouring brilliant red tracers into their chests and faces leaving big bloody holes, even exploding Warner's leeches. But they just kept coming. "Careful, guys" I screamed, "Don't hit Beverly!" The Japs were so fast and powerful they ripped through the thick jungle growth as if it were tissue paper. The deep mud didn't slow them, either. They were so powerful that each thick leg produced its own respectable wave, just like a ship's, as they tore through the muck.*

*I waved to the general. "Sir! Sir! They just keep coming! We're shooting them but they just keep coming!"*

*He calmly took the corncob pipe out of his mouth. Pulling off his sunglasses, he said, "That's good, son. That's good. We want them to attack us. We can defeat them more easily that way. Their weapons aren't as good as ours, so they try to into close quarters using the Banzai charge.*

*"Now, men, it is possible that I won't see a great many of you again . . . but I expect you to push through to all objectives regardless of cost."*

The nurse's damp cloth brought me awake with a start. I half sat up but then collapsed back as she said, "I think you must have been dreaming, Corporal."

The hissing Coleman lantern illuminated her face and transformed her frizzy brown hair into a tan halo. She tilted her head in concern and her voice was as soothing as the cool cloth with which she gently stroked the perspiration beaded on my forehead and temples.

"Wow, Ma'am, you better believe it was a nightmare. I seem to have the same dream every night, only with more shi- . . . pardon me, Ma'am . . . it just seems to be filled with more stuff each time I dream."

I was rigid with tension at first. But as I looked up into her kindly brown eyes, it just seemed to flow out of me. I felt my muscles beginning to relax. The nurse, a first lieutenant, must have been at least twice my age and she obviously was worn to a nubbin. But it was nice for somebody to care.

She frowned as she pushed a thermometer under my tongue, the alcohol flavor immediately filling my mouth.

"Would it help, Corporal, if I asked our chaplain to talk with you?"

With the thermometer in my mouth, I slurred. "I don't think I'd bother him about it, Ma'am. I've seen most of the guys here or over near Buna, all groaning in their sleep. Everybody seems to go through it."

She dimpled and nodded. "I'm sure you're right. But it might help to talk."

"Maybe you're right."

She pulled the thermometer from my mouth, read it, shook the mercury down and put it back in a stainless steel cup packed with cotton. She stepped to the foot of the bed to make a note in my chart.

Then she pulled a notebook from her breast pocket and scribbled in it.

"I'll speak to the chaplain," she said, smiling. "Try to sleep."

"Thank you," I said. "I will."

She picked up the hissing lantern and walked to the next bed, feet booming on the plywood floor.

I lay there trying not to sleep. I didn't want the nightmare coming back.

# Chapter 53
# Returning

Days later, the docs reported my wound had healed enough and my malaria was sufficiently abated. So I was back at Port Moresby's cargo strip boarding a C-47.

Twelve of us climbed aboard to find the plane had aluminum bucket seats facing inward, the sort I guess they used it for paratroopers. We waited, counting the slow tick-tick-tick as the plane's olive drab skin absorbed the sun's heat. Our sweat began to pour.

At last we heard a jeep drive up outside. The guy next to me said, "Well, it's about damn time."

We heard people saying "goodbye" and "good luck, sir." Then who should climb the ladder into the cabin but General Waldron? A captain, two lieutenants and a sergeant followed him, relaying and dumping their musette bags in the aisle. They then loaded eight 3-foot wooden crates, each labeled:

**2 Cart 105 HOW HE MI W/E M39**

After taking the vacant seat right across from me, the general made eye contact, nodded and said, "Well, Corporal, we meet again."

"Welcome aboard, sir. And welcome to that cannon ammo. Do we happen to have howitzers on New Guinea that will fire it?"

"A B-17 flew in our 105 howitzer yesterday and it should be assembled by the time we arrive. Along with more ammo."

I probably looked shocked at the idea of only one howitzer. He forestalled any more questions by asking, "What outfit are you with?" I couldn't answer because just then the plane's engines began their roaring start.

When at cruising altitude, I told him of being with a battalion headquarters in the 126th. He looked at me keenly and pointed to my waist where the bandages were visible through tears in the shirt.

"So how did you get that?"

I told him and he wanted to know why HQ personnel were taking place in an assault.

"Sir, we've very, very short-handed and we in HQ company are the only troops with any kind of night training." I explained how Lieutenant Irish prepped us before we got to New Guinea.

He seemed to want more information, but the captain pestered him with paperwork. So I tilted my head back and tried to sleep.

# # #

Our arrival gave me a huge surprise. In my absence, Dopodura had grown up.

Its natural airstrip now was in use as two wide runways. We were just touching down on one strip as two P-40 fighter planes roared aloft from the other.

As we descended from our plane into the steam, I counted four other C-47s circling to land. GIs were unloading two other planes. In fact, the base now looked like a good-sized supply depot. I saw 10-foot stacks of crates -- medical supplies, ammo, rations, weapons, equipment and God-know-what-else – sheltered under lines of brand-new tents.

Teams of Papuans were filing north into the jungle, looking like so many ants, each with a load.

"I can't believe what happened to this place," I told the clerk who issued me a beat-up M-1, a dented helmet, and a new suit of fatigues.

"Damn right," he said. "We been working practically around the clock."

I asked, "Do you boys happen to have American grenades?"

"Oh, you bet your sweet ass we do, Corporal. And, by the way, our pineapples are guaranteed to explode."

"Yeah? So what if a grenade doesn't explode?"

"Just return it, Buddy, and we'll double your money back."

"Jeeze, you don't do service calls?"

"Naaaah, we avoid the front line."

"Too bad. We could use you."

"No thanks, Corporal."

The Quartermaster jocks seemed to be working like beavers to supply the fighting troops . . . after first ensuring their own comfort. Their fatigues were dark with sweat and accented with white contour rings – the salt from their sweat. But none of them wore anything like the rags I saw on our infantrymen.

The engineers had graded well-drained pads for the camp's sleeping and storage tents and had hung Lister bags all around the area, ensuring everyone cool halazone-flavored water to drink.

A block-long mess tent was busy day and night serving real food, not just half C-rations.

They'd also cleared a half-mile perimeter, bulldozing scores of ultra-tall jungle canopy trees, not to mention enormous masses of vine and buttress root slabs. With so many trees gone, the place actually was getting some ground level breeze – welcome breeze, even if it felt like it came out of a kiln.

Another new feature along the runways was a series of pits each with its own long-barreled 40 mm gun, all manned and ready to fire in case Zeroes paid a call.

One thing about the brand new fatigues that the Dopodura Depot issued -- the Army had impregnated them with a dark green dye that supposedly made it harder for the Japs to see us in the jungle shade.

Whatever its camouflage properties, the dye made the cloth so stiff it quickly rubbed neck and wrists raw – not to mention the inner thighs – places where new jungle ulcers quickly began blooming.

# Chapter 54
# The Lone Battery

I joined a platoon of replacements – some recovered wounded, others off-the-shelf GIs – which began marching to the Warren Front, the new name for my combat zone.

Some genius had designated the New Strip-Old Strip-Duropa Plantation area to be the Warren Front. The other battle site, nine miles further north near Buna and Buna Mission, had been christened Urbana Front. I heard tell Urbana Front had an area – they called it The Triangle – that was as brutal to attack as our plantation.

Engineers had widened and corduroyed much of the Dopodura Road toward Warren Front. But still it was like being in a green canyon -- a very deep, narrow canyon of vegetation, blasted by torrid sunlight. The steamy airlessness made you droop, just like all the damned leaves on the trees, vines and bamboo surrounding us.

After three hours on foot, we came to a wider place in the trail. Ground had been cleared for some purpose. I fell out and took a seat on a fallen tree. Nausea was catching up with me as another malaria attack came on. My eyesight began blurring, so I tried to concentrate on bird cries and to ignore the drumming and ringing in my ears.

Perhaps an hour later, General Waldron and his party came into view along the track. They all looked a bit informal – shirts untucked and unbuttoned.

Behind them a truck, its wheels hub-deep in the mud, was dragging a stubby 105 mm howitzer. Pushing with their shoulders were two dozen natives and an equal number of GIs.

As I wobbled to my feet to salute, the general said, "Why are you here, Corporal?"

"Sweating out another malaria bout, sir. I'll be on the road in another hour or so."

"Well, sit yourself back down and let's talk about the training you received."

So he and I yarned as a very energetic and very sweaty second lieutenant oversaw positioning the howitzer while also directing the placement of ammo crates. He also had a crew of Papuans cutting down trees that looked tall enough to block the gun's trajectory.

General Waldron kept an eye on the gun's emplacement as I related how Lieutenant Irish coached our squad, and what we'd heard of his time in France and later, China.

The general's aide, the captain, also seemed deeply interested. Both officers wanted to know why the 128th hadn't progressed on the Warren front.

"Sir, the enemy has dug in deep and is very cunningly concealed, so without shelling, the only way to kill Japs is to catch them above ground, or to grenade them inside their bunkers. That usually means getting within an arm's length of those bunkers' firing slits which pretty much guarantees a wound." I also gave them a detailed explanation of the log-and-barrel construction of the first bunker we captured.

As I wrapped up, the gunnery lieutenant reported to the general, saying he was in radio contact with both the Urbana and Warren fronts and was ready to start registration fire.

The first blast sounded to me as if someone had slammed a gargantuan door, redoubling the ringing in my ears.

As I watched their very deliberate practice, it fascinated me to see how the howitzer's blast whipped the blades of Kunai on the ground, and tore at the fronds of nearby palms and banana trees. After my ears adjusted to the blast of the artillery piece, I could hear the shell rushing through the air as it raced off to the north.

"Are there any chances we'll get more of these guns, sir?" I asked.

"Corporal," he said, "it's a howitzer, not a gun. But no. This is it. We had a hell of a time getting a plane to bring this one in." He sounded bitter. "The air corps thinks aerial artillery is more effective. So right now, the rest of Battery A is back at Moresby and Captain Kobs is doing his best to send us ammunition every day."

"But . . ."

He gave a quick grin. "That's just the way it is right now. And we'd better get moving."

"I'm ready to move out, sir, but when you get near either front, I strongly recommend taking those stars off your collar. The Jap snipers seem to love targeting officers."

He grinned. "Thanks, Corporal Mays, but I think the troops need to know that we're not all back at the Officers' Club guzzling gin and tonic."

He and his little staff set off for Warren Front and I tagged along, bringing up the rear. We passed several Papuans carrying wounded men the opposite direction.

After two tiring, sweaty hours I could tell we were getting close to the line. At first it was the sound of popcorn. As we got closer we could hear the stutter and crackle of Nambus and Brownings and the occasional thump of a mortar.

We also were starting to pass small groups of GIs sitting or lying in the brush doing nothing.

I asked one man where his outfit was and he just looked away saying, "I don't know. I'm lost. Our platoons are all scrambled up."

"Are you looking for your squad?"

He looked away again.

"Well?"

"Just get off my back, corporal. I'm not going up there. It's fucking suicide."

## Chapter 55
## Back At The Plantation

The first time that I saw the plantation's palm trees, they were so thick that their green foliage almost blocked your view of the sun and sky.

But my first glimpse when I returned was different. Strafing runs had at least partially stripped the tops of maybe half the trees.

Portions of what had seemed like a thick, dark forest now was brightly sunlit. Scattered groves of palm trees lay amid clusters of bare trunks – many of them splintered. In fact, it looked like some of the photos from World War I where woods had been shelled to little more than naked vertical sticks.

But the battle lines stood where they were when Pop and I left. Debris from the trees now covered the ground even more thickly, adding to the Japs' camouflage.

Once we arrived at Warren Front, it took me about an hour to find Lieutenant Irish. He was working at the new headquarters, a cluster of map tables surrounding a giant hollowed tree stump.

He welcomed me and asked about Pop. Oh, and the latest news? General Eichelberger had relieved General Harding. Everyone was waiting for his replacement, the artillery commander of the 32nd.

"He's here," I said. "He just brought us a howitzer – a 105."

"One howitzer? That's it?"

"That's it. He said that's all the Air Corps agreed to fly in right now. General Waldron is his name and he seems pissed off about how little artillery we get, but there it is. Anyhow, he's a pint-sized little guy and seems pretty decent."

"Well, he sure as hell has his work cut out," the lieutenant said. "I think it's just now beginning to dawn on Eichelberger what a mess Harding had on his hands."

He told me that right after giving the boot to General Harding, General Eichelberger ordered his own medical chief do a quick survey of the troops.

"So the doc comes back and really shocks the general. He says, 'Sir, these soldiers look like Jesus just pulled down from the cross.' Harding hadn't left the area yet, so he gave Eichelberger a real pointed look."

"But nothing's changed?"

"Nope. Same problem. Troops are sick and still about half-starved. You can't see a Jap bunker 'til you're five feet away -- and then it's usually too damned late. We've had no way to shell them, and I don't think one measly howitzer will help that much. Mortars don't touch bunkers. No tanks, no flame-throwers. And so far the bombing has hurt us more than the enemy.

He sighed. "And every damned time we take out a bunker, the cost can be anywhere from a squad upward." He shook his head. "Yeah, in the last attack we thought we might have an edge."

"What was that?"

"The Aussies gave us five Bren carriers to take on bunkers."

"What the hell is a Bren carrier?"

"Well, it's a little steel box – a scout vehicle with tracks instead of wheels. It's about the size of a jeep and it carries a crew of two, a driver plus a gunner who handles the Bren machine gun, and two or three riflemen. It's a great recon vehicle."

"So it's like a tank?"

"Not hardly, Jim. The steel sides might stop a bullet, but there's no top cover at all. The driver and gunner and anyone else along for the ride are perfect sniper targets. Spam in a can.

"Anyhow, the carriers got anywhere from 50 to 100 yards into the plantation. The Japs busted one with an antiaircraft gun of some kind. And they got a couple with sticky bombs."

"Sticky bombs?"

"It's any container with explosives that you can stick to your target with grease or mud. Anyhow, that was it. Snipers got the rest. So the carriers are still sitting out there, about half-covered with debris. We retrieved some of the bodies and the wounded that night."

Lieutenant Irish said he thought the Bren Carrier attack was probably the straw that broke the camel's back, leading to Harding's relief.

"So, what's this Eichelberger planning?"

"Oh, the general wants to attack. He's *got* to attack. Scuttlebutt has it that MacArthur ordered him to capture Buna and the airstrips or not come back alive."

"Jesus."

Just then, a spare, white-headed man with three stars on each collar tab came into the headquarters clearing. Trailing him were several officers, including General Waldron. Lieutenant Irish and I braced and saluted.

General Eichelberger had the hard look of a man with a very short fuse. He compressed his lips and kept them turned down at the corners. Sweat, of course, beaded his face and forehead just as it did everybody. But he really appeared about to explode under some special kind of pressure.

And his fuse was hissing and throwing sparks.

"Okay, Irish," he rapped out, "who's this?"

General Waldron interrupted, "Sir, this is the corporal I told you about. He's just back from the hospital."

The general gave me a piercing blue-eyed glare. "For what?"

"Sir, malaria and wounds to the ribs."

"Okay, Corporal. Glad you're back. In fact I want to talk with you later. Right now though," he turned to Lieutenant Irish, "meet your new division commander, General Waldron."

# Chapter 56
# Night Patrols

General Eichelberger had seen Japanese troops in operation years before, so he invited Lieutenant Irish – who actually had fought against them – to meet with him and General Waldron.

The three of them came up with the plan that paid off.

Eventually.

General Waldron wanted and got a two-day halt in attacks so company officers could gather their outfits back together. "Too many people are hanging out back in the rear and nobody's got them under control," he said.

"That's good," General Eichelberger said. "And in the meantime, the troops can rest and get some hot meals and get resupplied. The medical people say the men all need salt tablets, vitamins, and quinine."

General Eichelberger also ordered Lieutenant Irish and me to start a school for night patrolling and night fighting. "Because beginning the day after tomorrow, I want every platoon to send out a patrol every night."

"I'll require that the patrol leaders report to me personally," Waldron added. "These boys have got to overcome their fear of the jungle and the night."

Lieutenant Irish snorted, ducked his head and thrust out his jaw. General Eichelberger caught the look. "Yep, Irish, I know. Should have happened two months ago. Enough said."

Lieutenant Irish nodded. "Right, sir." Then he added, "I've got one request, sir."

"What?"

"I think Corporal Mays here would be a lot more effective instructor if he had more rank. Besides, he was in on taking out three bunkers."

"That's a good point," General Eichelberger said, giving a glance at General Waldron.

General Waldron nodded and turned to me. "As of now you're a master sergeant."

*Damn!*

He looked at one of his aides, "See to the promotion orders."

# # #

It took a full afternoon, Lieutenant Irish overseeing, for me to get comfortable browbeating the men about slow, stealthy movement and resisting the temptation to slap mosquitos.

"By God, remember the three rules," I said. "And especially remember that if you don't keep dead quiet, you're just dead.

"If I hear you slap another mosquito, or even wave at it, you're going to dig a six-foot grave right here and now. No, not for the goddam mosquito, Dumbshit! For you! Your slap may kill the mosquito but it for sure will alert Corporal Sessue Pajamayama to drill your noggin.

"And, frankly, I'd rather dump your carcass into that hole than have to drag it all the way back to Graves Registration. Get me?"

Once night came, Lieutenant Irish and I teamed up in working with the men on peripheral vision, all the while pressuring them to be quiet, quiet, quiet.

"For God's sake, load your rifles and chamber a round before you get to the front. There's no way to do that quietly."

It was damn tiring work and the fear always gnawed me that I wasn't stressing slow movement enough – or riding them enough about turning eyeballs before rotating the head, or quiet breathing, or the other hundred things.

"Quit worrying," Lieutenant Irish told me. "We're opening their minds. And I bet if you think back, that's all I did for you and Pop. You took it the rest of the way yourselves."

Three mornings later, I began to see what Sarge meant.

I was with General Waldron when one of our pupils, a sergeant, reported to him about a nighttime patrol toward Old Strip. He had taken out three men for five hours and returned with no losses. And though worn out, he was animated.

"Sir," he said, "the Japs have set up double-apron barbed wire for at least 300 yards along the east margin of the runway . . . maybe even longer.

"It's staked in real solid and it's all covered over with coconut fronds and weeds and shit . . . oops, sorry about the language, sir."

"That's okay, son. Go on."

"Well, anyway, sir, it just looks like a long berm, but if you went racing into it you'd wind up all tangled and caught hanging on that wire like something in a spider web."

General Waldron, nodded, took a deep drag off his cigarette, and asked, "Could you tell whether those stakes are wood or steel or rods, or tubing . . . "

"Nossir," the sergeant said, practically bubbling over with his enthusiasm. "They're steel and at least an inch and a half wide but kind of bent down their centerline."

"Something like angle iron?"

"Yessir! Real strong. A fella couldn't hope to bend one. But the other thing was that – and I couldn't tell for sure because it was so dark – but on the other side of the wire, it looked like they've dug trenches right across the Old Strip runway, east to west. But not straight. It looks there are zig-zags in those trenches."

Nodding as he listened, General Waldron's questions were quiet but direct. He was frowning and speaking intensely, but acting just like one of the boys, no helmet, shirt wide open, streaks of dirt under the dog tags on his chest. And he still wore a star on each of his muddy shirt's collar points.

He should have listened to me

As the sergeant left, I turned to check our ancient aerial photo of Old Strip. The whiplash of a rifle and a noisy crack behind me made me duck.

The bullet's impact spun General Waldron like a top, then he fell flat.

His aide bent over him, saying, "General? *General*, are you okay? Gen . . ."

Clank!

The next shot penetrated the crown of the captain's helmet. He collapsed onto the general.

Lieutenant Irish had his rifle up, firing into a coconut palm 200 yards behind us.

I rolled the dead captain away and turned the general onto his back.

His face was contorted – the sniper's bullet had splintered his right shoulder. I packed a field dressing into the raw gap where his shoulder was supposed to be. It spooked me to see how fast that big gauze and cotton pad turned bright red.

Two of us lifted him gently as we could onto a stretcher, trying not to hear to his "Ahh! Ahhh! Ahhhhh!"

It spooked me even more seeing his right hand now resting below the level of his knee.

Then, carrying him as carefully was we could, we rushed about 300 yards to the field hospital.

By the time we got him there, the stretcher was starting to fill with his blood.

The first surgeon to look at him quietly said, "Oh, shit." They began work on him immediately.

And for the second time in three days, 32$^{nd}$ Division needed a new commander.

# Chapter 57
# The New Commander

General Eichelberger appointed his own chief of staff to command the 32$^{nd}$ Division. No long after, a sniper nailed him, too, so that in the end, Eichelberger had to do it all himself.

For a time, the lieutenant and I didn't see much of him because he became his own very rapidly constantly shifting headquarters.

But during training sessions we sure heard a load of complaints about him.

Patrol leaders who now had to report to him instead of General Waldron called him The Prussian. He was abrupt and demanding and he accepted no excuses for cutting patrols short.

But the men who found him so mean hadn't seen him break down and weep, as we did, about his own aide, another sniper victim -- a captain -- who'd been with him for a year. And he couldn't bear to visit the wounded in the field hospital

And they didn't hear him almost querulously tell us, "God, this place is a nightmare."

One of the GIs' gripes was that the general spent too much time popping up among the squads up on the line. They didn't like it one bit.

One Pfc. told me, "If the old bastard wants to get himself killed, that's fine. But I don't want to be shot right there beside him."

Another infantryman grinned as he said, "Let's say things are quiet and you're trying to get a bead on a sniper high up in a tree. You can see the Jap's arm and you're hoping he'll slide his head or body into view. Just then somebody splashes up behind you and says, 'What's going on here?'

"So I say, 'Get down, goddammit, and shut the hell up!' And then I see him and all I can say is, 'Oh! Holy shit! Sorry, General.'

"I mean, who needs that inspection crap when you're trading shots with snipers?"

Sometimes the problem was that the GI in question for once might be half-way comfortable, hiding behind the nice thick trunk of a coconut palm and a screen of Kunai. And I heard, 'That's when the boss waltzes up and expects me to stand up and report what's going on.

"My buddy and I was shooting the shit and I was telling him, 'You know, that old bastard ought to just stay back at headquarters with his goddam maps and leave us alone."

"And right out of nowhere I hear the general behind me and he says, 'Hey, soldier, I'm not so old'

"And there he is, big as life. Standing up, looking pissed-off, fists on his hips and all them stars just as shiny as can be. So I tell him, 'For Christ's sake, sir, you make a hell of a target. Get down or one of these Japs is going to kill you.'

"He gives a smirks and says, 'Thanks for your concern.'

"So I tell him, ''Concern my ass, sir! I don't want fire brought on my position.' So he just grins and walks off."

The general certainly won no friends when he passed the word that there'd be no relief at all for the 32nd Division until Buna and the airstrips were captured. He didn't explain that the decision came from general headquarters.

Now I've got to explain something about battle on the Warren front, particularly in the Plantation.

Fighting was sporadic.

We'd attack, firing like crazy. By now plenty of mortars were available, so the black smoke plumes or the white clouds of Willie Peter shells from those 81s and 60s would erupt on the ground or, occasionally, in tree tops.

And, now and then, we'd get some fire support either from our single 105 mm or from three Aussie 25-pounders – basically 90 mm howitzers.

None of the artillery damaged the bunkers much, but they must have made the occupants' ears ring real badly.

At any rate, it could be very noisy with everyone trying to assault while carefully doing their best to adhere to Rule No. Three – trying to stay out of sight.

But then after two or three hours, it might become dead quiet – almost as if everybody on both sides decided to take an extended coffee break, waiting for the general's next attack order.

And, of course, it was the luck of the dice that during such pauses GHQ observers would come traipsing around. Seeing no action and hearing no shooting, they figured the lads weren't trying.

I heard that during his first day at Warren front, General Eichelberger thought the same. But he changed his tune after he saw how hard the boys were trying and how hopeless it was for unsupported riflemen to dig out bunkered Japs.

But he still could be a bit caustic.

In fact, the general was so intimidating that, at first, just being around him kept me on edge.

But Lieutenant Irish smirked. "Look, Jim, he puts 'em on the same way you do. One leg at a time. He's under a hell of a lot of pressure – the big man is on his ass constantly. And he hates getting his men killed. So if he blows his stack now and then, don't worry. You're just another part of his staff and he knows he needs you."

What especially rankled with everybody – the general included -- was that MacArthur still was holding more than a third of the division back around Port Moresby. The 127th Infantry along with 99 per cent of the division's artillery were contributing not an ounce of support to the Buna Campaign where time supposedly was "of the essence."

Yeah, and we learned that meanwhile, the 41st Division had arrived in Australia. And they weren't building camps. They were living in the camp *we* built. And they were undergoing very intensive training for, guess what?

Jungle warfare.

Most of the boys made it clear that they thought the new division could benefit from some very realistic training experience right beside us on Warren Front.

Yet General Eichelberger's approach seemed to be working.

The men wished he'd stay away and they didn't like him or his questions. But they respected his guts for being on the line so much with those silver stars catching the sunlight – and they were impressed with the improvement in supplies.

For one thing, they now were getting full meals – sometime hot ones. And they were American meals instead of Aussie mutton. And, yes, even if they sometimes were watery powdered eggs with a few twigs and flies mixed in -- their flavor was vaguely familiar and they were warm and filling.

Moreover, American grenades were the hot kazotsky. They worked. Every time.

Even Aussies began to appreciate U.S. pineapples. And we now had link-belt instead of fabric-belted machine gun ammo. Any jams or stoppages now were our fault, not that of jungle humidity.

Something that impressed me as I ran classes was that I saw less and less of the oh-don't-hand-me-that-bullshit attitude on the faces of my audiences – especially when talking to men who'd been on a patrol or two. They didn't want to go on patrols, of course. Nobody did. But their experience made them more accepting of what we had to tell them.

Lieutenant Irish and Riegle and I migrated away from the Duropa Plantation to spend more time working with the men around the inland end of New Strip. They were the boys who had to live in swamps.

Many of them were terrified at first of snakes and crocs. But after we'd hiked them through those morasses four or five times without incident, they calmed down.

"So, Sarge, what if a croc does sneak up on you at night?"

"Well, for God's sake, unless you want to be dinner, shoot the bastard between the eyes. You've got a real powerful rifle there."

One thing really rattled me, though. We'd be swamp-swimming as we called it, when we'd come upon a tidal zone filled with mangrove trees.

With the tide out and in that dim light or especially when silhouetted by flares, those black glistening mangrove roots looked exactly like enormous spider legs.

They jutted upward from where a gargantuan spider's body would be, and then bent sharply downward with their tips in the water or – if the tide was out – that black mud.

The swing and sway of flare shadows accentuated the spidery impression. But even in daylight, mangrove roots still were spooky. Whenever we approached, dozens of critters -- snakes, baby sharks and baby crocs – would panic dart out between those roots.

It gave me a couple of high-sweat nightmares about platter-sized tarantulas crawling up to wrap me up in web strait jackets.

But as disgusting as jungle swamps could be, it was starting to dawn on the men that the fastest and only way out of the horrors of New Guinea was to kill Japs – every damned one of them. The men were learning how to hate.

# Chapter 58
# First Successes

One night we surprised a squad by switching from training to what Lieutenant Irish labeled a practical field exercise – not a scouting mission, but their first night combat patrol.

Riegle, the lieutenant and I and our class of six sat on logs as he wrapped up his lecture. But instead of dismissing us, Lieutenant Irish said, "Tonight, men, we're gonna do to the Japs what they've been doing to us. We'll spook them by killing a few. We'll make them jumpy . . . wear the bastards out."

One of the men said, "Well, sir, we're already pretty wore out ourselves."

Lieutenant Irish, who looked gaunt and displayed a raw jungle abscess on his left forearm, gave a sour grin. "Johnson, I feel sooo sorry for you! It just purely makes my heart pump piss."

Changing to a snarl, he went on, "Yeah, we're whipped and tired. We're sick, too. I have the shits so bad that I wonder if it wouldn't make sense to just cut the seat out of my pants. But believe me, buddy, it's just going to get worse unless and until – Get that? – *until* we whip them.

"So quit your goddam bellyaching and just accept the fact that we've got to kill these bastards – ever' damn one – before they kill us."

# # #

We had asked for weapons other than M-1s, hoping to get two or three BARs. None was available. But Lieutenant Irish had some Aussie NCO friends who gave us a Bren gun.

I didn't like the idea.

The Bren's .303 ammunition was different from the .30-06 fodder for our M-1s. And when it's pitch dark, who the hell needs to be sorting through cartridges looking for the right kind?

But the lieutenant was all for it.

"Look, the Bren is excellent," he said. "I'll take it over a BAR any day. It's the firepower you need. It's got a 30-round magazine instead of a 20. And a quick-change barrel. It feeds from the top which is a lot better than the BAR's bottom-feeder magazine.

"And I think the best thing is that, even though it's a little heavier than the BAR, it's got that nice wooden carrying handle. Believe me, if you're in the dark and you try to pick up a BAR that's been fired for a while, it'll sear the skin right off your palm."

He assigned me to carry a Bren for an escapade that I think he'd planned for some time. He detailed each of the other six men to carry a loaded magazine for me. Riegle, the back-up gunner in case I got the hammer, carried two mags.

Once it was dark, we started moving gradually into the swamp west of New Strip. We moved five yards apart in a shallow arrow point with me second from the right.

It turned out to be Johnson, over on the left flank, who gave a short, shrill two-fingered whistle. The lieutenant moved to him, and the rest of us crouched.

Stuttering bright orange fire on our left lit up a firing slit. It was the lieutenant's Tommy gun blasting 180-grain slugs into the bunker.

A second later came a brief flash and "whump!" Johnson's grenade exploded inside.

I screamed, "Duck!"

It seemed like 50 Nambus – probably only five or six -- began blasting from the jungle. Each of those glowing tracers illuminated the ground as it whipped past us. So we kept still, turning our eyes and heads very slowly in order to ID other bunkers.

Another "whump!" echoed behind us. Somebody tossed a grenade into another Jap firing point – a trench. Very high-pitched screeches came from it.

*Good to hear one of you bastards scream for a change.*

Through all the racket, Lieutenant Irish shouted, "File left! File left!" It was our signal to move out of the area in his direction, keeping low and slow.

The Nambu firing slowed, but enough tracers still flew that they silhouetted a Jap patrol moving through the swamp.

Perhaps the tracers robbed them of night vision. Perhaps they just weren't paying attention. Or were sick. Anyway, four of them, carrying rifles with fixed bayonets, seemed oblivious as they crossed behind us, slightly overlapping each other.

I had the Bren's pistol grip in my right hand. The sling over my shoulder supported the bulk of the gun's weight. A tight grip on the carrying handle, now swiveled down to the left, gave me perfect control.

I fired two bursts left to right in a narrow arc embracing the line of Japs. Despite the noise, I heard the empty casings – ejected downward from the action -- hissing as they splashed just in front of my knees.

The quartet collapsed into the swamp. One of my shots must have hit a rifle because it sparked and cartwheeled a good 10 feet before splashing into the muck.

A brand-new farrago of Nambu fire erupted around us and we all crouched again.

A metallic thump knocked Riegle out of his crouch.

"Riegle? Riegle! You okay?"

Stupid question. He'd been hit. He wasn't okay.

# Chapter 59
# Paying The Price

I grabbed Riegle's arm and hauled him upright.

As water sloshed off of him, he hissed, "Leave go of me, you big ape."

"I thought you got hit."

"It was just one of your damn Bren magazines that got hit. I think I'm just bruised as hell."

He stepped away from me and then collapsed. "Jesus," he sputtered. "Maybe I am hit. Feel like the damn wind's has been knocked out of me."

I grabbed him again, this time by the cartridge belt. "Come on. You and I are getting out of here."

Somebody fired from behind us – an Arisaka -- and a bullet sang past us.

I let go of Riegle, turned and fired. I didn't see anybody and I don't know if I hit anybody, but that Bren sure churned up a lot of swamp geysers. I threw away the exhausted magazine and fitted my spare into its place.

"Come on, Charlie, let's go."

He didn't answer, so I grabbed his arm again and dragged him.

Twice, our sloshing legs and the sucking sounds of mud provoked more Nambu fire. So I had to duck and drop Riegle in the muck. I bellowed that he was a no-good lazy asshole. He mumbled back, sound as if he was only semi-conscious.

Suddenly, I heard splashes beside us, headed our direction. "Gimme a hand, dammit! Riegle's hit!"

Between us, we got him back to our lines. A medic was waiting, so we just dragged Riegle right onto his stretcher. Two men picked him up and headed for the field hospital. A minute later Lieutenant Irish arrived, coated in muck just like the rest of us.

"Who was on the stretcher?"

"Riegle."

"Hit bad?"

"I hope not. He seemed about half-conscious."

"I hope he makes it," the lieutenant said. "We lost two other men."

I had quit praying long ago but that night I prayed for Riegle. Long and hard. I kept dwelling about how much I'd miss the little wiseacre . . . how much I already missed his constant wiseass talk and bullshit.

In the midst of praying I suddenly found myself thinking about killing Japs and my Bren gun.

See, I wondered ever since enlisting how I'd feel about killing another human being.

So it seemed a bit odd to me that I never felt so much as a twinge of guilt or remorse about shooting those two Jap machine gunners back on the beach. I mean, it was a clear case of kill or be killed.

And, thinking back, it was the same about the tree sniper who hit Pop.

Maybe I didn't feel anything was because I was in such a panic both times.

But I had to admit to myself that hosing those four Japs in the swamp gave me a deep, surging animal thrill. In a way, it felt just as good as charging the net and feeling the ball bound off the racket's sweet spot.

I know. Killing people isn't supposed to be sweet. So maybe it was the Bren that was sweet. It was my racket – exciting, rattling power in my hands. It made a threat disappear, four threats -- leaving them for the rats and the crocs in that stinking black water.

# # #

At dawn, I went to the field hospital and felt a gust of relief at seeing Riegle alive.

They'd cleaned him up and he was pale but conscious. They had a plasma tube running into one arm and his upper chest was bandaged.

"Hey, Jim," he whispered. "I was lucky. They said I had an entire cartridge – you know, an unfired cartridge -- jammed right into my chest just under my collarbone. Whatever hit me must really have broke up that Bren magazine.

"They said that it cut some blood vessels, but also kind of squished them in place so that I didn't quite bleed to death."

He grinned. "Lucky them docs don't know .303 cartridges from .30-06 cartridges. Otherwise, they might arrest you for using the wrong weapon. Send you to Leavenworth."

"Oh, yeah, and Jim . . . thanks for hauling my butt out of the swamp."

"Oh, crap," I said, "I'd do the same for any shipmate from the *SS Vomitorium.*"

"Even Warner?"

"Well . . . I don't know as I'd go that far."

He began blinking rapidly and tears started to stream from his eyes. "I had some crazy dreams while they was working on me, Jim. I dreamed Sis and I was outside the house making angels in the snow, and then building snowmen. Do you ever do that in Seattle?"

"No. We don't get much snow. Usually it's just drizzly and chilly, but that's about it. You can see lots of snow up on Mount Rainier way southeast of town and the other Cascades, but not in the town."

"Too bad. Jimmy. Man, it's so fucking hot here that I really miss the cold and the snow. I used to bitch about it when I had to get out of bed at 4 a.m. and put my bare feet on that cold floor. But I wouldn't mind now at all."

"Hey, Mister," I said, "you want cold feet, come see me in Seattle after the war and dip your toes in Puget Sound. It runs right around 50 degrees all year round. Turns you blue to the knees real quick."

"Well, Jimmy, I'd give my ass to be able to do it now. The fact is," he went on, "I just miss home . . ."

"And the Sunday Funnies?"

"Oh, God, yes." He started sobbing. "Damn, I miss the farm and my folks. And Sis. She has the biggest, bluest eyes you ever seen. I bet she's a real beauty by now. Oh, God, how I miss them."

"Well, play your cards right, maybe this wound will get you a furlough home. There's snow on the ground in Michigan now, I bet."

"He nodded and grinned. "Oh, yeah. And it's cold, buddy. Around Christmas the cows and horses puff out so much breath that each one carries his own fog with him."

One of the medics elbowed me aside.

"Okay, now, let him rest, Sarge. He needs it because as soon as this IV is finished, the boys are going to start hiking him to the Dopodura airstrip."

"How's he doing?"

"Oh, he'll make it. I bet he'll be back in two or three weeks."

# Chapter 60
# The Butcher Bill

I let the lieutenant know I had become a firm believer in Bren guns.

He grinned and told me to keep the weapon out of sight. "Otherwise" he said, "some army bureaucrat will raise Cain about your unauthorized equipment."

"Hey, sir, as long as I'm killing Japs with it, they can't get too worked up about it. Right?"

He just grinned. "The further they are back from the front, the more stupid people get about these things."

# # #

Meeting with a group of company officers and NCOs the same day, Lieutenant Irish said we needed to make more hit-and-run combat patrols.

"I'd like to see every company with a junior officer or an NCO who can lead a patrol and an attack like ours every night. We'd start getting a twist on these bastards for a change."

"What good does it do?" a lieutenant snapped back. "You went out and cleared a bunker and then came back. So what? The Japs probably occupied that bunker again and we're no better off than we were."

"That's where you're wrong," Lieutenant Irish said. "No, we can't get up and march to Buna. Not yet. But put yourself in the place of the guys who had to clean all the blood and guts out that bunker. And imagine how they'll feel tonight. Ever' little noise made by a land crab will have them jumping. I guarantee they ain't going to be getting a beauty rest.

"Who knows?" he went on. "The Japs might even be rattled enough to attack us. Wouldn't it be a nice change if they got up out of their holes and tried a banzai charge or two against us?

"But the main thing is that we've got to attack and keep attacking to kill some of them and rattle the rest."

I wasn't so sure about that. It seemed to me that all we were accomplishing was an even trade, life for life.

# # #

Two days later, we got a surprise that scared hell out of us at first. Flight after flight of big silver twin-engine Jap bombers roared over practically at tree-top level.

Actually, they didn't fly directly above us, but a bit to the north. And instead of bombing, they parachuted supplies to their own troops.

After the scare, Corporal Benson said, "It'd sure be nice if the Air Corps would do that for us."

Lieutenant Irish said, "Close your hole, Corporal. The Air Corps is doing just fine by us. Now that they've got a good airstrip at Dopodura, I hear they've been sinking Jap resupply vessels right and left."

The corporal wilted.

He had rejoined us a day earlier. It put him in kind of a foul mood to see that the lieutenant, his old NCO supervisor, now was an officer. And it didn't help that I – once one of his clerk-typists -- now ranked him by four grades.

"Don't worry," I told him. "With all the casualties we're taking, you'll probably wind up a sergeant major by next week. As for the Air Corps, quit bitching and be damn glad they flew you over here. The guys who had to hike over the hump to get here still haven't recovered."

He and Riegle suddenly were looking wide-eyed over my shoulder. They came to attention.

I turned to see General Eichelberger had just showed up. Being in his usual mean frame of mind, he could have cared less about military courtesies. But he brightened when Lieutenant Irish reported to him about the Jap airdrop.

"Men, this is great news," he said. "They could have bombed hell out of us, but instead they're using valuable combat planes as delivery trucks. That's desperation. It tells me the Japs are running short. They're sick and they're hungry."

Sometimes I wonder about generals.

I mean, at first what he said seemed to make sense. But think about it.

If the Japs are resupplied, maybe they're no longer hungry. Right? And what does an airdrop have to do with whether they're sick? Most Japs we'd seen looked in pretty good shape – like that miniature Mr. Atlas who almost finished me off hand-to-hand in Maggot Marsh.

And then something struck me.

After the general left, I got Lieutenant Irish off to the side.

"Look, sir, if the Air Corps now is flying fighter planes *and* bombers out of Dopodura and if they're sinking Jap shipping like the Japs did to ours, and if they're attacking Jap air bases and hitting Rabaul, then why the hell do we need to capture Buna and these airstrips?"

He gave me a sour grin.

"Really, sir, why can't we just wait the Japs out – or just leave a small enough garrison to keep them from using these airstrips. I just don't see why we've got to rot in this jungle to capture something that we don't need."

He gave me a grim look. "Jim," he said, "you're talking strategy now and you're catching on. But I can't answer you. So go ask MacArthur why we just don't let the Japs starve. He's the big dog in charge."

Yeah. Sure.

# # #

Thanks to continued pressure from MacArthur, General Eichelberger ordered a new attack all along the entire nine-mile dug-in crescent from Buna to the airstrips and Duropa Plantation.

The attack quickly stalled.

It showed that regardless of whether they were sick or hungry or both, the Japanese still could feed ammo and pull the triggers on large numbers of rifles and machine guns.

And they sure as hell were not skimping on ammunition, either.

Despite modest support from our artillery – the Division's lone 105 used up all 100 rounds at its disposal – plus heavy mortar fire including barrages of white phosphorous, the Japs stopped us cold, adding generously to our butcher bill.

They still remained hunkered out of sight in a checkerboard arrangement of bunkers and pill boxes and those bunkers and pill boxes still dominated our only lines of approach.

That afternoon, we heard the Warren Front CO tell the general, "Well, sir, we hit them and we bounced off."

I didn't hear General Eichelberger's reply, but "bouncing off," wasn't quite the term I would have applied – not after seeing another column of Papuans bearing our newest casualties off toward the airstrip at Dopodura.

The only good news was that Pop came back to us with a slight limp and a pair of heroic-looking star-shaped scars.

# Chapter 61
# Regardless Of Costs I

That same night we knew of at least three patrols going out into Warren Front. One was a new group we'd been training – eight men led by a shaky lieutenant backed up by a buck sergeant who seemed rock solid.

The patrol eased its way into the pitch-dark brush and swamp right after the tropics' typical high-speed nightfall.

Perhaps 15 minutes later heavy firing broke out right to our front. "Shit!" Lieutenant Irish said. "That's too damn soon and too damn close."

Small arms fire that is, say, a quarter mile off sounds something like popcorn. And we could hear that particular noise well off to our right.

But the fire-fight in front of us was much noisier – close enough that we took to our holes when Nambu tracers began slapping through the trees and brush near us.

"Looks like our boys didn't keep quiet," I said.

"Maybe, maybe not," the lieutenant said. "Maybe we got the Japs worked up enough that they decided to set up an ambush. You know, the Jap always gets a say in what's going on."

"So, how about if we request some 105 fire?" I asked. "Just anywhere so as to shake up the Japs and maybe make them take cover."

"The howitzer is out of ammo. Besides, Sergeant Mays, you don't start shelling 'just anywhere.' 'Just anywhere' might be where another one of our patrols happens to be.'

"Oh."

"What's more," he added. "the officer running that howitzer ain't going to listen to you or me. They probably won't take a fire mission from anybody below a company-grade forward observer."

It was impossible to tell exactly what was going on to our front, but the firing intensified. In addition to those slow peckerwood Nambus, we could distinguish M-1s and tommy guns.

And there wasn't a damn thing we could do about it.

# # #

The firing in front of us still hadn't subsided when we heard someone gasp the password. "Applied pulley! Applied pulley!" I had chosen the phrase, believing no Japanese could pronounce the two words anywhere near correctly.

"Advance and be recognized."

We heard rustling in the brush ahead of us, but then a flare burst overhead and the movement stopped.

As the flare descended, I yelled, "Dammit! Advance and be recognized!"

"I can't. Can't walk. I'm wounded and I'm trying to crawl."

"What's the password again?"

"For Christ's sake, man, it's 'Applied pulley'."

"Say it again and, this time, pronounce it really slowly and clearly."

He did, with good Midwestern pronunciation along with some more swearing.

"Okay. Keep your shirt on!" As the flare died, I crouched and pushed forward into the vines and brush. "Where the hell are you?"

A hand scrabbled at my leg, so I grabbed his hand and started pulling. "Jeeeeeeeesus. Damn, that hurts!"

"Sorry, Buddy, but I've got to get you out of this crap before I can get you to the doc."

"Be careful! I'm an officer!"

"So, you want an egg in your beer?" Then I said, "Sir!"

I pulled him out of the muck and through the undergrowth. When I lifted him into a fireman's carry, he resumed some very energetic cussing. It seemed to me like a good sign. Minutes later, I was able to lower him into a stretcher at the field hospital where a medic took over.

Under lamplight I could see he was the nervous lieutenant.

"Sir, where's the rest of your patrol?"

"I don't know. Still back there, I guess."

"You *guess*?"

The medic interrupted me. "Where are you hit, sir"

"It's my lower right leg. Be careful, for God's sake."

The medic slit and then ripped open the lieutenant's trouser leg to reveal a bloody scrape down his shin. The medic pressed the scrape with his thumb.

"This it?"

"Yeeeeoww! Damn you, you're killing me!"

"Well, sir," the medic said in a sardonic tone, "I'm a-gonna fix you right up." He tilted a bottle of alcohol, pouring a generous glug or two onto a gauze pad. He gripped the leg with one hand and then, with the other, slapped the soaked pad into the middle of the scrape.

The lieutenant screamed and tried to kick the medic away.

A surgeon, his mask all adangle, bent over us. "What you got here, Eddie? Traumatic amputation?"

The medic, keeping the gauze and his grip clamped on the squirming leg looked up in disgust.

"Naaa, Doc," he yelled over the officer's screams. "Simple abrasion."

The surgeon snorted, straightened up and walked away.

I did the same, heading back to Lieutenant Irish.

# Chapter 62
# Regardless Of Costs II

When I got back from the hospital, Lieutenant Irish and a medic were working by flashlight on the rump of a wounded man face down in the dirt.

The buck sergeant, who had a field dressing on the left side of his face, grimly watched over Lieutenant Irish's shoulder.

I looked closely. The flashlight showed the man's left buttock ripped away, dangling beside his naked hip by a twisted strip of skin. Where his left butt cheek should be about all I could see was gristle and bone splinters.

The sight made me gag but Lieutenant Irish snapped me out of it.

Yanking me away with a vice grip on my arm, he hissed "Damn you, don't do that! He's bad off enough without you adding to it."

He gave my arm another hell of a jerk. In a fierce whisper, "Now just stay away until you're settled down."

I swallowed, told him I was sorry. I took a deep breath and returned with him.

The wounded man audibly was gritting his teeth. Then he gave out a harsh whisper of his own. "Yeeoooooow-zerrrrrrr! You bastard! What the hell are you doing -- digging for gold?"

The medic, sweat beaded on his forehead and dripping from his nose, said "Not really. Sorry this hurts so much. As soon as we get these bleeders clamped, I'll give you morphine and we'll get you to surgery."

"Will I lose my leg?" the soldier said.

"Hell, no. Now quit your fussing."

I asked the sergeant, "Anyone else make it back?"

"Chuck here and me are the only ones. We run into a real buzz saw."

"Well, one other man got back," I said.

Peering at me he said, "Let me guess. Was it our fearful leader?"

"Yep."

Lieutenant Irish looked at me. "Was he wounded?"

"Yeah. Something scraped some skin off his poor shin."

Chuck, face downward, rocked his head up, "That little pussy! I heard this splash and somebody squealed like a stuck pig. I bet it was the lieutenant – little Mr. Peebie Shit himself. Next thing you know every Jap in the world is blasting us."

I guffawed. "You really you call your CO Peebie Shit?"

Chuck said, "Damn right. That's his nickname. He's nothing but a prissy little turd. Wouldn't make a wart on a real officer's ass – let alone a good sergeant."

Starting to get to his feet, Lieutenant Irish said, "I believe I'm going to report this."

The sergeant grabbed his sleeve and whispered, "Wait a second, sir. I wouldn't bother. No point in starting anything official. We can just settle it ourselves."

The sergeant and Lieutenant Irish exchanged glances. "You're an old NCO, right?" the sergeant said. "Get my drift? For the good of the service, right?"

The lieutenant finally nodded and settled back down. "Yeah. Okay."

The medic by now had some of the soldier's flesh back in place and covered with a field dressing.

"Now, my friend," he said, "you just stay right here. I'll get a stretcher and we'll haul you to the surgeons. They'll make a new man out of you."

"Okay, Buddy. And thanks for the shot. I feel better already."

The sergeant and I toted Chuck through the darkness to the field hospital. The place was scurrying like a disturbed ant hill.

A nurse glanced at our patient and pointed to an open spot on the ground next to another patient who grinned up at us. The left side of his skull was yawning wide open.

As he took a drag on his cigarette, he said, "Boys, just set him down easy now! Easy! The docs will get to him pretty quick. They checked me out and they tell me I'm headed back stateside."

We congratulated him.

Walking back, the medic said the butt-shot soldier probably would be going back to the states, too.

"He's likely to lose everything from the left hip down," the medic said, "manhood included."

# Chapter 63
# A Blow From Home

Lieutenant Irish gave us electrifying news the next morning. Last night a platoon on the Urbana Front – led by a sergeant – penetrated through the Jap line to the ocean. The survivors dug in on the beach and were standing off repeated frantic Jap counterattacks.

Another platoon was trying to get through to them with more machine guns and ammo.

The outfit achieving the breakthrough was part of the battalion that had suffered so heavily crossing the mountains last month. Now – thanks to exhaustion, sickness and heavy combat casualties – it was down to fewer than 200 die-hard scarecrows.

Because of those losses, General Eichelberger began making demands that headquarters at last release the entire 127th Regiment to him.

"From now on," he told us, "we're changing things. The 128th here on the Warren Front will just hold until we can get some tanks. Harding was right -- no attack down here ever can succeed without more artillery and some armor.

"We'll use the 127th plus the Aussies and what's left of the 126th against The Triangle up near Buna and Buna Mission. Now that we've got some penetration up there, we should able to start pushing the Japs out."

He ordered us to keep up our training, but said we should ease off on night patrols for now.

# # #

At that point, thanks to fragments of a letter that seemed to be a Dear John, I could have cared less.

That was the day we finally got mail, if you could call it that.

The mailbags that the natives hauled to headquarters were mildewed and stained, as if they had rested in some ship's bilge water all the way from San Francisco . . . and then maybe a swamp or two.

The mail officer opened the first bag, looked in and just stared. He turned gray and then began opening the other mailbags in quick succession.

His face still ashen, he glanced at his Pfc. clerks and just said, "You won't believe this." He reached into the first bag with both hands and pulled out a thick, dripping glob of letters. "Christ," he said, "look at this. Looks like the all the names and addresses have run."

He and his boys dumped out the bags onto the ground and had a hell of a time the next two days peeling and sorting through those sodden masses of mail. The bulk of it was little more than stained pulp. Humidity and constant rain, of course, made it hopeless to try drying that mildewed mass.

I received two pieces of mail. One was a damp but intact letter from my kid brother. He had typed it so that it remained fairly legible.

Stevie reported that Dad was recovering okay from an accident on the line at Boeing. Mom had been given leave to help nurse him at home. Meanwhile, Stevie was having a good season as a guard on his high school football team. Upon graduation in spring he planned to enlist in the Marines.

I immediately wanted to write to him not to do it, but first tried to open the other letter . . . the one from Beverly.

The envelope fell apart as I tried to peel open the flap. The contents were pulp. It took 20 minutes to separate the damp tatters of lined paper. The ink had run so badly I could make out only scattered phrases. Afterwards I wished I hadn't tried to read it, because all it did was torture me.

One scrap said she was very, very sorry. I found another piece saying ". . . to get pregnant and . . ." Then I found a reference to ". . . Naval officer in the South Pacif . . ." and finally, just above the blurred signature, ". . . your forgiveness, please."

Lieutenant Irish and Pop both asked what was bothering me so much and I told them to just leave me the hell alone.

At first I was in a black fury.

The one goddam thing I had to look forward to had fucking deserted me. I wanted to go back and read through all my old letters from Beverly to see if they contained any clue that would verify an affair with some asshole swabby ensign. But those letters disappeared with my old ripped-up uniform when I was wounded.

Then I remembered something. When I found out that all those treasured letters from Beverly were shit-canned with my blood-stained gear, I really hadn't felt that torn up about it.

At length, I had to admit I deserved it. In Adelaide, I had been disloyal to Beverly with the little redhead . . . and my memories dwelt far more on the redhead's beautiful body and the pleasure I took from it than upon my memories of Beverly's gorgeous smile. So, yes, I was an asshole to be sore at Beverly for doing to me what I already had done to her. In either event, we hadn't even been engaged.

Still, it tortured me. My mind paced endlessly back and forth as if in a cage that Beverly and I . . . and the redhead . . . had fabricated all these months.

Finally I let Pop know I had received a Dear John letter.

He tried to sympathize with me by snarling and asking how that bitch could let me down that way.

His comments just made me angry at him. And that, in turn, led me to feel even more guilty.

I toyed with the notion of standing straight up and marching north across New Strip into the Jap guns.

Came close to doing it, too, but hardly in such a calculating way.

# Chapter 64
# Meeting Some Allies

Lieutenant Irish stuck me with the job of briefing an Aussie major and a company of soldiers called a commando, a term new to me.

The major ordered his men to sit in a semi-circle in front of me, all the officers joining them. Many of them began waving off mosquitos with their broad-brimmed bush hats.

"Gentlemen," I said, "this won't take long because there's not a lot to tell you.

"The main thing is that the Japs have burrowed themselves into scores of bunkers – very stout log and steel construction. Or else they position themselves under what we call cages – these trees that stand on stilt-like roots that form kind of an upside-down bowl. The interior is quite dark so they're hard to see until they start shooting. They also dig in among those fan-like buttresses of giant trees. The buttresses make great cover and they're usually thick enough to stop a bullet.

"Anyway, they cunningly set it up so that all those fire points are mutually supporting. Howitzer fire doesn't seem to damage bunkers and something to remember is that the Japs inside a bunker often will let an assault group pass them, and then they start shooting from behind. We've learned that sometimes they'll wait several days to do that."

The major asked, "What about direct fire from something like anti-tank guns?"

I chuckled. "If we ever get such weapons, sir, I'd love to be the first to try firing them directly at the bunker firing slits. Those are the only vulnerable points.

"About the only way we've found to get at the Japs is by tossing grenades or shooting Tommy Guns through those firing slits. We would all value the chance to use flame-throwers," I added, "but so far we don't have any."

The major and his officers listened politely. Then the major asked, "What about getting inside and using the bayonet?"

I said it didn't seem practical because every assault always came under fire from supporting bunkers or firing positions.

He said, "I see." The Aussies looked at each other. I thought I saw a few smirks.

I really didn't think the major was serious because he and his assault experts supposedly had arrived to support us when our tanks arrived, supposedly any day.

They certainly were an impressive bunch, each armed with that go-screw-yourself Australian grin. They also brought several Bren guns with them. Many of them carried Enfield jungle carbines, and some were armed with the odd-looking Owen submachine gun.

I call it odd because it had no wood. Just a wire handle. And it looked like a plumber's nightmare with a mottled green and yellow camouflage paint job. It also had a top-loading magazine, just like the Bren. But instead of firing the .303 rifle cartridge like the Bren, it used a pistol bullet, the 9 mm. I'd never heard of it.

"It's a damn fine round," Lieutenant Irish told me later. "The Germans developed it years ago for the Luger pistol. It's about the same as the .38"

"Oh."

More or less running the commando show day to day was a staff sergeant named MacKenzie.

Mack, as his men called him, was shorter than me. But deep-set hooded gray eyes made him a forbidding-looking character.

He got me off to the side to ask about our tactics.

I explained we were running our boys through training that they had never received – jungle training and nighttime stealth practices. The idea was to help them overcome their fear both of night and swamps.

"Good-oh," he said. "And how much bayo time?"

"Bayo?"

"Yeah, bayonet training."

The bayonet again. I grinned. "Oh, hell, Sergeant, none of us has had any bayonet training at all since basic. And then only for two or three hours."

He seemed genuinely shocked. "We take bayonet drill most seriously indeed," he said. "My chaps have their bayonets razor sharp. It's the only thing when you charge Jap positions."

"Sounds suicidal to me, Mack."

"Well, yes Jim, we always lose a few diggers," he admitted. "But that's war, innit? You also have losses when you don't do anything at all, right? Better to attack those bastards than just sitting around waiting for it."

"Sounds like pure death wish," I said.

"Please come with me, Sergeant," he said. "I want you to see something."

It turned out to be the most monumental event of my life . . . and damn near the end of it.

# Chapter 65
# Bayonet Work

As MacKenzie led me along a muddy jungle track, we heard the repeated clatter of a Nambu.

Bullets began snapping through the foliage above us, so Mack crouched and I followed his lead. We came to a clearing where a large party of Aussies sprawled on the ground behind a broad stretch of Kunai.

The machine gun rattled off a burst in our general direction every minute or so, but the shooting was high, harmlessly shredding the tall tops of the grass.

A freckled corporal rolled to his side and looked up as Mack and I knelt.

"They got two of the lads an hour ago, Mack. Now I think they're just teasing us."

"Where are they, Bluie?"

The corporal nodded toward the area beyond the grass. "They look to be holed up in the buttress roots of that fig tree over there. That tree's gotta be 200 feet tall, so those roots are head-high."

"Ooch, the mussies are turning your vision bad," another soldier said as he reassembled his Bren gun. "The buttresses are maybe chest high, if that."

"Mussies?" I asked.

"Yeah, sport, the bloody mosquitos."

Mack asked the corporal, "How far is it?"

"Maybe seventy yards . . . muddy, but a lot of palm frond and grass lying over it. Not too bad for runnin'."

"Naah," the argumentative soldier spoke up again. "It's a scant sixty yards. Almost grenade range. Piece of cake."

As the corporal and the sergeant debated, I looked at the men around us.

One lay on his back, smoking and cradling a Mills bomb on his chest. Most lay on their stomachs or sides, rifles or Owen guns pointed in the Japs' direction.

Without anyone saying a word, the men with rifles and carbines began fixing bayonets.

Once his bayonet was fixed, the man on his back cradled his Enfield in his right arm, the bayonet's blunt edge lying on his shoulder.

Several soldiers were teasing him about his height and skinny build. "Mike, if you run straight at the beggers, they'll get you. But if you scamper sideways, Tojo won't be able to keep you in his sights."

Mike laughed. "What a pack of flamin' wombats." The other men chuckled with him.

"Okay you characters," I said. "Translate please."

Mike looked up, "What I'm sayin' is that they're wombats -- all just little fellas. They're lucky. They're so short that the Japs shoot over them, mostly."

McKenzie spoke up, loudly. "Well, cobbers, they got Herb and Graham."

One of the soldiers pushed himself to his knees and then stood up. "Duty first."

Just then a very young-looking Aussie showed up. "Are we ready?"

Mack said, "Yes, sir. We are. And, sir, we have an observer, Master Sergeant Jim Mays, US Army."

The soldier's uniform had no rank insignia. But the deference shown him by Mack and the other led me to conclude that he was an officer. So I figured he had to be a lieutenant. "Leftenant," I said, "It's a pleasure."

He nodded. This close to the line, nobody saluted anybody.

Another digger grinned as he arose. "Looks like this will be a one-section job."

"What do you mean," I asked.

"That means probably ten of us will get through."

"Get through?"

"Yeah, mate -- without getting shot."

The man with the Bren stood up, checking to see the magazine was firmly locked into the receiver. He shook his head. "I'd say six of us will get through . . . maybe eight."

"Oh, what a bloody optimist you are."

The Aussies' chatter about their own lousy odds made my blood run cold.

"You guys are going to charge that goddam machine gun with bayonets? Seriously? In broad daylight?"

One digger frowned at me. "Well, not really, Sarge. Down here in the weeds, we ain't getting much daylight at all, now are we?"

Someone answered, "Not broad daylight, any roads."

As the other men rose, checking their weapons, MacKenzie met my eyes. "Jim, you coming?" The others had their eyes on me.

"Yeah Yank, are you a fobbit?"

"A fobbit?"

"A stay-behind."

A day ago I had been considering suicide. But now I wasn't so sure.

My heart started pounding and I know my voice got shaky. "Oh, hell no, not me! I wouldn't miss this for anything. So, you crazy bastards, what's the drill?"

Corporal Bluie nodded and said, "Well, Sarge, it's quite simple, really. You run fast as a bloody hound, scream like a bloody madman and, when you get there, you stick the little barstids."

The lieutenant looked at me. "You needn't come, you know."

"Yeah, well – I've got to uphold 32$^{nd}$ Division's reputation, I guess."

Mack said, "All right. Check your weapons -- one up the spout, right? Spread out a bit. Mike and Ted, take your Brens to cover our flanks. Keep the crossfire off us, right?"

"Right!" Mike and Ted nodded. We stayed low, crawling through the grass, stopping just inside its edge.

The lieutenant looked right and left. "Let's get stuck into them."

The men nodded.

He bellowed, "GO!"

Twenty-three of us – two Australian infantry sections plus Staff Sergeant MacKenzie, his lieutenant and yours truly terrified, tore through the Kunai grass to race across the misty ground toward that monster tree.

I never in my life wanted to do anything less.

But since we were trying to outrun the Japs' trigger fingers and dodge their aim, I guess mob psychology took over.

It was just like being in a football game kick-off, and it was over just about that fast.

I don't recall fear . . . just racing, screaming, rifle pumping diagonally across my chest. I don't recall shots but I certainly heard bullets strike among us. People grunted and fell right and left, some landing flat, others rolling over and over. As I heard the first slugs slam into them, I cringed. Something slammed my own M-1 against my chest, almost bringing me to a stop. *My God! Run! Run! Catch up! With them . . . catch up . . . with them.* No more cringing.

The man in front of me, the lieutenant, pitched backward as if struck in the face. I dodged him and in five strides we were there -- a dozen of us, more maybe – screaming like banshees as we plunged among those wave-shaped 6-foot roots.

A Jap reared up in front of me, rifle up, eyes wide. I pulled the trigger. Nothing. Still running, I butt-stroked his head with all my weight behind it. Something hit and smashed apart my M-1. I grabbed up his Arisaka with that lonnnng bayonet. A heavy, alien feel as I tried recalling bayonet drill commands.

*Block right! Horizontal butt stroke! Short thrust and hold! Retract! Vertical butt stroke . . .*

A screaming Aussie soldier showed me how. He blocked his opponent's bayonetted rifle and then skewered him, yanking out the bloody blade before the man's face even registered eight inches of cold steel transfixing his aorta.

As Target One collapsed to his knees, Corporal Bluie bashed in the face of another Jap coming from his right. I dropped the rifle, jerked out my .45 and aimed at a pair of Japs frantically trying to clear their jammed Nambu.

Three quick head shots splattered orange brain matter into the corner formed by two huge moss-coated root buttresses.

I heard two more shots in the vicinity and a quick burst from a Bren.

Suddenly it was quiet.

I staggered, looking for a place to sit, or maybe lie.

# Chapter 66
# Relief

Bluie slapped my shoulder, laughing. "Bad form, Yank. Bad form. You're supposed to bayonet the Jap barstids. It ain't sporting to shoot a kneeling Tojo."

"What? What?"

"Now corporal," Mack chided Bluie, "maybe you didn't see the sergeant bash that devil who was taking aim at you." He turned to me. "Well, Jim, what do you think of bayonet charges?"

'I think I need a cigarette."

What did I think?

I didn't.

I just reveled in a soft, pink soft cloud of euphoria. I was alive, not noticing a big sore spot on my chest where the M-1 slammed me when a Jap bullet hit it.

Alive! Shaking like a leaf, but gloriously alive and very grateful. No suicide thoughts. Not now.

Soon, however, the mingled stench of sweat, swamp, gunpowder and rotting bodies intruded on my senses again. I counted. Eleven Aussies still walking.

So it had been a one-section attack.

Still trying to get my breath, I discovered a double bullet hole in my left pant leg and another in the left sleeve of my shirt. I told Mack, "It was damned lucky that their Nambu jammed."

"Yeah, it often happens," Mack said. "It's not luck, though. Their machine guns just aren't as reliable as ours. Under pressure, they often have trouble fitting the next strip into the action. And if they're feeding cartridges into one of those hoppers, dirt and brush often fall in and cause a stoppage.

"The ammo belts for our machine guns are much more reliable. And changing magazines on a Bren is a piece of cake."

Totting up, we killed 18 Japanese and captured two, because they were wounded. We had sustained seven wounded, two badly, and five killed – the dead included the scrawny soldier, Mike, and the young lieutenant whose name I never heard.

As Mack spoke, two of the survivors and lightly wounded started going through the Japs' pockets. The other men had their Brens and rifles up, eyes sweeping back and forth on the rustling tree tops.

"Eddie," one digger said, "I believe I spy a Tojo in that banana-looking tree to your right. About 80 feet up, I'd say. I believe he has his eye on us."

Looking up, Eddie moved five steps, raised his Owen and ripped off a burst almost vertically. The palm fronds above rattled and an instant later the sniper took a swan dive from his tree. He landed head-first ten feet from us with a satisfying "whump."

"Be alert, now," Mack cautioned. "That kind of kill often provokes more sniper fire."

"Right, Mack," one of the men said.

"Now, Jim," he said to me, "the point is that we take casualties because, no matter what, these Jap bastards aren't like the Afrika Korps. The Krauts had all the sand anybody would want, but if their position was hopeless, they'd do the smart thing and surrender. The damned Japs won't. So we feel we're better off charging, killing them all and getting it over with."

He turned to his men.

"Okay, any documents for the dart-throwers?"

Two looters held up wallets and notebooks I looked at him in puzzlement.

He grinned at me. "I'm referring to the Army Intelligence boys."

Bluie looked at the lieutenant who had been shot in his upper chest. "Too bad about Mr. Nietz and him not even wearing his birdshit."

Mack told me, "That's slang for the pips a lieutenant wears on his shoulder straps."

"Right!" he went on. "Bluie and Scotty, you're rear guard. Each with a Bren. We'll carry the wounded and the dead.

"Jim, your rifle's kaput and you seem to fancy the Owen. Would you mind carrying one and being our point man back to the Kunai?"

"If I can rip off a burst first, just to get the feel of it."

He nodded. I fired a burst into the treetops. Because of the compensator at the end of its barrel, the gun had very little recoil. "Love it," I said.

As I turned to lead the diminished team, I looked back. "Mack, I think you've made a believer out of me."

Mack, with the lieutenant's body in a fireman's carry, gave me a thumbs up.

# Chapter 67
# Reflection

When I got back to meet with Pop and Lieutenant Irish, I wasn't exactly bubbling over with good humor, but I certainly was excited to talk with them.

"Well, Jim," Lieutenant Irish said, "how was your first bayonet charge?"

"You dirty bastard! You set me up for that, didn't you?"

He gave a slight smile, shaking his head. "No. I just wanted you to see how the Aussies deal with these situations. I figured you might go along, but I wasn't sure. By the way, Sergeant Mays, it's against regs for you to call your superior officer a dirty bastard."

Pop said, "Yeah, you dirty bastard."

"Look, *Sir*," I said, "you told me you were always a bastard. And being in New Guinea, you sure as hell are dirty.

After he and Pop chuckled, I went on, "But, I must say, that kind of assault seems to make sense. And it would make a lot more sense if we had some pack howitzers, or anti-tank guns or tanks . . . even more white phosphorous mortar fire.

"The thing is," I added, "it's terrifying before you charge, but it's over with so damned fast."

Speaking behind me in his raspy voice, General Eichelberger said, "It's fast if you live or you're killed. But if you get a bullet in the guts or, say, the knee, it's not over fast at all."

I turned and saluted and he just nodded and took off his cap. For the first time he looked old.

"I was just at the hospital," he said. "Seeing those boys really takes it out of me."

He looked up at me. "So you were in a bayonet charge?"

"Yes sir. I was amazed they were so willing to do it. And before the charge, they were talking just very casually about their odds being two-to-one at best. I couldn't believe it – using ordinary everyday betting math when you're talking about your own life?"

"Jim, those Aussies are combat veterans," Lieutenant Irish said. "I can tell you this -- they tend to assume they're already dead. It's not 'if' to them but 'when'. Veteran infantrymen are downright cold about their chances."

Pop said, "I don't know if our boys feel that way. I think charging with the bayonet – or at least a tommy gun – makes sense. But I don't know how our troops would feel about it."

The general nodded.

Lieutenant Irish said, "I don't agree, Pop. I've spent quite a bit of time with the boys in the last few days here and on the Urbana front. They're sick and they're bitching, but they're finally getting some decent chow. And I think morale is picking up because they're learning. And, believe me, they're fighting.

"The longer we're in this hellhole, I think the more willing they'll be. For damn sure the only way out of here is by finding and killing every Japanese soldier along this whole strip of coastline.

"And do you men hear that noise?" General Eichelberger said.

Pop said, "Yes, sir. Sounds like a jeep."

"No, it's a truck. The engineers finally got a road through to us.

"It's corduroyed -- log surface rather than asphalt – so it's bumpy as hell.

"But now we can get the wounded to Dopodura fairly quickly. And very soon it will help us give the Japs a nasty surprise."

"What's that, sir?"

"Later."

# Chapter 68
# The Cavalry . . . At Last

Among the many unpleasantries about New Guinea – at least the Buna area -- was the glue-like mud.

When you had to crawl in it or try to walk and pull your legs out of its sucking depth, it was midnight black. But once it dried clinging to your uniform or boots, it became a sickly gray and turned hard.

I was using the back of Ishimoto's knife to whack away chunks of that caked mud from what was left of my boots when somebody behind me with an Aussie accent said, "Right awful stuff, innit?"

"Yeah, dammit," I said. "It's a real bitch to get off. Maybe if we stuck it in a kiln it might good for making ceramic tile or pots or something."

The man gave a wheezy laugh. I looked up – red tabs on the collars, three pips and a crown on the shoulders.

I jumped to attention and saluted. "Sorry, General."

He was something you just didn't see in New Guinea.

He was fat.

He had a very round face perched above a humpty-dumpty body. Everybody else had lost so much weight that our cinched-in belts gave our pants very unmilitary pleats.

This new officer, however, looked a bit like the proverbial John Bull -- treble chin bulging above his collar, his gut bulging both above and below his belt.

But like John Bull, he also looked bulldoggish with gimlet eyes and an expression that said he was ready to bite.

"Stand easy, Sergeant," he said. "Just a brigadier, actually, not a general. I've just come up here to have a look at things."

Several other officers – Aussies and a couple of Americans, including Lieutenant Irish -- clustered behind him.

Still at attention, I said, "Sir, I'm with General Eichelberger's headquarters. Can I take you to him or be of assistance?"

"No thanks, Sergeant. He and I already had a conference back at Dopodura. He should be here any time."

He turned to his major.

"The engineers will have to do a better job of work on that road. Needs much wider corduroy. Now," he turned back to me, "how far are we from New Strip?"

"It's not visible from here, sir, but it's only about 400 yards right up this track. It leads just past the west end of the runway and then another 300 yards to Old Strip.

"Right. And Cape Endaiadere is about 800 yards beyond that?"

"More like 1,000 yards, sir – that is, northeast of where we stand now. It's not visible to us and we only know it by map. And I beg pardon, but who are you, sir?"

Genially, the major told me, "Sergeant, you are addressing Brigadier Sir George Wootten, commander of 18 Brigade of the 7th Division."

The designation rang a bell. "Didn't the 18th take out the Japs at Milne Bay? First ever defeat for the Japs?"

The brigadier grinned, "Exactly right, Sergeant. We're going to lend a hand up here. General Eichelberger has given me command of Warren Front."

We heard a jeep bouncing over the road's corduroyed surface. Minutes later General Eichelberger joined us. For the first time since I'd seen him, he seemed close to grinning.

"Come to take a look-see, George?"

"Right, sir. We'll need a few more hours' work on some of the corduroy and then we'll be able to stage them to break out over on the beach.

He added, "A morning attack might catch them with their knickers down."

General Eichelberger asked, "Okay, now how do you think you want to do this?"

"I think the main thrust first will be north along the beach through the plantation directly toward the cape."

*Good luck, buddy. I'm not going along on that one.*

"Once we get to the cape, then we wheel west to pinch them out between the plantation and Old Strip. But at the same time I want a secondary push straight west between New Strip and Old Strip. Your patrols have reported many bunkers there."

General Eichelberger nodded and pointed at Lieutenant Irish and me. "These are the boys who organized those patrols. And the sergeant just came back from work with one of your commandos."

"Excellent." He glanced at my skeptical look. "Maybe you'll find this approach more rewarding since we now have tanks."

Now that was exciting news. "Tanks, sir! We've tried to get them for weeks."

"Right." The brigadier said, "They are American tanks which will have Australian drivers and gunners. In the desert, we named the tanks Stuarts after your Confederate cavalry leader."

Brigadier Wootten and General Eichelberger walked together to the tables where I'd just weighted down the brand-new up-to-date maps that arrived yesterday.

I turned to Lieutenant Irish who had a grim smile on his face. I whispered, "So what's with fatso?"

He frowned. "Easy, sergeant. He's fat, but only from the neck down. Brigadier Wootten is one sharp cookie.

"He's been there – fought in Gallipoli and France during the World War I. After the war he became a lawyer in civilian life.

"But then he rejoined the army and was leading a brigade in North Africa against Rommel.

"He had general staff training in England and he knows what he's doing. He's put in a lot of time on this assault.

He organized shipping the tanks here, got them barged to shore and meanwhile had the engineers working to build ramps for them to get ashore and to corduroy roads for them.

"The guy's a hell of an organizer."

I asked about the tanks.

Lieutenant Irish said, "They're light – only 14 tons – so they can operate in the plantation. But they're decently armored and they have three machine guns plus a 37 mm main gun that can hit the bunkers up close and cause a lot of grief inside.

"I don't think the Japs will be prepared for the Stuarts."

# Chapter 69
# Tank Attack

Late Dec. 17, in the midst of another downpour, we guided the brigadier's eight Stuart tanks into concealed positions at the jungle's edge. Meanwhile, to cloak the tanks' engine noise, the brigadier ordered an intense mortar and artillery barrage of the plantation.

After that, Pop, Lieutenant Irish and I helped guide a battalion from the Aussie brigade to the assault phase line. Then Pop and I attached ourselves to a section of Aussie infantry.

At dawn Dec. 18, I yawned as I told Pop, "By God, this better work or we'll still be fighting in this shithole until 1950."

The Aussie sergeant commanding the section grinned at us. "No worries, Sarge. Tanks and infantry together will shift Tojo very nicely. We protect the tanks. The tanks blast open the way for us. Just you watch."

A heavy air strike started and the three of us stuck our fingers in our ears and cowered behind a tank. Peeking toward the plantation, Pop yelled, "Well, for once, the fly boys are on target."

Heavy blasts shattered trees and hurled up plumes of earth and smoke where we knew enemy bunkers to be. Then, along with the bombs, howitzers and mortars began shelling the plantation, the sign for the tank drivers to crank up their motors. Kneeling behind a tank, I convulsed in a brief coughing fit after getting a healthy blast of exhaust in the face.

As the barrage ended, the Aussie battalion and seven tanks broke from cover. The eighth tank remained in reserve.

Five of the tanks began their rattling, squealing advance north into the smoky plantation. Two others, supported by First Battalion of the 128th, turned west toward the gap between New Strip and Old Strip.

Pop with his M-1 and I with my Bren gun joined the northbound force, sticking with the sergeant's section beside one of the tanks. As we began walking, I mentioned wanting to bring in a POW or two.

The sergeant sneered and spat. "The bastards murdered some of our cobbers at Milne Bay," he said. "And we heard that at Rabaul they tied diggers to trees and used them for bayo drill.

"They're naught but bloody roaches," he said. Grinning nastily, he added, "And we're exterminators."

Following the tanks and Aussie infantry was another force -- Third Battalion of the 128th, staying 300 yards behind us to mop up and to intercept Japs who habitually managed to infiltrate behind any attack.

Every one of us, Aussies and Americans alike, looked like hell – tattered, worn, gaunt, eyes sunken and exhibiting crusted weeping jungle ulcers. But today everybody also managed to look eager, even excited.

As we entered the plantation through the barrage smoke, I could see Jap soldiers at listening posts popping up and catching sight of us. I couldn't make out their features at that distance, but each stood straight, did a double-take, crouched and whipped around to sprint north. They disappeared into trenches, bunkers or bomb craters.

Pop yelled, "Wooooie! Look at that! A bunch of cottontails spooked by beagles. It's a whole new ballgame, Tojo."

Tank machine guns began a manic yammer. Some panicked enemy soldiers jumped into view and ran. At first, the Jap gunners seemed paralyzed at seeing the tanks. "Maybe they can't believe their eyes," I said.

But as we and the tanks pressed into the first rows of trees, they opened up with all they had. We often had to hit the deck, diving into muddy craters or sopping, ankle-deep palm detritus. Twice Pop and I sheltered briefly with Aussies in craters or trenches. As fire shifted, we got up and dashed forward, ready for another dive.

At first the Japs' fire seemed fruitless. Showers of tracers simply caromed off the tanks' turrets and frontal armor.

Looking like cumbersome black beetles, the tanks – each with its party of infantry -- moved deliberately across the areas where so many men had died. Each would slow, its turret turning briefly. The coaxial turret machine gun would fire into a bunker's firing slit.

"Look out, Tojos," Pop yelled.

Then the main gun would blast.

The first shot cracking from our tank's main gun detonated in a bunker's interior with a disappointingly dull thump. But smoke spewed from the bunker's apertures. Seconds later, several stunned, bleeding Japs staggered outside.

We mowed them down.

But the enemy in other bunkers and firing points neither retreated nor surrendered. They fought viciously. Tracers zipped among our infantry and Aussie troops began to fall. Yet as the Stuarts clattered up to and into the Japs' positions, we and the tanks took them under fire and killed them.

I soon had to fit a third magazine onto my Bren gun.

Under cover of the tanks, our infantry were able to drop white phosphorous grenades into bunker air vents. We saw some grim nods and thumbs up at the shrill screams coming in the wake of low-key but fiery explosions.

For the first time on New Guinea, our tanks forced Japs out to face hardened veterans – old hands who knew how and when to take cover, when to assault, how to maneuver under fire and when and how to concentrate their fire.

The tank gunners kept blasting the sources of tracers, forcing the Japanese out into the open where at last they were forced to meet us on an equal footing. Jungle carbines, Owen guns and Brens kept up a constant rattle, fire rising to crescendos as cannon fire rousted more Japs.

We advanced north through the plantation by fits and starts. "It's still not a cakewalk is it, Pop?"

"No, but it's mighty good to be walking along with Bunker Blaster here."

"What's Bunker Blaster?" the sergeant asked.

"That's our nickname for this tank."

Each time that we riflemen and Bunker Blaster crossed enemy trenches, the sergeant ordered us forward to clear the trench either by firing or throwing grenades into it. "See, we don't want to leave behind any flamin' sacrificial lambs to shoot us in the back or to grenade the tank."

As we tackled the trenches, the tank machine guns fired at any enemy showing themselves among the trees beyond us.

We'd been moving and fighting about an hour and were just about to the Cape Endaiadere beach when we paused before a trench with radical zig-zags. Two grenades flushed a covey of enemy who scrambled up, firing at us from point-blank range. Bullets buzzed through our line like hornets as our 10-man section fired back. A three-second firefight killed all four of them and cost two of us.

But we missed one die-hard.

Just as the tank approached the lip of the trench, he tore into sight from one of the diagonals. Shirtless, a sweatband around his forehead and his face contorted in fury, he screamed and hurled a big Sake bottle at the tank. The bottle was stoppered with a burning rag.

Pop and two Aussies nailed him, but too late to stop the Molotov cocktail from smashing near the drivers' hatches. The exploding fireball singed all of us. The commander vaulted out of the turret and the gunner, blazing liked a comet, came right behind him.

I tackled the gunner and rolled him on the sodden ground to extinguish his burning clothes. He bellowed curses the whole time because Bunker Blaster's drivers were trapped inside screaming as the blaze roasted them. I prayed for them to die quickly but it took forever. Ammo inside the tank started cooking off, so that cordite stink slightly and the odor of kerosene overrode that of broiling flesh.

A medic raced to us, but the gunner brushed him off. He only wanted a firearm.

"I'm infantry now," he snarled. "They fried me mates and I'll see the buggers in hell." He and the tank commander joined us, picking up weapons from the section's two dead infantrymen.

Just then, an Aussie major came tearing past, waving an Owen gun and blowing a whistle. "Turn to, lads! We reached the cape. Now we attack toward Old Strip. Don't give them time to recover!"

# Chapter 70
# Into The Fire

The major led us inland to support the tanks' attack toward Old Strip. Our sergeant yelled and waved, "Come on! We're winning, but we ain't finished them yet!"

At first, it felt to me like the bayonet charge all over again -- the same racing, football kick-off excitement.

It didn't last.

This time we were charging toward an objective not 60 yards but 300 yards away. And trying to run carrying a Bren gun was a hell of a lot harder. With full 30-round magazines, the load seemed about four times that of an M-1.

Pop yelled, "Good God, look! That whole damn runway must be a bunker."

I saw what he meant. This time we were weren't charging a single machine gun nest.

Bright yellow flashes flickered along most of Old Strip almost as if it were decorated for Christmas shopping. Those machine guns made the air around us twitch and smoke with nasty little glow-worms and vicious invisible bees and hornets.

"Take cover for God's sake!" Pop and I dropped into a bomb crater. An instant later, bullets chopped the earth above us, flinging dirt and palm splinters onto our backs.

Like us, the rest of the Aussie section wisely melted into the ground.

After groveling for a minute and getting my breath, I peeked over the crater's edge. Downed palm logs lay all around us. *Thank God for all the bombing.*

As the zip and whine of bullets around us diminished, Pop and I jumped from our shell crater. We both fired toward Old Strip and then raced to drop behind a tangle of downed coconut logs. Bullets drummed against our shelter, but we were safe and thirty yards closer to the airstrip.

All around us, Aussie troops were doing the same, advancing in alternating rushes.

The tanks had slowed, their drivers not wanting to advance without infantry protection. They continued chopping away at Old Strip's Nambus, but then, one-by-one, they pivoted south, heading for New Strip.

"Sergeant," I yelled. "What's with our armor?"

He yelled from our right. "Seems they're needed down on New Strip. We have to carry on without them. We're getting help soon."

A voice came from my left. "Hey, are you guys Americans or what?"

Pop prepared to pull the pin on a grenade. "Who wants to know?"

"We're with the 128th. We was following the Aussies that was with the tanks. What's going on now?"

"We're Yanks working with Aussies. Now we're assaulting toward New Strip. Fire and movement, just like your training."

"Jeez, we ain't done that in a while. But we're with you."

We kept working our way forward, log to crater and crater to stump, stump to logs, the men from the 128th now advancing in line with us on our left.

With a tearing rush in the air, the help arrived -- artillery and mortars began slamming along Old Strip. The shelling – particularly the mortars' white phosphorous – killed Jap gunners or forced them under cover. Either way, Nambu fire declined sharply.

The sergeant yelled again, "Let's go! Let's go!"

Now we could run fifty yards or more before machine guns began tearing into the ground and logs around us.

Pop and I and one of the Aussies jumped up together to charge forward. My right foot went into a bottomless hole and I fell my full length. Pop and the Aussie disappeared into the ground, leaving a large gap in the earth.

Pop shouted practically beneath me and then came a burst of fire from an Owen. I twisted to look down at where the hell they'd gone and the ground gave way beneath me. I fell into the hole together with a shower of dirt, bamboo and dead palm fronds.

I landed painfully on the unforgiving steel of my Bren, but I was facing the caved-in skull of a Jap soldier. Crouching beside him, the Aussie said, "Look, mate! It's a flamin' tunnel." He had his Owen submachine gun pointed toward a six-foot black hole in the earth.

Pop, pointing to another hole in the opposite direction, shouted, "We got Japs down here! They're running." I checked the body's ragged uniform. It had the double star of a lieutenant so I patted him down and found a thick notebook in his back pocket. *Diary maybe!*

The Aussie section leader appeared above our hole and bellowed at us. "Will you buggers quit skulking down there. We've got a job of work."

"It's a Jap tunnel," I yelled. "I think they're trying to infiltrate behind us."

"Leave off. That's the work for the 128th!" he yelled. "Now get your brains out of neutral and scramble back up here. Just toss them a couple of grenades."

We helped each other up. We just got to our knees on the surface and were starting to pull the pins on our grenades when two Japs scuttled beneath us, racing over their officer's body. They glanced up in surprise and plunged into the tunnel's other hole. I fired a burst after them.

The sergeant, now with a bleeding left arm shouted, "Come ON! The Yanks'll take care of them."

We tossed grenades into both tunnel entrances and raced to join the section, now down to six men. But our charge had to end. We were emerging from the west side of the plantation and running out of cover. No more logs and fewer craters.

The earth sloped down from the plantation toward the creek we'd patrolled. You might say it was a nice tilted shooting gallery for the Japs.

Worse, the ground became boggy underfoot and then swampy. And it's hard to dodge or dive for cover when you're calf-deep in muck.

At least, we found muddy cover in a few bomb craters.

A burst of Nambu fire hit the sergeant as he jumped up to lead a new rush.

He fell out of sight and a rose-colored mist slowly dissipated in the air behind him.

# Chapter 71
# Withdrawal

A corporal immediately jumped up, trying to race west with his men toward the creek.

They hit the dirt and Pop and I jumped up and suddenly found the creek lying before us – six feet wide and, now at high tide, probably eight feet deep.

We found cover in the brush and bamboo along the creek bank which was only inches higher than the water's surface. The brush may have made us hard to spot, but it wouldn't stop bullets. Worse, Old Strip now was uphill from us, 15 or 20 feet above sea level. Not only that, with its barbed wire apron and firing pits, Old Strip was still a good 100 yards beyond the creek.

"Corporal," I called, "we're sitting ducks here. And when the barrage quits, we're dead ducks."

"Right," he yelled. "We can't do any good here."

"Okay," I called back. "How 'bout we just ease back into the plantation?"

"Right-oh, sergeant."

The artillery still was flashing and blasting among Old Strip's defenders, but some of them still were shooting. So we withdrew, shooting, in alternating rushes, just as we assaulted earlier

The corporal led the last dash to the plantation. Now he had only five men with him. He yelled. "They got another of us. You two blokes better split when you rush next."

"Will do! You hear that, Pop?"

"Yeah, I got it. You go left and I'll angle right, okay?"

That's how we did it.

The instant I was up, a Nambu on Old Strip fired a burst. The Aussies fired back at the gun.

I ran to the left and then dropped.

"Pop? You okay?"

No answer.

I crawled back and found Pop on his back in a depression in the tall grass. The Nambu had riddled him.

I turned and screamed, "Medic! Medic!"

He grabbed my sleeve. I think he tried to say, "Don't bother." But starting the second word made him cough blood up onto me. I could tell that it alarmed him to see his blood spatter my face and uniform. He frowned.

In gasps, he said, "Ssss . . . sorr . . . eee."

"Shut up, will you? Medic's on the way. You'll be going back to Brisbane, maybe even get to Adelaide and meet up again with that long, tall lady."

He gave me a derisive smirk and shook his head. "Jim! Don't dump . . . my body in . . . Maggot Marsh."

"For Christ's sake, Pop, don't talk that way!"

I turned and shouted again for a medic.

When I looked back down at Pop, blood bubbled from his nose and lips as the life and the air left his body. Right there in front of me, his body just seemed to subside.

"Damn you, Pop! Damn you!"

He and I stood side by side – still in our civvies -- when they swore us into the Army at Fort Ord's reception center February 19. We'd been side-by-side for 10 months to the day . . . not a long time to know someone.

But when you're shared so much concentrated misery with someone who has saved your life, someone whose life you've saved, someone whose reactions are timed to yours and vice versa, you know him better than you'll ever know anybody ever again.

So I had a hole in my life, but I had no time to mourn because bullets started whipping above me from a fire-fight flaring 100 feet behind us further inside the plantation.

A squad from the 128th had found Jap soldiers popping up in bunkers we overran earlier with the tanks.

Linking up, we slowly moved back over the ground we took earlier, this time carefully checking every bunker. So now we and other men around us were a conglomeration of units – Corporal Benson would have called it FUBAR.

But we were a united team spending the rest of the day hunting, trapping and killing Japs. We even looked alike, because Yanks and Aussies were equally filthy. The only way you could tell us apart was by our accents or whether we wore steel pots or bush hats.

When the sergeant of the American squad saw my six stripes, he offered command to me.

"No. You know what you're doing. I'm just trying to be a half-decent rifleman."

I don't know whether I helped. I used up my last Bren magazine and abandoned the gun for some dead man's M-1 and two bandoleers of loaded clips.

And, as the saying goes, by then I was so damned tired I didn't care if school kept going or not.

I was so tired I forgot about what happened to Pop – until I cracked a joke to him.

And he wasn't there to laugh.

# Chapter 72
# Resting Up

By about 1900 I made my way back to headquarters to turn in the Jap's diary. Lieutenant Irish was there looking as whipped as I felt. His left arm, hit by some shrapnel, was in a sling, but he actually seemed pleased.

"Boy, the tanks really did the job today, didn't they? Do you know how many bunkers we found between the two airstrips? There was two dozen of them. Literally. And there also was four steel and concrete pill boxes. We never could have captured them with infantry alone.

"We had to blast the little devils out of there one-by-one. The tanks had to back off to twice for more ammo. The Japs just won't quit. Like digging out a bunch of damned moles. Some times it can take five men to kill a single hold-out. We took pretty heavy losses."

"So, they're all cleared out?"

"Nope. Brigadier Wootten says the plantation is clear. So is all of New Strip, but the Japs still hold Old Strip."

"Yeah, tell me about it."

He gave me a look. "Where's Pop?"

"They got him."

"Damn."

We just listened as the rain started hammering down again. After a while he said, "So it's just down to the two of us."

"Right. Until maybe Riegle gets back."

I sat there a while, head down. Then I asked, "So do we get some rest tomorrow?"

He nodded. "Yeah. I hear tell that Eichelberger is running tomorrow's attack up at Urbana Front. He'll lead the 126th in together with Aussies from a different brigade. Japs are in bunkers all over the place up there, but the Aussies and the 126th have carved out several pockets right to the beach. It has fragmented the Japs and they've starting attacking and are getting slaughtered right and left.

"And the really good news," he added, "is that GHQ finally released the 127th to Eichelberger. The Air Corps flew them in from Port Moresby so Urbana Front now has three fresh battalions. And they've had a hell of a lot of jungle training. "

"Who arranged that?"

"The training? Eichelberger. He demanded it. Didn't want more troops coming in here without knowing what to do. And, boy, is he spitting mad."

"Even madder than usual?"

Lieutenant gave a huge smile. "Boy, you had better believe it. Sutherland showed up this afternoon with a letter from MacArthur. First, Sutherland announced that MacArthur is white hot because we *still* haven't captured Buna and the airstrips. He told Eichelberger that MacArthur authorized him to take over command of the 32nd if he deemed it necessary."

"My God, I can't believe that!"

"No, that's smoking hot gospel. One of the general's aides said the old man told Sutherland, 'Fine. I'll hand over command to you right now. May I leave this minute? Or should I wait until you bring your sweetie WAC captain here?'"

My mouth dropped open. God, what a story for Pop. "No shit! What did Sutherland do?"

Lieutenant Irish chuckled. "Well, my friend, you can bet your last dollar that General Sutherland doesn't want a combat command. Especially not this one. I hear he muttered something about not being too hasty, that he also had this personal letter of advice from MacArthur."

"A letter?"

"Yeah. I haven't seen it, but it went something like that instead of two or three hundred men in his attacks, Eichelberger should attack with two or three thousand. It also said our casualties, compared to our total numbers, have been 'slight'."

"Slight?"

"Slight."

"After that, I hear they had a knock-down, drag-out shouting match. Eichelberger said trying to attack with two or three thousand men can't work on jungle trails that are three feet wide. Besides, how was he supposed to put two or three thousand rifles into attacks when GHQ kept a third of his troop strength out of his control?

"Eichelberger said he could not believe that MacArthur – having actually commanded in combat – actually wrote the letter.

"He said he believed it was composed by Sutherland himself, whom he called a multi-starred paper-pusher who never commanded so much as a platoon in battle.

"He advised Sutherland that for reasons of personal safety it might be wise for him to leave this combat zone."

"And?" I asked.

"Oh, he left."

# Chapter 73
# Scheming

Fighting on the Urbana front was several miles away, so when the wind was right we could hear the *whuf-whump* of mortars or artillery and sometimes the stutter of machine gun fire.

I tried not to think about it because I felt more lousy than usual. Something more than malaria.

*Hook worms? Jungle typhus?*

There was no time to worry about it because we were unscrambling our infantry units on the Warren front while resupplying them.

Both the Aussies and the 126th had to send patrols into the plantation to comb the remaining trees for snipers. They also had to dig out small groups of Japanese who somehow managed to infiltrate back into the area. We heard at least three allied soldiers were shot in the back by enemy troops who had never left the plantation, or who snuck back in after we rolled over it.

Later, Lieutenant Irish and I met with a Nisei lieutenant to have him translate the last few pages of the diary I brought in. What the late Lieutenant Eiji Higashi wrote elated us:

"At first the Americans were stupid and fearful like the Chinese. They wasted much ammunition at night shooting at nothing but jungle sounds. And they made much noise and even lit their tobacco at night so we could shoot them.

"But they learned quickly. Now they sneak quietly as fog and suddenly spring into our positions like great cats. Their weapons are like ours and have great power. But how good are our weapons when the men who fire them are sick and starving? We know some of our high officers have deserted on boats taking comfort girls with them. Once they told us ships would come from Rabaul to reinforce us. Then they told us ships would come from Rabaul to rescue us. All we know now is moldy rice, bitter tea and that we will die for the Emperor in this filthy place."

It was good to know that at least one Japanese soldier had come to respect and fear his American adversaries.

Lieutenant Hamada looked up at me from the report he was typing for G-2. "Other than that, I'd say the guy was really crying the blues. Sounds like he felt deserted."

"Yes sir, but I'd bet you'd also say that he wasn't about to surrender."

"Oh, hell no! These guys are so wrapped up in the *Yamato* myth and the old Shinto ancestor worship that they can't even begin to think about that. And of course they fear we'll torture them if we capture them."

He told me he had interrogated three wounded Japanese who, even after treatment, believed they were being saved for torture. He was quiet a minute. "There's something else. These guys realize that their command is abandoning them."

Lieutenant Irish said, "Yeah, so?"

"Well, look at it from their standpoint. They can't retreat. They can't surrender. So they're doomed. I think it's utter despair for them.

"All they have left is to die -- while killing as many of us as they can."

# # #

Assorted distant explosions told us the next day that the Urbana Front battle was still underway. We heard the Japs literally were fighting to the last breath. Aussie and American attacks were costly, but were splitting the Japs into smaller and smaller pockets.

Meanwhile, we on the Warren Front got ready to make a two-prong assault to capture Old Strip.

The key to the attack was Bugle Boy Bridge. Warren Front had to capture it first and then strengthen it for tanks. The tanks then would charge onto Old Strip, and bust its bunkers and strongpoints.

The 128th had seized everything up to the south end of the bridge, but dug-in Jap machine guns and riflemen north of the bridge had cut up every attempt to repair the bridge.

Late the afternoon of Christmas Eve Lieutenant Irish casually asked me to join him in looking over maps and new aerial photos of Old Strip and the bridge.

When we got to the tent, Brigadier Wootten and an Aussie major were waiting for us.

The brigadier asked, "Right. Is this the bloke who patrolled the creek and the zone around the bridge?"

"Yes, sir," Lieutenant Irish said.

"Ah, yes, Sergeant, I remember meeting you just a few days ago. So you know that sector?"

"Well, sir, I can't really say I know it. I did sneak around there on patrol late one night."

Lieutenant Irish said, "I recall you telling me of a bunker just a short distance from the bridge."

Pointing, I said, "Yes, sir. It was just about here and at least three others plus some firing trenches that sort of screen the flank of that long stretch of double-apron barbed wire."

"And that barbed wire runs where?"

"It parallels the runway, east side -- maybe 40 feet from it – just upslope from the creek."

He gave me a pencil to sketch in the obstacle on the map. The brigadier said, "Excellent. What do you think, Stanley?"

The major looked at me. "Sergeant, my lads and I have been trying to find a way across the creek. But the opposition has been too much. Now, do you know of a ford?"

"Well, sir, I do recall a shallow maybe 200 yards downstream from the bridge. What I don't know is whether it extends all the way across."

Lieutenant Irish asked, "Do you think you could spot it from the plantation?"

"Yeah, maybe."

The major grinned, glanced at the brigadier, "Ripper! Do you suppose we could get you to scout for us? At night, of course. I know it's a crook job, but we've got to get across somehow to take out those Nambus."

All I wanted to do was go somewhere and sleep. I swallowed. "My dad was with the Army in the Philippines and he said never to volunteer – for anything."

The major said, "I see." The brigadier gave me a grim stare.

"But," I went on, "I suppose that if I didn't volunteer you'd probably order me to scout, right?"

Both men and Lieutenant Irish grinned.

"So, supposing I do this, can you give me an Owen gun?"

"I think we can arrange that, chop-chop," the major said.

"One thing worries me," I said.

"Only one?" the major cracked.

"Well, no sir. Actually, the whole damn thing worries me. But, assuming we capture those bunkers, how long do we have to hold off the Japs before the engineers fix up the bridge for tanks."

"Fair question," the brigadier said. "In fact, an excellent question. In point of fact, the engineers have all their bridging material in place. The job should take no more than two hours before the first tank can cross.

"Meanwhile, two batteries of 81 mm mortars will be covering you and – if we need it – the 105. As a matter of fact, thanks to my rather strenuous representations, your Air Force wallahs have flown in extra shipments for 105 ammunition for days, so we'll have no limits on the support the 105 can give you."

"That's terrific, sir. Then, a final question, Major. How many men are we taking across to assault these bunkers?"

"One understrength company – about ninety men."

"Can they move quietly?"

"Sergeant Mays, my men have learned to move like ghosts."

# Chapter 74
## Shoving Into Enemy Territory

He was right. The Aussies moved very quietly.

I barely heard a faint rustling from them at dusk as we deployed north into the plantation. With full darkness, we turned west toward the creek, stopping at the plantation's edge.

Faces blackened, Staff Sergeant Wallace and I crawled from the plantation to the creek bank.

We eased into the water and I had to guide him downstream about 50 yards before I found the shallows.

Crouching, we slowly waded toward the creek's west bank, me expecting any second to step in over my head. But it never happened.

We were almost at the west bank below Old Strip when Wallace grabbed my shoulder, urging me back to the east bank of the creek.

Once there he whispered, "Crikey, this is wizard! This is a bleedin' artificial ford! Jap sandbags. Can't you feel 'em under foot? They must have used it all this time for infiltration."

I could almost feel his grin. "Now we'll use it against the dirty little dingoes. Wait here. I'll be back with the company in half a mo."

I crouched, leaning against the bank and trying not to doze off. Soon, Wallace and a lieutenant startled me, arriving together with a squad of men.

As the Japanese diarist wrote, they came like fog. They all just sort of emerged from the brush around me.

The lieutenant and Wallace came back across the creek with me. We huddled just below the west bank as the lieutenant whispered, "Sergeant, get us to the first bunker. We'll take it and then . . ."

He clamped his mouth shut as a Jap soldier walked downhill from Old Strip to the creek bank. He stopped right above us, unbuttoned his pants and started to take a whizz into the creek.

Wallace muttered something foul, reached up and yanked the man's feet out from under him. I swear he and the lieutenant killed the poor bastard before he even landed on the bank. Other than the thud of his fall and a wheezy gurgling from his slit throat, it was very quiet.

The lieutenant snapped, "Quick! Now where the hell is the bloody bunker?"

Shaking my head to keep myself awake, I moved downstream about three minutes until Bugle Boy Bridge was in sight.

I noticed we had company. The Aussie squad had followed the lieutenant across the creek. I pointed out the bunker.

Crawling like giant ungainly spiders, the Aussies surrounded it and then swarmed inside. From outside I heard the kind of "ooff" you get when slamming all 190 pounds into an unsuspecting halfback. Then somebody knocked over a bucket.

The lieutenant emerged and hissed, "Next?"

I just started to lead them to the next bunker when somebody called, "Okada! Okada? Doko ni masu ka?" Okada! Where are you?

Okada might have been the poor dink who started to piss on us. We never found out. The guy calling for him didn't either.

An orange burst flared in the dark from an Owen gun, shutting him up forever.

The lieutenant said, "Bloody hell! Too soon! Come on, men!"

And then it all became chaos. Nambus began spitting tracers from Old Strip and from the bunkers below it.

The lieutenant shouted, "Go! Go!" Some Jap launched a mortar flare to reveal dark forms churning the creek to froth as they raced across it.

But others already had crossed.

They bellowed and screamed as they raced up the slope toward Old Strip. That line of Aussies was in among the bunkers, shooting into or rolling grenades through the firing slits. Amid the crackle of automatic weapons and the thump of grenades, the squad which crossed with me pushed north.

More by accident than design, we were running kind of a V-shaped attack into maybe an acre of bunkers

Even feeling woozy and a dizzy, I found it exhilarating to be among bunkers instead of downrange from them.

Bunkers seem impregnable at a distance, but they're pathetic when fed-up, pissed-off veteran infantrymen are right on top of them – especially in the dark when overlapping fields of fire don't work well.

In fact, to a soldier close by or atop it, every time a bunker fires at night, it merely reveals itself. And such men ache to destroy it.

Gunners inside bunkers are pretty much blind and can't defend their flanks, their entrances, their firing slits or even ventilation vents.

After ten chaotic minutes of burst and counter-burst, screams and wails, a new flare revealed something joyous that I'd never seen – a jumble of demoralized, unarmed Japs, taken by surprise, running uphill, trying to escape up to Old Strip.

The major was among us, cheering and yelling, "Dig in, men! Get Into those bunkers and clear out the cockroaches! Get ready for counterattacks!"

Mission accomplished. Now American engineers would be able to strengthen the bridge.

I ran back and practically fell into Bugle Boy Bunker. Seven Jap bodies and two dead Aussies lay inside. I started to haul the enemy corpses out to form a barrier of flesh west of us and Sergeant Wallace soon joined me.

"Capital idea," he said. "Might make their little hearts go pitty-pat when they see this."

Trying to catch my breath, I said, "I just hope the tanks get here early."

"Yeah," he said. "Tojo's going to be browned off once he knows what we've done to them here."

# # #

Once we'd discarded all the bunkers' oriental occupants, we formed a defense line – part bunkers, part foxholes -- facing west to Old Strip then curving to face the still-occupied bunkers north of us on Old Strip's east flank.

It was daylight before the Japs organized their first attack.

About 0600, they sent a few squads straight down from Old Strip to probe toward Bugle Boy Bunker itself.

# Chapter 75
# Christmas Eve

Sergeant Wallace and one of his men welcomed the Jap probe with a series of short bursts from our captured Nambu.

Our Aussie neighbors in the adjoining bunker also blasted the visitors.

The surviving Japs retreated. I was woozy and my ears were drumming like Gene Krupa's long solo in *Sing, Sing, Sing*. Even so, I managed to hoot at the sight of fleeing Japs

"Don't celebrate yet," the lieutenant cautioned. "I guarantee we're to receive some presents from Father Christmas."

"Yes, indeed," Sergeant Wallace added, "for what we are about to bloody well receive we thank thee, Dear Lord."

"Oh, great!" I said.

Sure enough, Japanese mortars started dropping near us, so we pulled the machine gun and ourselves into the safety of the bunker.

The next few minutes taught me that "safety" was a dubious word. Though a bunker may stand up well to mortar bursts, a mortar barrage is still a damned unpleasant experience for the people sheltering inside.

"Yank," Sergeant Wallace said, "you'd better keep your mouth open to equalize the blast pressure for inner and outer ears. Otherwise, it's goodbye eardrums."

I felt what he meant when a shell exploded on our bunker roof. It was a hell of a loud bang and which raised a cloud of dust, half of which seemed to coat my tongue and teeth.

The rest settled into the sweat on my face and in my ears.

"And you'd better crouch low and keep your head down," he added.

"When a mortar bomb goes off opposite a bunker entrance or firing slit, even its debris tear inside like a load of buckshot.

"Shrapnel is bad enough," he said, "but I've seen a blast of ordinary dirt, grit and pebbles take off a man's eyes and face."

As we coughed and spat, the lieutenant said, "I hope that our friend Tojo soon will learn that it is more blessed to give than to receive."

"I hope so," I said. "I can't tell if it's mortar blasts or my malaria, but it's making me sick."

"Just keep it off me, Yank."

I was able to guffaw with the Aussies in our bunker as the mortar batteries of the 128th started dropping Willie Peter shells onto the Jap positions along the south end of New Strip.

And, just as Brigadier Wootten promised, howitzer shells also began whopping in, exploding among the bunkers north of us.

"Ho-Ho," said the lieutenant. "Now I appreciate that. It looks as if your 105 battery finally got its hands on delay fuses. Turning bunkers into pits."

"Delay fuses, sir?"

"Up 'til now," he said, "all that they had were instantaneous fuses so those shells exploded right on top of the bunkers' roofs. Didn't seriously hurt the Tojos inside.

"But a delay fuse detonates a shell maybe a tenth of a second after it strikes earth. That gives it time to penetrate the bunker before exploding, causing serious distress and woe to the occupants."

Sergeant Wallace grinned, "It's a right bitch. Saw it working on some Jerries in the desert. Time to grab your harp, Tojo."

Thanks to all the artillery, we had to do little fighting – at least until 1000 hours when the first tank came beetling and squeaking across the bridge.

As lousy as I felt, the sight made me want to start singing *The Star Spangled Banner*. Four tanks got onto Old Strip and began blasting forward with us infantrymen in company.

I quietly thanked God that, for once, we would have an easy walk-over.

Unfortunately, God was busy somewhere else that day.

Our artillery had taken out several bunkers. They looked like giant divots, where shells collapsed their roofs, leaving little more but mud puddles. But the further we advanced, Jap resistance hardened.

Pushing with the tanks through the brush and grass, we found the old runway to be a fortress all its own. First, we came upon enemy trenches zig-zagged clear across the airstrip.

We were using grenades to clear the second trench when our tank practically blew apart, its turret flipping upside down in front of us.

With that explosion, every Japanese machine gun in the world began clawing at our ranks. Men dropped right and left. The same was happening to our left where the 128th also was attacking north, paralleling us west of Old Strip.

The fire was so intense we had to take cover in the trench we had just cleared. And that was when the Japs started dropping mortar shells in and around the trench.

One shell exploded inside our trench, a few yards to my left.

It must have knocked me unconscious for a few seconds. As I was shaking my head and trying to gather my wits, it slowly dawned on me that Sergeant Wallace and his lieutenant had saved my life.

Standing between me and the mortar impact, the two men absorbed nearly all its shrapnel. That storm of steel ripped both men into bleeding shreds mingled with the rags of their jungle-green uniforms.

The surviving Aussie sergeant told me, "Hey, Yank. You're doing a bit of bleeding there."

He pointed at my left leg and side. Lesser shell fragments had merely peppered me. I was too rattled to really give a damn at that point.

When our own mortars and artillery began pounding the northern reaches of Old Strip, the Aussie sergeant urged our section out of the trench to push north.

It was painful for me to move, but we were making progress forward toward the third trench. Fire from the tanks seemed to be keeping the Japs' heads down.

Then, somehow, the enemy managed to destroy two more of our tanks.

The only good thing about it was that tanks and their crews burned with thick black smoke. It cloaked us from Nambu gunners long enough to scramble into the third trench.

The Japs began shelling us again, but I just fell into grateful sleep, huddled in the mud at the bottom of the trench. After dark, they evacuated several of us wounded.

# Chapter 76
# The Christmas Present

This time the medics sent me to the Tenth Evac where I was diagnosed with septic superficial shrapnel wounds, acute malaria, double pneumonia and inanition.

So while I was asking what the hell "inanition" might be, they started an IV with a new wonder drug called penicillin and flew me for extended treatment to the 4th General Hospital at Melbourne.

As near as I recall, they said inanition meant something like "half-starved" which, by now, probably applied to almost every man on both sides in New Guinea.

Stupidly, I had very mixed feelings.

God knows it was wonderful to leave that filthy stinking charnel house of an island.

But without my comrades – including Aussies whose names I never got to know – I felt alone and abandoned.

I admit, though, I very much looked forward to the pure luxury of a canvas cot under mosquito netting.

We landed after an interminable, dull flight. Imagine the surprise, then, to find myself and three other stretcher cases being carried indoors into a real gleaming hospital.

I mean it, it was a modern civilian-style hospital. Except it temporarily was the U.S. Army's 4th General Hospital staffed by a U.S. Army medical outfit from Cleveland.

It was a shining white hospital and ten stories tall. Its nurses wore fresh white uniforms. And it had real beds with crisp white sheets and white porcelain railings.

Most enjoyable to me were antiseptic hospital odors overriding my memories of perpetual stench.

And the hospital – started before the war and turned over to the Army in spring -- was so brand new that its construction still was underway on the top three floors.

Lying on an honest-to-God mattress in the sweet breeze of tall floor fans, I could hear the clatter and roar of machinery outdoors – the motors of cranes, cement mixers and, far below, trucks delivering building materials.

Some of the nurses complained about the noise.

Not me.

Compared to mortar blasts and the rattling of machine guns, it was heaven. It didn't even startle me when some clumsy yokel now and then dropped large pieces of steel upstairs with an echoing clang-bang.

I was just glad they weren't using rivet guns.

I was the first man in my ward, so for two days I received all the tender loving care that Sister Alda had within her.

Sister Alda wasn't a nun, but a giggly young Aussie nurse. I just gather that Aussies call nurses "sisters." Anyway, she was the day-shift nurse. I can't remember the night nurses because, between nightmares, I slept like a log.

Sister Alda seemed to think her prime duty was to build me up with mounds of good food. And when I found out my weight was down to 162 from 190, I started making a pig out of myself.

Sometimes she'd help me into a wheel chair and then roll me out to the balcony which ran the whole length of the building. Each floor had its own balcony. It was great just to sit there in the sun and feel the breeze.

I certainly felt better and my breathing was easier by the time they started bringing in new patients – from the 126th and 128th and from the Aussie brigades.

They all looked deathly pale and pitifully wasted, just as I had, Sister Alda said.

She and the other nurses lost no time cutting off and discarding their filthy uniforms and treating their skin ulcers, not to mention caring for the incisions where the surgeons had repaired bullet and shrapnel wounds.

Some of the Aussies had massive godawful ulcers on their calves and knees, the results of wearing desert shorts amid the thorns and biting insects of the jungle.

Most of our GIs had similar ulcers, the result of wearing trousers stiffened with green dye.

As each new patient came in, he brought us up to date on the decided but slow-as-ever progress around Buna.

One kid from the 128th got his leg wound – a bad one that broke his thigh bone -- after they'd discovered a semicircle of bunkers stretching clear across the north end of New Strip.

"That was New Year's Day morning," he said. "You could tell the little peckers was desperate. They came charging out of there just running flat out -- headed straight for our CP. Must have been 50 of them and only about 20 of us shooting at them.

"Well, a few of them got into the CP. Killed the skipper and a dozen other guys. Got me in the leg. But there wasn't one of them left alive. Bastards!

"As the medics got me out of there, they said that was the last resistance on Old Strip.

"There's another plantation right along the coast," he said, "and then there'd Buna itself, or maybe Buna Mission. I never got them straight."

It came as an explosive a shock a day later when one of the men received a big package in the mail – did I mention we in the hospital were getting regular mail?

His package contained the front section of the Dec. 15 *New York Times*. When he read it, he screamed.

The banner page one headline of the two-week old paper read:

### ALLIES TAKE BUNA IN NEW GUINEA

The first words from everybody reading it were, "What? *What?*"

The article reported a headquarters communique claiming that American troops had scored their first victory over Japan for General MacArthur, when they "captured Buna yesterday."

"Yesterday? So what did we do? Give Buna back to the Japs a day later?"

Not a word in the HQ communique about the Aussies fighting on New Guinea long before we got there – those Aussies who had taught us how to fight Japs, and whose tank tactics alone started breaking the Japs.

Oh, on an inside page near the end of the report, the story mentioned that Japanese forces at Buna Mission still were holding out.

No shit.

And of course those Japs were sending more casualties to us daily.

# Chapter 77
# And A Happy New Year

The Buna battle, or whatever you want to call it, didn't actually end until Jan. 22.

It had taken two months for us and the Aussies to extinguish all Japanese life along a miserable 10-mile stretch of beach, swamp and jungle.

I was out of the hospital by then, back at Camp Cable having a quiet reunion with Lieutenant Irish and Charlie Riegle, both pretty much recovered. At the NCO Club, we drank a toast to JB, Hofstra, Pop, Muskiewicz, Drexel and Svoboda.

Riegle and I tried to recall some funny stories about them – especially about Hofstra's transition from 'sufferin' succotash!' to more soldierly expletives. The lieutenant didn't say much.

"Boys, I've been through this before. You remember the good guys for a while. Then they fade along with the hurt."

So we just sort of sat there sipping our brews when a half-drunk war correspondent from Chicago came over and asked to buy us a round.

He seemed angry, saying he wanted to "make it up to the boys in the 32nd."

So we thanked him but he didn't seem to hear us. He sat down at the bar beside Riegle, slapped him on the back and said "I don't care if the bassards kick me out. Don't gi(hic) give a rat's ass any . . . anymore. I'm sick of it."

It took a while but he explained that GHQ threatened to yank his press credentials because he protested a new communique about the Buna Campaign.

I nodded over my beer and said, "Oh, I get it. You're pissed off because they declared victory in mid-December."

He gave me a blurry close-up look and said, "Nope, son! It was somethin' a lot worse."

"Well what the hell could be worse?"

"Can't tel . . . (hic) tell you boys. They'd pull my credentials and it'd get you in trouble."

So we let it go, but after two more drinks he said. "Awright. I c'n tell you in conf . . . conf'dence."

"Okay," Lieutenant Irish said, "so spit it out. We're not going to spill the beans."

"You sure?"

"Damn sure we're sure."

"Okay, men. Here it is: the real scoop. Gen'l MacArthur (hic) jus' announced yesterday that losses in the Buna campaign were small because (hic) an' I'm quoting now -- with fine accuracy -- because 'the time element was of little importance'."

We turned our heads, looking at each other. You could have heard a pin drop.

"Are you shitting me?" I asked. "He said losses were small?"

"That's wha . . . thass what the man said."

Lieutenant Irish added, "And time was of little importance. What a filthy fucking lie."

He took a sip of beer, looked at Riegle and me and gave a nasty chuckle. "Boys, don't say a goddamned word. Otherwise you'll wind up in Leavenworth."

After a bit, Riegle said, "Well, what now?"

"Well, they'll start bringing the boys back from both fronts to get rested," Lieutenant Irish said. "And we'll get replacements and we'll put them and ourselves through a hell of a lot of training."

"An' then," the correspondent said, "the next stop will be the Philippines.

"You boys are going to take Big Bad Doug back so he can keep his promise to return."

# Epilogue

Nearly all 11,000 men of the 32$^{nd}$ Infantry Division who were directly involved in the two-month seizure of Buna were casualties.

The butcher bill to conquer 10 square miles of jungle, swamp and beach was 690 killed in action, 1,689 wounded and 62 missing.

Another 7,125 men were listed as non-battle casualties, most from malaria.

Of those disease cases, 2,334 were so severe that the division dropped those sufferers from the ranks as unfit for combat. All told it was an 86 per cent casualty rate – one of the war's highest.

The Australian forces fighting in the Buna Campaign – more numerous and fighting for a longer time -- lost 1,602 killed in action and 3,359 wounded. Malaria also cut a swath through Australian ranks.

After Buna, the Aussies spent much of the rest of the war besieging similar Japanese garrisons dotted along New Guinea's torrid north coast, then going on to invade and destroy Japan's forces in Borneo.

After the Buna campaign, the 32$^{nd}$ Division was slowly returned to Australia. New draftees filled the gaps in its ranks. They, together with veterans of Buna, underwent intensive training for future battles, including the Philippines campaign.

When the 32nd landed in the Philippines it was a toughened veteran outfit . . . fortunately so, because it faced the same incredibly tenacious enemy in jungles and stinking swamps, not to mention narrow mountain jungle trails, mud, slime and ghastly tropical weather.

By VJ day, the 32$^{nd}$ Division had logged 654 days of combat, more than any other U.S. infantry division during World War II.

# The Generals

**Douglas MacArthur** vows "there will be no more Bunas." Accordingly, he puts into practice – and claims credit for – the Navy's innovation of by-passing and isolating numerous Japanese island garrisons, leaving them to starve. When invading the Philippines, he often outmaneuvers the Japanese. Considering his vast force – larger than the allied D-Day Normandy invasion – his army's casualties are relatively low. After the war, he heads the United States' Far East Command and virtually rules Japan, a duty he discharges with remarkable success. In 1950, he devises a brilliant stroke -- the Inchon invasion -- nearly destroying the invading North Korean Army. The Chinese Communist Army, however, stuns and defeats him that same year. Soon after, MacArthur publicly attacks the policies of his commander-in-chief, President Harry Truman, who fires him.

**Albert Waldron** – The general's wound leaves him without a right shoulder joint, forcing his retirement. He is appointed the administrator of a Veterans Administration Hospital in California. After retirement he keeps busy as a Republican Party organizer and, despite his infirmity, becomes an avid sportsman who also specializes in carving and painting duck decoys.

**Charles Willoughby** advises MacArthur that there is "little indication of an attempt to make a strong stand against the Allied advance" in Buna which he estimated was held by about 1000 sick, starving Japanese. The number turned out to be 5,000 veteran troops in expertly designed fortifications. MacArthur retains Willoughby on his staff through World War II, the subsequent occupation of Japan and the early months of the Korean War. At one point, MacArthur says, "There have been three great intelligence officers in history. Mine is not one of them." In 1950, despite ample evidence, Willoughby predicts North Korea won't invade South Korea. Wrong again. Later, despite ample evidence, he predicts Communist China won't come to North Korea's aid. An Army of 300,000 Chinese hands MacArthur one the worst defeats any American commander ever sustained. Willoughby retires shortly after MacArthur is sacked.

**Richard K. Sutherland** serves throughout the war as General MacArthur's chief of staff. But where the two at first were a close team – Sutherland almost functioning as MacArthur's alter ego -- operational and organizational differences come to divide them. Too, Sutherland repeatedly defies MacArthur's angry orders to leave his mistress, an Australian national and U.S. Army captain, in her homeland. He retires shortly after the war and is reconciled with his wife.

**Robert Eichelberger** is appointed to command Eighth Army before and through the Philippine Campaign. The 32$^{nd}$ Division is part of his army. Eichelberger is embittered about his superiors' attitudes concerning fighting troops and how such officers often try to glorify their own accomplishments. In a post-war letter he speaks derisively of MacArthur as "the great hero" who never bothered to visit the Buna front "to see first-hand the difficulties our troops were up against." By contrast, Eichelberger habitually stalks the front lines throughout the war. He also scorns victory communiques that state "only mopping up" remains. He advocates banning the phrase "mopping up" from military and news reports because so many soldiers die or suffer hellish wounds during such operations. Eichelberger retires in 1948 after administering the occupation and disarmament of Japan.

**Edwin Harding** is given soothing assurances by MacArthur that no disgrace will attend his relief from command of the 32$^{nd}$ Division and that he'll receive a new assignment in the Southwest Pacific. It never happens. Unlike his many noted West Point classmates – including William Simpson, George Patton and Bob Eichelberger -- he receives orders to return to the States and later is given commands in the Panama Canal Zone and in the Caribbean. In 1945, he's named Director of the Historical Division at the War Department for the Joint Chiefs of Staff. He retires after spending a year planning the Army's comprehensive history of World War II.

The End

# A Message From The Author

Dear Reader

If you found *The  Green Hell* interesting and enjoyable, I hope you'll consider writing a brief review and posting it on Amazon or any other site. Satisfied readers such as you are the best way to spread the word.

Sincerely,

J. Scott Payne

## About the Author

J. Scott Payne is a retired newspaper reporter and editor who began his career in the early 60s at the *Kansas City Star*.

Part of his professional life involved city hall plus the police beat where he got to know cops, dicks, dispatchers, judges, chiefs, ambulance-chasing lawyers, and sheriffs' deputies plus a four-legged officer with long glistening white teeth.

He later served in Korea, Vietnam and Washington, D.C. as an investigator with the Army Counterintelligence Corps. It was work requiring basic journalistic skills: You ask. You watch. You listen. You write. Just the facts.

Journalism nowadays, however, seems to require a different skill set: You ask "gotcha" questions. You never let facts get in the way of the political you want to perpetuate.

Scott finds it more fulilling to write pure fiction from his lower-level office looking out on the woods in Allendale, a little college town in western Michigan. He and Jane feed and watch birds, walk their pooch and adamantly refuse to move to Florida.

15163860R00157

Made in the USA
Lexington, KY
11 November 2018